A [illegible]ettia Paradise Christmas

A Poinsettia Paradise Christmas

A Love in El Dorado Romance

Janine Amesta

TULE
PUBLISHING

A Poinsettia Paradise Christmas

Tule Publishing First Printing, October 2023

The Tule Publishing, Inc.

First Publication by Tule Publishing 2023

Cover design by Elizabeth Mackey

ISBN: 978-1-961544-15-4

Dedication

Para mi familia

And to anyone who's felt like a Halloween person in a Christmas family and vice versa. I see you.

Content Note

Dear Readers,

Never forget that your mental health is important. As a note, this book does contain family strife, including feuding parents, and feelings of unworthiness. Also, there is strong language and open door love scenes. But always know that a happy ending waits for you at the end.

Chapter One

NATALIE GONZALEZ-TORRES WAS not a Christmas person.

People assigning themselves holidays, as though it was a personality trait, was, in itself, silly. It's not that she hated Christmas, she simply did not understand why it was treated like the Super Bowl of holidays, especially when Halloween, an infinitely better day, was right there. But she didn't consider herself a sentimental person and, therefore, couldn't care less about the most sentimental of all holidays.

Her youngest sister, Carla, liked to tease her that this preference proved she was part villain. Natalie didn't care. It was one more thing her family didn't understand about her, and to be fair, she didn't necessarily always understand them either. She accepted being a Halloween person in a Christmas family.

It wasn't that Natalie didn't love her family. She wasn't that much of a villain. It was just…her family was constantly together and up in each other's business all year long, not just during the holidays. So unless she got stranded on a deserted island by herself, there wasn't much of a reprieve from either the Gonzalez side nor the Torres side.

Case in point, her cousin Diego. He knew of her low

tolerance for Christmas music, especially when it came on the direct heels of Halloween. Was nothing sacred anymore? It took an hour into her shift, and the discovery of absent-mindedly humming a bar of Bing Crosby's "White Christmas," for her to realize her cousin had snuck into the manager's office and switched from their normal station of inoffensive coffeehouse music to one featuring Christmas tunes.

"Ugh, Diego. Seriously?"

The kid, who was a year out of high school with thick, shaggy hair, turned his head toward her with the appearance of complete innocence. "What?"

Natalie was not the owner of Pony Expresso, a small coffee shop located in the heart of the historic downtown area of Placerville, California. This title belonged to her Tío Enrique on the Gonzalez side. She was, however, the manager, giving her ultimate control over when sentimental sap, such as holiday tunes, was allowed to infiltrate the workspace. She was hoping to push this until at least the week before Christmas, because there was no reason to rush into this type of music commitment.

Fortunately, she had no problem telling off any employee, especially when they were young, cocky, and happened to be related to her. This was exactly what she did, making sure to chew Diego out in Spanish, so most of the customers would remain ignorant of the situation, as she relieved Crystal at the register for a break. Her cousin responded to her early morning music tirade by smirking and rolling his eyes as he returned to his work at the espresso machine. He was Tío Enrique's son and had the unearned confidence of a kid who could get away with most things.

"Yes. What can I get for you?" she said, flipping to English, and raising her gaze to the customer standing there. She had to raise her eyes quite a bit more than she was used to as he was very tall. Natalie wasn't sure if it was his large presence or something else, but she immediately felt overwhelmed by him. Perhaps he felt the same because the man froze, as if he was dumbfounded to find himself standing before her.

The spell broke when an older man in his twilight years, jabbed the younger one in his side. "Mason. Wake up. Whaddya want?"

"Oh. Uh… Sorry. Let me…uh, let me have the…" The man's eyes darted across the chalkboard menu on the wall and appeared to be approaching a panic in his attempt to order something. "What do you recommend?"

Oh, for the love of—It wasn't as if they had a very lengthy menu. Compared to places like the local Starbucks, their menu was quite small. And while there were times she enjoyed playing this guessing game with customers, today was not that day. She had a lot to do, there was a long line of customers, and there was still Christmas music playing. She wasn't in the mood.

"I recommend that you know exactly what you want by the time you get to the register," she heard herself saying before she could think better of it. Definitely not A+ customer service this morning. Her villain side showed up at the most inopportune times.

She expected the man, Mason, to demand to see a manager after her inappropriate and sarcastic comment. Instead, those hazel eyes connected with hers again and his lips lifted in amusement.

"Just get him the same as me. Small coffee, black. For Daniel," the older man injected while pulling out his wallet to pay and shoving a few bills into the tip jar. "We also have a meeting with Enrique." Then Daniel yanked the younger guy out of line who almost tripped and said some word she didn't quite understand. The whole encounter was a lot more awkward and flustery than ordering coffee ever should be.

Weird.

Natalie was never happier than when Crystal reappeared and retook her position at the register, letting Natalie return to her previous job of restocking the supplies and yelling to her uncle that he had visitors. She glanced up as her uncle came from the back, wearing slacks and a soft burgundy sweater, rather than his usual everyday uniform of track pants and long-sleeve T-shirts. The one thing ruining the professional businessman illusion was him lightly dusting pastry crumbs from his chest and mustache. He shook Daniel's hand before doing the same with Mason, but he was much more openly friendly with the former. They clearly knew each other well. The younger guy met her eyes again before quickly moving his gaze away, as though he didn't want to be caught staring.

Natalie wanted to giggle—No, strike that. Thirty-year-olds didn't giggle. Natalie wanted to laugh because the look Mason gave her was clearly one of interest. While she was no stranger to receiving attention, even in her place of work, she wasn't used to the attention-giver being so flustered. Casually flirting and asking her out was one thing. Tripping all over himself like she was a gorgeous woman in possession of large boobs, instead of a chest that aspired to be a B-cup, was definitely more unique.

He was Caucasian and not only was he tall but also broad, although he didn't appear muscular under his clothes. His physique gave the impression of something softer, like he was on his way toward establishing a dad bod and gave great hugs. He had close-cropped hair that was a medium brown with some reddish undertones. His jawline was in the process of growing a beard but, at this stage, the follicles weren't long enough to hide a cleft in his chin. The eyes weren't quite brown and not quite green but a swirly, hazel combination of both. She had to admit, this was exactly the type of guy she tended to gravitate toward, and maybe she found herself sneaking glances at him as well.

Except there was already a strike against him.

He was obviously a local guy.

Natalie made it a rule never to get involved with local guys. The less chance she had of running into someone she might want to eventually avoid, the better.

Also, he was clearly too nice. It was a mistake for *too nice* guys to get involved with her because what they wanted and what she wanted was not only not in the same ballpark, it wasn't even in the same sport. Her needs were very simple. As long as she didn't have to commit to an actual relationship, she was good. Anything else wasn't worth the hassle either for them or for her. Plus, the older she got the less Natalie enjoyed shredding hearts. She may have been a villain, but she didn't have the stomach for any organs, let alone the beating ones.

Okay, that was two problems. He was a local. Too nice. Oh, and he had trouble making decisions under pressure. There was probably a lot more she could list but their encounter had lasted two minutes and she wasn't psychic.

Hmm. That did make her think, though. Daniel had ordered for him, ordering the same drink as himself. Except there was no way Mason was a black coffee type of guy. His vibe was reading something entirely different. Also she was feeling a tad guilty about being rude earlier. She could at least do something for the guy. It wasn't as if he was the one forcing Christmas music on her. The only person who earned her contempt so far was her cousin.

"Are you working on that order for Daniel yet?" Natalie asked Diego.

"Just getting to it now."

"Make only one a black coffee. The other should be…a Nutella latte."

He studied the ticket. "That's not what this says."

"I know because that's not what they ordered."

Diego stopped his activity, his brows pressing together. "Are you sure you want to do this? I don't want to get in trouble for wrong orders while my dad is here."

She waved him off. "It's fine. I'll take it over to the table and take responsibility for it. You're not going to get in trouble." And it wasn't as if Mason hadn't asked for her suggestion to begin with. Her answer to his question was merely delayed.

Shrugging, Diego did as she instructed. With the drinks in hand, she strode to the table with confidence. The group of men all acknowledged her, although it was Mason's eyes that stayed on her the longest. "Okay, here's a black coffee," she said, placing the drink before Daniel. "And a Nutella latte."

"We didn't order that," the older man said. "Mason should have got—"

"It's okay. I'll drink it," he replied, taking the offered cup, and gulping a large sip as if he expected someone to come along and snatch it away. Yeah, this guy was definitely in the way too nice category.

Her Tío Enrique sent a stern look in her direction, but she clasped her hands together and smiled sweetly. "Natalie—"

"Wow, that's really good. This might be my new favorite drink." Mason stood, reaching into his pocket. "Do I owe you something extra?"

"It's fine. Fine," Enrique answered, waving away Mason's wallet. "Don't worry about it. For you, my friends, it's on the house."

Mason continued standing, staring at her, before appearing self-conscious and sinking into his chair again. "Okay, thanks."

She glanced downward to see if her boobs had suddenly grown overnight. Nope, they were still small. Also her hair was a mess, and the only makeup she had hurriedly swiped on this morning was some tinted moisturizer. She didn't know what he saw but she wondered if the guy was due for an eye exam. Small boobs aside, Natalie had always been okay with her body but even she wasn't *that* confident.

"What about her? Could she do it?" Daniel asked and

suddenly she regretted coming here instead of sending Diego. If there was one thing she didn't like, it was being roped into things, especially when her uncle had a bad habit of volunteering people regardless of whether they were his own offspring or extended family members.

"My niece is the manager here and she's great, but she's a bit…" Enrique studied her as if she was going to finish this description and save him the trouble. Natalie crossed her arms, giving her uncle a flat look. This was going to be good. If there was one thing her family wasn't afraid of, it was being honest to the point of rudeness.

Enrique waved a hand in her direction. "Yes, exactly. Natalie is like that," he replied as if she'd made his point with her stance and current attitude. "Diego would be a better choice for this business plan," her uncle continued. "He has more of the right attitude for…"

Excuse her? Enrique was going with Diego for whatever this was? *Over her?* Diego? The kid who thought it was hilarious to make fake fart sounds when the coffee shop was dead quiet—which was sometimes funny—but that wasn't the point. For one thing, she'd been working at Pony Expresso for a long time, at least since she was Diego's age. Plus, her cousin was willing to overlook an order and be talked into making something else entirely just because someone told him to. Did that sound like a leader? No, it did not. She was the manager for God's sake and actually wanted to be the owner of her own coffee shop, if she ever had the money for it or could get Enrique to give her a chance. She wasn't fooling around, doing this job for spending cash.

"I can do it," she interrupted.

All eyes turned to her again.

"I don't think you'll want—" her uncle started.

"I can handle it," she assured him. "What is it?"

Natalie got her first sign that maybe her ego wasn't the best at making rash decisions when a smile, one that could only be described as devilish, slipped from beneath Tío Enrique's mustache. He spread his hands as if to say, *Well, you asked for it.* "Daniel and I think it would be a good idea to have a small Pony Expresso coffee truck at Poinsettia Paradise, their Christmas tree farm in Apple Hill."

"Oh." Apple Hill was an area located in a town called Camino just outside the city of Placerville. While Mason could technically not be considered local-local it was definitely close enough. Too close.

Although, she had a bigger problem to worry about, because after hearing it laid out, everything her uncle said, especially about Diego, made a lot of sense. The kid would love to escape the coffee shop and goof off in a Christmas tree lot, a place where he wouldn't have constant supervision and could make all the fart noises he wanted. In fact, fart noises were probably more appreciated in a place like Poinsettia Paradise. "Okay, well, now that you mention it—"

"Actually, you know what? Maybe you are exactly the right person for the job," Enrique said, leaning smugly against the chair back. "It'll be good for you."

Being surrounded by Christmas trees and cheer and cold and all that stuff? Yeah, none of that sounded like the kind of change she was looking for. How could Natalie be the right type of person for this job when she wasn't even a

Christmas person? Time to pump the great attributes of her younger cousin, who happened to be a star employee and never complained about cleaning the bathroom, even though it took him a weirdly long time to do it. Oh, and he had a great sense of humor and did exactly what the manager told him to do. "Yeah, you know, Diego—"

"Great," Daniel added, appearing pleased about Natalie volunteering herself. "Both Mason and I will look forward to seeing you around. Isn't that right, Mase?" He planted a hand on Mason's shoulder, giving him a light pat.

"Yeah, sounds good," he replied. "When do you want to come by to pick up a tree?"

"Uh, what tree?" she was at a complete loss and her whole world was shifting out of control. Damn Enrique. She was calling her tía right after this to tell her all about him sneaking pastries for breakfast after promising he was going to eat healthier.

"They're giving us a tree for the shop. Isn't that great? We still have some ornaments in storage around here, right?" Enrique asked.

"I guess." Cheap ornaments from the Dollar Store were stashed in a supply closet somewhere. She wasn't looking forward to adding *decorating a tree* to her list. "I'm sure whatever tree you guys bring will be fine. Although, it seems like a bigger hassle than it's worth."

Mason frowned, tilting his head. "It's no hassle at all. But it's probably better if you pick it out yourself. Picking out the right Christmas tree can be very personal."

Huh? Did one type leave fewer pine needles than another? This was her biggest requirement, considering she was being forced into this tree-hunting situation in the first place. Getting a Christmas tree wasn't the same as getting a puppy. There was no way Natalie was getting attached to a silly tree, especially one that would only be hanging around for a few weeks.

Her negligence of houseplants was the reason she had earned a reputation for being a plant killer. The one plant she'd kept alive was a tiny potted cactus Carla had brought from her job at the florist and gifted as a joke. She made sure to inform Natalie the cactus type was called Old Lady. *Ha, ha, Carla.* Regardless, she named the plant Thorny, and, at three years, it had been her longest committed relationship. Maybe the cactus started off as a joke, but Thorny and her got along great. Neither enjoyed being fussed over, preferring negligence to smothering. Maybe instead of a Christmas tree, she could bring Thorny in and spear its spines with colorful pom-poms. That was the type of holiday festivity Natalie could get behind.

Except it was becoming clearer she wasn't going to be able to weasel her way out of this, not when Enrique had already made the decision and had his mind set.

"ARE YOU KIDDING me with this whole Christmas tree farm thing? You and I both know I'm not the most bubbly person," Natalie said to her uncle as he was gathering his items from the manager's office.

"It'll be great for business. And *you* said you really wanted to do it," Enrique replied, slipping his arms into his jacket sleeves.

"Oh, stop. You know I don't. You just tricked me into it. Besides, I can't do it, because I have my state-line vacation set for the week after Thanksgiving, so I'd be missing at least two big weekends."

He slid her a flat look. "You're really gambling right before Christmas?" Enrique and Tía Sonia were more religious than her own immediate family. They never bluntly told her gambling was a sin, but they had no qualms implying it, usually disguising their opinion as either a joke or an invitation to join them for Mass at St. Anthony's.

Except Natalie only took two vacation weeks a year, one in April and one in December, when tourist season was less busy. Also, she wasn't actually gambling. It was a little white lie that started as a joke and then stuck. She thought it was funny, so she never corrected her family's assumptions regarding her Tahoe trips. She even owned a T-shirt reading *Queen of the Machine* with an image of a slot machine. There was no way something this hilarious could bite her in the ass, and it was better if the family (especially the really religious side) didn't know the truth.

"Of course. Gambling might be the only way I'm ever going to get enough money to buy Pony Expresso from you," she replied.

Enrique rolled his eyes. "You should come to Mass with me and Tía."

"If I go with you to Mass, can I skip out on this whole Christmas tree lot scheme? Diego has a better personality to fit in with that whole scene anyway."

Her uncle's thick brows pushed together as he studied

her. "Look, I love you like you were one of my kids, but sometimes I don't know what you're thinking. What exactly do you want, Natalie?"

"I want to go on my damn vacation and not have to work at some damn Christmas tree lot."

He shot her a look, translating to *cut the bullshit*. This, and the fact he didn't say something about her swearing, indicated his seriousness about the situation. "No, what do you want from all of this? Do you still like working here?"

She took a deep breath because though she joked plenty of times about being the true heart-and-soul owner of the coffee shop, she'd never had an honest and open conversation about it with him. "Yes, I do. I want to be like you. I don't want to be a manager of a coffee shop, I want to be an owner. You know I could do it too. I've been running this place for almost ten years now. I know everything about it. I just don't have the money to do it."

His expression softened. "You want to be like me?" He studied her while tapping the keys in his hands, taking longer to think about what she had said. "You talked to my brother about this before?"

Natalie shook her head because her parents only cared about her having gainful employment and possibly settling down to start a family. She took care of the first one, but they'd been waiting a long time for the latter. While she didn't mind kids, she was convinced it wasn't worth chaining herself to someone in order to have one.

"I want you to do Poinsettia Paradise."

This wasn't the response she was hoping for, but she didn't know what she had expected. Her family could be

What could she say? He was giving her the opportunity and she had to snatch it. "Yes. Okay. I can do that." Giving up her vacation wasn't a huge sacrifice when so much was on the line. She could go through her dry spell a little longer for the greater good. Sure, she still wasn't looking forward to being surrounded by festivities and Christmas and all that, but she could definitely manage.

"Great," Enrique said. "It'll be good for you."

"Okay."

She could do this.

With the discussion over, she returned to the front of the shop, only to discover Mason was still there. He stood as soon as their eyes connected. Her heart did a small flutter but she did her best to tamp down this reaction because heart flutters were a waste of time.

He approached, his head ducking and his hands stuffed into the pockets of his coat. "Hi again. Sorry. We never figured out when you were going to come get the tree. We can also exchange numbers and set something up later if you're too busy to do it now."

Her suspicions rose. This was all her fault. She did one nice thing, like giving a guy a Nutella latte, and now he thought she was a friend or open to receiving unsolicited dick pics. "That's okay. I'll just stop by sometime after work or something. Thanks anyway."

He blushed, which was kind of cute. She wished she hadn't noticed that. It made her want to be nice instead of smart.

"Oh, i-it's not..." Stumbling with his words he tried again. "I just mean we're not officially open to the public yet.

I want to make sure someone will be there to help you. Unless, of course, you're a certified lumberjack. In that case, I apologize. I shouldn't have presumed. But I'll need to see your certification. It's a tree farm liability thing."

He said this with complete seriousness. She had to work hard to school her features, hiding her amusement, which would only encourage him. "Is getting lumberjack certified something I can do online?" she asked while also playing it straight.

"Probably not in time to get a tree this year."

"Darn. I'm sure that's something that really comes in handy too."

"It might be easier if I just help you." Mason pulled his phone from a pocket, waiting expectantly.

She became nervous, feeling trapped. Taking control, she retrieved her own phone. "How about I text you when I know my schedule better? What's your number?"

Natalie was about to inform him that this was about getting a tree and nothing else, to set expectations exactly where they should be, when he continued after rattling off his number.

"I don't want to make things weird but I just want to say that even if you ask, no, I am not willing to send you any dick pics. Don't even ask because it's not going to happen."

This took her by complete surprise. She wasn't about to beg for one… But her curiosity had become piqued, because who was this guy? "You get asked for a lot of dick pics?"

A smile slipped from his lips, warming his whole face, as his eyes crinkled in the corners. "No, but I figured it's probably because I've stated up-front that I'm not going to do it. It's just better if I cut the request off from the start. This way there are no expectations, and neither one of us is disappointed."

This time a small laugh did pop out, the back of her hand pressing against her mouth to hold some of it inside, but it didn't escape Mason's notice, his smile lines becoming deeper. "Okay then. Natalie." Her name reverberated in his husky voice as though he was trying the syllables on his tongue, testing them, getting used to the feel of them. "Well, I better head out. I'll see you again soon."

"'Kay." Her own brain felt somewhat scrambled at this point. A lot had already happened today, and it seemed she'd used up all her words because she couldn't think of anything better at this point. But she did her best to push him from her mind after he departed and return to her day. Natalie had to get her focus because she had a partnership to earn.

And the last thing she needed was a distraction in the shape of a local nice guy.

Chapter Two

MASON LAVIGNE LIKED to play games.

Well, some games, like actual board games. Other types of games like those involving women and dating and love, not so much. And while the love game could involve strategy, this wasn't the type of strategy he was good at. His preference were games that had clear, up-front rules, rather than ones that require the skill of bluffing—another thing he wasn't very good at.

But every once in a while, Mason came across a person who made him want to try the love game again, like the woman who worked at Pony Expresso. A woman so gorgeous, he stopped in his tracks as soon as he saw her behind the counter. His father, Daniel, had to pull him into line after his morning thoughts had been completely hijacked by her.

Natalie was about average height with an athletic frame. When her black T-shirt rode up her arms, her biceps looked strong and firm, revealing more of her light brown skin, giving him the balmy, glowy impression of summer in cold, gray November. Her dark, glossy hair was haphazardly pulled in a half bun, half ponytail thing. There were strands making their escape, but the majority remained away from her face. Even so, it was clear the hair was beautiful and thick and probably soft and nice-smelling. Things that smelled nice were his favorite, like when jasmine first started blooming in the greenhouse or the first honey harvest of the season.

When those dark brown eyes had turned their focus onto him, he stopped functioning altogether. Her gaze stunned him, like discovering the richest, deepest velvet.

Again his dad had to rescue him from this potential manmade disaster of epic proportions as his heart panicked, trying to come up with anything witty or intelligent or at least something resembling a drink order. Not only was he unfamiliar with this particular coffee shop's offerings, (he had only come because his father invited him to the meeting with his friend, Enrique), but it was as though he'd become unfamiliar with the concept of coffee itself.

In one great attempt to impress her at the end of the transaction, he'd attempted to say something amazing. But as he lacked the necessary caffeine to make anything resembling a coherent sentence, what came out was, *Greanks*. If he was being generous with himself, he was probably either trying to say *great* or *thanks* but it sort of merged together in a Frankenstein mess of a word that was neither impressive nor amazing. He thought he blew his opportunity for sure, especially when he nearly tripped over his own feet and almost knocked the tip jar from the counter.

Wow. What a disaster.

Thankfully, he got another chance to speak with her, one which he was a little more prepared for. Mason could use all the chances he could get. He left the coffee shop that morning like he had a lottery ticket in his hand potentially worth millions and—

"Hey. Mase. Stop daydreaming and looking at your phone. Why the hell are you so distracted tonight? It's your turn."

"Sorry," he said, apologizing to Gemma before grabbing the dice and rolling.

The pretty Black woman with curly hair and glasses rolled her eyes, muttering, "You're the one who picked this game and now your head just isn't in it. What's going on with you?"

"Nothing." He took a resource card before handing two more cards to Damon and one to Isaac. Isaac was a Latino man with expressive eyebrows. His husband, Damon, rarely said much at all, allowing him to almost disappear within the group, but this might have been his gameplay strategy as he won most of the time.

Isaac laughed. "You know he picked this game because it's the only one he wins at. He cheats."

"No, I picked this game because it's my favorite and, because Jay isn't here, we actually have the proper number of players for it. And how do you cheat at Settlers of Catan? Do you think I'm hiding resource cards in my sleeve or something?"

"Or something," Isaac said while reorganizing the cards in his hand.

"What do you want to do? It's still your turn," Gemma said.

"Oh. Let's see." Mason studied his cards. "Isaac, do you want to trade one lumber for a grain?"

The man crossed his arms. "Uh, no. Nope. I'm not helping you."

"Are you joking? You do this every time. You can't hoard your resources like Gollum over there. And then you get upset when someone rolls a seven. This is why you always lose."

"It's called strategy."

"I'll do that trade," Damon piped in.

"Thank you," he said pointedly while swapping cards with him. "And I'm going to build another road." Mason placed a road game piece on the board. "That gives me the longest road, so I'll take that victory card. And I'll play a knight card, moving the robber here, and will take one of your cards anyway, Isaac."

Gemma barked a laugh as though she couldn't believe Mason's audacity but there was a reason Settlers of Catan was his favorite board game.

"He cheats," Isaac stage-whispered behind his hand to Damon.

"I know, baby," his husband murmured back.

Board game night had been a regular thing for the last few years, and usually fell on a Thursday. Mason had gone to school with Gemma and Isaac. After high school, they all separated, focusing on their individual education and careers. Except Mason, who continued working for his parents at Motherlode Nursery and Poinsettia Paradise tree farm, located amid the natural beauty of Apple Hill. There were times he wondered if he was missing out on something, for not going off as his other friends had, but the truth was he couldn't imagine himself anywhere else. Mason wasn't the type of person who liked having his days ruled by a strict schedule or spent in an office.

Gemma got her teaching license and came back to become a high school math teacher. While Isaac became a dentist and had the sparkling perfect teeth to prove it. He eventually met and married Damon who worked in IT. The three of them met up as adults at a bar called Gold Rush Bar & Grill in downtown Placerville where they'd all gone to participate in a Pop Culture Trivia Night. Their friendship re-sparked and board game night was born.

"Where's Handsome Jay tonight?" Mason asked, inquiring after Gemma's husband who was, in fact, more handsome than any human had a right to be.

"He's on call tonight at the hospital." She slid some of her cards on the table, exchanging them for a single development card. "Someone has to make that money so we can buy a house. I'm not going to do it on my teacher's salary."

"Handsome Jay would be making that house money faster if he took my idea and just became a hair model or something. That man has the finest hair I've ever seen," Isaac said.

"Mm-hmm," Gemma agreed. "Don't be jealous."

Mason wasn't going to say it out loud because he didn't need to give his friends any more ammo on things they could tease him about, but he may have been a little jealous of Jay's hair. At twenty-seven, he was at least lucky to maintain most of his original hairline but he didn't have anything close to the dark, luscious Italian-stallion locks of Handsome Jay. If he had hair like that, he probably would have already heard from the gorgeous barista from Pony Expresso by now. Speaking of which, he better check his phone.

"All right, what's going on? Are you expecting an important call? Did you go viral on TikTok or something?" Gemma asked. "I swear, I have never seen you so invested in the status of your phone before."

"It's nothing," he started but, at Gemma's raised eyebrows, he sighed. "I met this woman when I was with my dad at a coffee shop yesterday."

"Oh boy, here we go," Isaac replied.

Gemma shushed him. "No, wait, I wanna hear this." She leaned her chin into her propped hand resting on the table. "You know I keep trying to push you to get out there, Mase. Does she like board games? Find someone to bring to game night so I don't have to be the Smurfette to this clown show every week."

"I keep telling you, you're free to bring any of your other friends."

She waved him off. "And I keep telling you, none of them want to play. So I'm depending on you to bring another lady into the group."

"I just met her."

"So?"

"Right now, I'd be happy just to get a text message from her so I can set her up with a Christmas tree."

"Oh God," Isaac replied. "You're way too nice, Mase."

"No—"

"Yes, you are. You deserve to be with someone who isn't using you to get a free Christmas tree."

"*You* use me for a free Christmas tree," Mason replied to him.

"Yeah, because you're too nice. You never say no. I'm

one of your oldest and dearest friends. Besides, I thought I was doing you a favor by taking one of your sad reject trees."

"Okay, first of all, none of our trees are sad—"

"So, can I have one of your sad, reject trees for free this year?"

"I'm thinking about telling you no."

"And?"

"Okay, you can have a free tree, but just know how badly I wanted to say fuck off."

Isaac lifted both hands in the air. "That's progress but still proves my point."

"Are you two going to stop at some point? Damon and I are tired of putting up with these constant interruptions," Gemma said.

"Yup." Damon played one of his cards.

"I'm just looking out for him, Gem. I don't want another Dakota to grab hold of him."

Mason leaned against the back of his chair, crossing his arms. "This situation is completely different. And I'm different." And, most importantly, Natalie was nothing like Dakota.

THE REALITY OF the Dakota situation, once Mason had finally moved past the fog of love and could see it for what it really was, was a shock to the system. He'd met her at a bar, and she'd been a sparkling, flirty blonde with whiskey-colored eyes. Mason was instantly swept away. He couldn't believe she had let him buy her drinks and food all evening, and she'd made Mason feel like a charming guy who could finally hold the attention of a beautiful woman. He thought he'd hit the jackpot when she'd reached out to him days later and coyly asked if he wanted to take her to dinner or shopping.

His friends were the first to grow suspicious, wondering why Dakota was never interested in doing something simple like coming to board game night, but, like some of Gemma's other friends, he assumed she didn't like games, and it was okay for them to have different interests. Except it was weird she never wanted to just hang out and watch a Netflix movie or do something that didn't require him to spend a lot of money. Mason made okay money working at Motherlode, but he wasn't rolling in cash. When he asked his new girlfriend out for a simple picnic dinner date one summer evening, she made her decision quickly.

"That's okay. I think I'll ask Aaron if he wants to take me to Tahoe for the weekend."

"Aaron? Who the hell is Aaron?" He'd been caught off guard.

"You know. Aaron. I've talked about him before. He's one of the other guys I'm seeing."

"Wait. You're seeing other guys?"

"Well…yeah. We've never talked about being exclusive. Why are you making this weird, Mase? If you can't afford me, that's fine, but I have to look out for myself. You're a nice guy and everything but I'm afraid you're just going to work at your dad's little plant shop and it's never going to be anything more for you. You can't expect me to take this seriously when you seem to just be floating through life."

Her words had sent a verbal spike into his gut. The first part might have been partially his fault. They had never talked about being exclusive. Mason had assumed he'd been enough for Dakota. The second part of her statement was crushing because he realized how loose of a hold he actually had on her. He'd always been fairly laidback, which could be mistaken for floating through life, but he didn't think her observation was fair. He was working, earning a living like everyone else; he just didn't have the aspirations to become a millionaire. Even so, he wanted to hold on for as long as possible, to give her exactly what she wanted because that was what Mason did when he really liked someone.

And then he made the worst mistake of his life.

"I can afford you," he heard himself saying as though he were in a tunnel and his conscience at the end was getting further away.

"Oh?" Her voice turned sultry. "Do you want to take me to Tahoe, Mason?"

He quickly tried to estimate the amount he had in his bank account, which hadn't been much in those days, considering he hadn't been financially smart back then. When he realized it wouldn't be enough, he borrowed some of the money he had access to from the nursery. It wasn't a lot, only a couple hundred dollars, but it didn't take his father long to discover what he'd done. And, though Mason had quickly paid everything back, the damage to his father's trust in him had been done.

Mason had been spending the last two years trying to reclaim it, to make his work at the nursery something his dad could count on and to make his dad proud of him again.

And his relationship with Dakota? After all that, it hadn't been worth it. She still left him to be with Aaron or one of the other people she'd been seeing. In Tahoe, when he asked to be exclusive and said he loved her, she'd merely laughed at him. He'd never felt so small in his life.

His friends knew most of the story—except for the money part because he was too embarrassed about that fact. Maybe Isaac had a point that he needed to be protected from himself, but he didn't like it. He wanted to believe he had become wiser and less of a doormat.

"YOU MAY HAVE changed," Isaac said, "but there are some things you can't change, like being too nice, and I just don't want this coffee lady to take advantage of you."

Mason sorted through his cards before making a play. "To be clear, this is something my dad set up. He offered to give the shop a tree because they're going to have a coffee truck at Poinsettia Paradise this season. So, if anyone started this whole thing, it was my dad, and I'm just the middleman making sure she gets the tree he promised. That's all." Plus, Natalie had resisted exchanging numbers like he was asking for her bank card PIN number, so if she was trying to take advantage of him, she had an unusual tactic.

"Oh," Isaac replied.

He finally got the satisfaction of shutting Isaac down. He didn't get to live with his smugness for long though.

"But she's pretty?" Gemma asked, not about to let the matter go. "You like her?"

Mason thought about playing it cool, but who was he kidding. He wasn't able to hide much of anything, and he wanted to talk about her. "She's beautiful. She has this gorgeous hair. Oh, and I'm pretty sure she's Latina."

Isaac perked up. "What's her name? Maybe she's a relative of mine. And if she is, you're not allowed to date her because I'm not introducing someone who cheats at board games to the rest of my family. We take winning very seriously."

"Too seriously," Damon piped in, scraping fingers through longish brown hair before using a hair tie to pull it into a ponytail.

"Excuse me?" Isaac said, faking outrage. "See if I let you play on my charade team this Christmas Eve."

"Her name is Natalie and she works for Pony Expresso. And, as I said, she's beautiful. So do you know her? Is she related to you?" He wasn't sure if this would be a good thing or not. Isaac could provide him with more information and maybe put in a good word for him. They were, after all, the greatest of friends—and Isaac owed him something after all those free Christmas trees he'd been given over the years.

"Oh, so just because we're both Latino we must be related to each other?" Isaac wasn't able to maintain his bluff before he broke and a laugh escaped him. "As far as I'm aware she's not a relative, so I guess we're not going to be family by marriage anytime soon."

"Ha! Joke's on you. I don't need to get married to consider you family," Mason replied.

"God damn, Mase. Even when you're trying to snap back at someone you're still being wholesome about it. I'm touched, man. Seriously. And I take it back. You can marry any of my cousins you want. Maybe forget this other woman."

But he couldn't forget her because at that moment his phone buzzed. "I got a text!" He didn't mean to shout this. "Okay, everyone, calm down. Just calm down." The only one who needed to follow his advice was himself as everyone else was quite calm. Gameplay froze while everyone watched him read the text and respond before putting the phone in his pocket.

"Well?" said Damon.

"What happened? You know we're dying to know," Gemma added.

"Oh, uh…she just asked if she can stop by the farm after work on Tuesday and I replied, okay."

Isaac was aghast. "What? Are you serious? After all that, that's all you wrote? I take it back again. You're not allowed to go after any of my cousins because you clearly have no game."

"I'm trying to play it cool." Wasn't this the best course of action? After how their first conversation went, he wasn't about to add further evidence that he was weird or awkward.

Isaac shook his head. "That might have been too cool."

"Like I'm supposed to know the perfect balance between cool and too cool. I hate these games. Why can't flirting be more like Settlers of Catan? Clear-cut rules where I can trade her a grain card for a date or something. Easy."

"You need to invite her to board game night, honey." Gemma put a game piece on the board. "I don't want to be the Smurfette anymore."

"You should have at least thrown an emoji in there or something," Isaac said, blowing out an impatient breath.

Regardless of his lack of game, Mason had decided, when it came to the love game, he was ready to put his piece back on the board again.

Chapter Three

"THANKS FOR GOING with me, Mia," Natalie said to the driver of the old red truck currently traveling North on Highway 50 toward Apple Hill. Natalie's tiny compact seemed insufficient for Christmas tree transportation, and she had no problems roping her best friend into this errand.

"I haven't been to a Christmas tree farm since I was a kid. Do you think we're going to be greeted with hot apple cider? I adore hot apple cider. Ross and I will have to come back and get our own tree later." Mia was part nerd, part charmer and all heart and sunshine. Her golden-brown hair was in a neat ponytail and she sported her signature black-rimmed glasses while wearing a dark gray peacoat.

Natalie did her best to not roll her eyes at her friend's enthusiasm. She loved Mia, she did. The biracial Latina woman was great in so many ways, but not everything warranted such a positive outlook. Some things were a chore, and it was okay to treat them as such. Picking out a Christmas tree was just one more errand, putting it on the same level as grocery shopping and finding a birthday gift for her abuelita.

She checked her phone's navigation for the next direction before turning to her best friend again. "They're not even open yet so don't expect any hot apple cider. I'm only doing this because my uncle asked me to."

"I'm happy to come along. Maybe I'll find a new business that needs social media images. I've always been a 'two birds, one stone' type of lady. By the way, how is Enrique doing?" Mia had worked for a short time at Pony Expresso when she first returned to Placerville after years away. Of course, Enrique loved her because she'd been a model employee, and almost everyone liked her, even more cynical individuals like Natalie. Probably because Mia made Natalie's work and life easier, not harder. Plus, she was charming. Everyone should have at least one charming person in their life, because good luck followed them.

"He's fine. The same. Although, I'm currently mad at him for forcing me into this coffee truck thing by dangling a business partnership in front of my nose."

"I don't get that at all. You know more about his business than he does. You're almost always there. You've been working at the coffee shop since forever. You've earned this. You shouldn't have to prove anything else because you already have done so time and again." And this was how she got the position of being Natalie's best friend, because she was the most supportive person in the world. See? Charm.

"He said it was because of my supposedly *bad gambling habit*." Natalie did lazy bunny air quotes with her fingers around the words *bad gambling habit*.

"Oh."

Out of all the people in her life, Mia was the only one who knew the truth, because she wasn't a blabbermouth and knew how to keep secrets. Most importantly, Mia wasn't judgmental, unlike her uncle. If Tío Enrique thought gambling for a week was bad, then he *really* wasn't going to like what she actually did. There was no nice way to twist the truth so it was better to be blunt about it.

Natalie picked up guys.

Yes, she went to Tahoe for a week in December, and in April, for the exact purpose of picking up men to have a little no-strings-attached fun. She didn't always sleep with them, and sometimes it was more hanging out and heavy make-out sessions, but she also wasn't opposed to sex, if it felt safe and she was feeling it.

Natalie never made it a secret that she never planned to marry. Even if there were other men who shared the same frame of mind, it actually wasn't the ring or the marriage certificate or even men themselves that were the problem. She didn't want to be in a relationship. Period. She liked things to be easy, no hassle, nothing that couldn't be forgotten when she was ready to move on. There wasn't any point to go further than that.

Lake Tahoe had no shortage of guys who came from all over to have a boys' trip or were participating in a bachelor party. As long as they weren't in a relationship, Natalie didn't care. She took all the precautions she could with protection and never exchanged last names or other personal details, as she never wanted to run into them or be found again. Hence, her rule of no local guys. She preferred the type of guy who was a little bit of an asshole. In fact, having asshole tendencies made everything easier. Plus, she was almost positive serial killers couldn't be an asshole douche in public and also be successful at serial killing. Mia always insisted Natalie stay in constant contact in case there was ever a problem. Fortunately, besides bad sex, she hadn't yet gotten into any trouble.

While her private life was no one's business, she was also holding on to this dark secret, one she'd probably never be able to tell her family. While Enrique's side was extremely buttoned up and traditional, the other side wasn't much more open-minded about an independent, thirty-year-old Mexican-American woman doing what she wanted with her own body and not caring much about old traditions. And it was because of old traditions that she was leery about relationships and marriage in general.

When she was young, her mother would warn her daughters about the danger of falling for someone too quickly, using her own history as a cautionary tale. Rosa had married Miguel one week after meeting at a party, running away to elope at the state line against the wishes of all their family. As her mother told it, she saw Miguel and fell instantly in love with him. He had been the most handsome man she'd ever seen.

But everything that glitters isn't gold.

"Appearances aren't everything, mija. Don't be like me," she told Natalie time and time again. "Be smarter. Don't let your emotions prevent you from seeing the truth." And maybe they had been deeply in love or lust or whatever they wanted to call it. One thing was quite clear. It hadn't lasted, and both claimed it was the other's fault.

Regardless of the reason, the Gonzalez-Torres household only knew peace when her parents were not in the room together, preferring to bury themselves in their own interests on separate ends of the house. Interactions quickly unfolded into arguments or with them sniping at each other.

She once had a disagreement with her mother, when she felt Rosa was being especially unfair to Natalie's father. In a moment of exasperation, she had shouted, "What's the point of all this fighting, Mamá? Why did you just never leave?"

Her mother, equally frustrated, had responded, "You know why."

Natalie did know. It was because she'd become pregnant with her soon after. Her mother could point to wanting to do the best thing for her children by sticking it out or say it wasn't allowed due to her Catholic faith, but it didn't matter. Her daughter was the first link in the chain holding her in place. Her mother's love for her was part of the reason she had become stuck.

"Was it worth it?" Natalie had asked.

Rosa had only sighed before half-heartedly shrugging a hand in the air. "It is what it is."

In the end, it didn't matter. Even if her mother had replied it was all worth it, she might not have believed her anyway. Natalie knew the answer because it had almost happened to her.

She'd found herself nearly swept away in her own whirlwind relationship when she'd first started working for Enrique. She had foolishly let Stephen have sex with her without protection and considered eloping with him when he asked. She could have easily become sentimental over him. History would have repeated itself. But it hadn't. She'd gotten lucky. Stephen had been incredibly disappointed in her, telling her she wasn't the girl he thought she was; she wasn't worthy of all his effort. She'd been more disappointed in herself for being so foolish in getting caught up in the haze of infatuation. They fell out of love so quickly, there was no way it could have been real at all.

Because of this, she'd learned Rosa's lesson well. Don't get stuck. No matter how charming someone was, it's not worth it because it'll never last. Her relationships with men became much more pragmatic, and she didn't think she was truly missing anything. She didn't need anything else from them. She was okay with how her life was. Why mess with a life that was fine as is?

Tahoe would always be there to give her exactly what she needed and to leave it at that.

Except this December.

This December she wasn't going to Tahoe. She was spending the holiday season working at a Christmas tree farm, where she'd serve countless cups of hot chocolate and coffee to cheerful people similar to Mia.

"Maybe you can tell him, *just kidding, Enrique. I'm obsessed with camping*," Mia said, interrupting Natalie's internal thoughts.

She slid a look at her friend. "Camping? In December?"

"Okay, then maybe you're going skiing?" she suggested next.

"Then why do I always go in April?"

"Camping and skiing. A person can have more than one hobby."

"It's no use. My uncle is not going to be any more receptive to me saying, *Oh, by the way. I've been lying to the whole family all these years and I'm actually a huge outdoor activity aficionado. And the reason I lied is because I'm embarrassed of my walking sticks.* What kind of sense does that make? Besides, lying is probably going to put me in the same position in the eyes of my uncle, so I might as well keep my mouth shut and work the truck. I'm not going to be happy, but I can do this."

"Do you want to borrow my Christmas sweater? It has a reindeer on it with ornaments hanging off his antlers. It's really cute."

"No, thanks. But if you find a Christmas sweater with something like holiday spiders, I'll consider it."

Mia laughed. "Okay, I'll keep my eyes open."

They took the recommended exit and drove a couple miles off the highway, following the large green signs advertising Motherlode Nursery. While the weather was getting colder, the lack of snow and the surplus of evergreen trees kept the area looking quite green. With some decent precipitation, it was only a matter of time before the area became a winter wonderland.

"I thought we were going to Poinsettia Paradise," Mia said.

"Motherlode is the nursery part. Poinsettia Paradise is what they call the Christmas tree section, at least according to my uncle. It's all on the same property."

When Mia pulled past the wooden fence line, there was a small shop to the left called Motherlode Nursery with the same color green sign. Behind the shop were two large greenhouses and a farmhouse in the distance. To the right was a large lean-to with a blue banner reading *Poinsettia*

Paradise and it included the days and hours of operation. Mia parked the red truck in one of the designated spots belonging to the nursery and the women walked toward the lean-to.

Mason, dressed in a gray flannel work shirt, boots, and a navy-blue knitted beanie, was bent over, helping another man position a wooden post. At the sound of crunching gravel, he turned his head, standing to his full height and removing work gloves. He patted the other man, saying something before walking toward them.

"You guys find the place okay?" An easy smile spread across his face, but the expression wasn't limited to his mouth. Every emotion the guy had went straight to those hazel eyes. When his gaze fixed on hers, her heart reacted with a funny tiny hop. A slight jab in Natalie's side snapped her back.

"Hi," Mia piped in, reaching a hand toward him. "I'm Mia, Natalie's friend. We didn't have any trouble finding you. You guys have a lovely farm here. I'd love to come take pictures here someday. Oh, and I like your hat."

Mason shook Mia's hand. He pulled off his hat, and nervously twisted it in his hands before he returned it to his head. "Thanks. My mom is a big knitter. I keep telling her she should make things to sell for our little holiday marketplace, but she says that would only remove any joy she gets from the hobby."

"Yeah, I get that. My mom was a big quilter and would have probably said the same thing," she replied with a light laugh, showing off her single dimple. "Hobbies are only fun when they're not a job, right? Luckily for me, being a business marketing consultant isn't a hobby and is in fact my job… In case you're looking to update any images on your website or social media or whatever."

"Oh, yeah, maybe. I'll have to talk to my dad." He snuck a glance at Natalie who had yet to say a single word.

She was currently planning how to sneakily let it be known that Mia was married. This was a simple favor to Mason because it wasn't right for him to be fooled into thinking her friend was flirting. She wasn't—this was how Mia befriended everyone, (and got new freelancing jobs). Natalie could clear her throat and point an obvious finger at Mia's left hand. Or Natalie could attempt to beat Mia at her own sparkle. Except, when she opened her mouth, instead of sparkle, all that came out was: "I'm here for a tree," which did a great job of turning the light interaction into something more awkward. That's when she realized her brand of straightforwardness would never sparkle.

"Yeah. Yeah, sure," he responded. "I'm, uh, just going to grab a saw and then I can take you through the farm."

"You don't have any pre-cut trees?" She knew the farm offered people the option of choose-and-cut, but she expected there to also be the option of a grab-and-go Christmas tree, which was what she preferred.

He ran a hand along his neck. "Uh, no, sorry. It's still a little early in the season. We don't like to offer harvested trees until Thanksgiving weekend. But, trust me, picking your own tree is part of the fun."

"Great," Natalie said.

"Well, I can't wait to see more of the farm," Mia said, her dimple returning, and Mason left to retrieve whatever tools he needed.

Natalie gave her best friend a light pinch in her upper arm. "Knock it off, M."

"Ow! What?"

"He probably thinks you're flirting. I'm already getting the tree for free. I don't need you to charm your way into extra discounts or anything."

Mia's mouth dropped, clearly offended. "Because I said I liked his hat? I do like his hat. I wasn't flirting."

"Save it for your husband and tone it down a little."

Mia released a delicate snort. "Oh, so you're going to carry the conversation? You're doing really *great* so far."

Her best friend wasn't wrong, and this didn't make Natalie feel any better about her natural lack of sparkle. "Whatever. I'm only here to get a tree, not a date."

Mia looked at her with a spark of amused suspicion. "Why would you bring up dating? Do you also like his…hat?"

"No! I—Knock it off. You know my rule about local guys."

Mia laughed at her fluster. "This is Apple Hill, not Placerville. Does it still count as local?"

Mason soon returned with a lightweight, battery-operated saw and a large yellow Labrador he introduced as Bentley, his father's farm dog. Bentley greeted each of the women but became more focused on sniffing the tops of Mia's Converse sneakers.

"So, what kind of tree do you like?" Mason asked.

Bentley barked at a nearby bird before sprinting toward a dirt path, disappearing among trees. Natalie and Mia followed Mason toward the same path.

Natalie hadn't thought about trees at all and now understood why Mason had panicked picking a drink at Pony Expresso, because her brain scrambled to come up with something. "Oh, um, I guess if I have to get a tree, I prefer the ones with the metal pole running down the center that are pre-lit. So if we can go directly to the spot where you grow those, this can be over pretty quickly and we don't have to take up too much of your time."

A glint appeared in those hazel eyes, telling her he had a sense of humor and wasn't insulted by her pedestrian Christmas tree opinion. "Got it. You like Christmas trees of the fake kind." He stopped, his neck stretching as though he was searching for something, and he even did a few hops as though trying to see over the tops of trees. "Yeah, I don't think we've grown any of those this year, but maybe I can convince you of the benefits of a real tree."

She ran her hand along a nearby branch, the needles soft and pliable against her fingertips. This resulted in a stronger scent of fresh pine in the air as she passed through. Natalie tried not to dreamily sigh it into her lungs. Instead, she crossed her arms, demonstrating how hard it would be to convince her of anything. "You can do your best. I've heard all the talking points from Big Christmas before, and it hasn't swayed me yet."

Mason barked a laugh, and it was a pleasant, deep rumble. He set the lightweight saw to his shoulder, carrying it like a lumberjack with an ax, as if he'd never been more comfortable than when he was working among the trees. He was different than he was in the coffee shop. More at ease with himself. For whatever reason, this left her nervous, as though she needed to guard herself more or she might start considering Apple Hill an acceptable distance away from Placerville to be considered "not local."

"Big Christmas?"

"Mm-hmm. A very powerful lobby. I believe they follow G.I.F.T. Growers…uh, Implode…Fake Trees, or something."

"Implode? Are we farmers and anarchists?"

"Definitely the worst combination of professions," Natalie said, exaggerating her level of dismay. She didn't want to admit it, but maybe her day at the tree farm wasn't the worst chore she ever had to force herself to go through. It was turning out to be more entertaining than grocery shopping at least.

"Why isn't it Growers Against Fake Trees?" he asked seriously, as if her Christmas tree conspiracy theories were to be taken sincerely and were not the most outrageous thing he'd ever heard.

"Because that spells G.A.F.T. and I don't think that's a real word."

"But being against fake trees is something I can actually get behind. I wouldn't even know how to implode a tree unless it involves a black hole or something."

"*Ha!* And I *knew* you were prejudiced against fake Christmas trees. I can see it written all over you." She waved a hand over his torso to indicate what she considered all of him.

He shrugged, but the glint of amusement was still there. "I wasn't trying to hide it. I want that sweet Christmas tree cash and someday this farm will be mine. But I can see that I have my work cut out for me as you appear to be a customer of discerning plastic taste. Luckily, I'm a Christmas tree expert so you just tell me what you like about a fake tree and I'll see what I can do to make sure you're just as happy with one of ours."

While she did her best to maintain her poker face, he intrigued her in spite of everything. "Okay, fine. Fake trees are more economical. I don't have to buy them every year."

"I don't think you're getting more economical than this year, because I'm giving you any tree you want. For free."

"Hmm. I guess you're right. Okay, fake trees are more environmentally friendly, because you don't have to cut a tree down just for the sake of decorating the inside of your house for a few weeks out of the year."

"We practice eco-friendly harvesting, which means we utilize stump culturing. So, when we cut a tree, it's never at ground level but above some of the lower branches. This keeps the tree alive and allows it to grow another top. Do you know if the energy and resources going into creating your *fake* tree are environmentally friendly?"

Natalie slid a glance at Mia whose only response was to raise a single eyebrow, which meant her friend was impressed with the man. She had to work to keep her own jaw from jarring apart. Okay, he didn't come to play, and, despite herself, she liked it.

She considered going with the argument that putting away fake trees was easier. Natalie hardly gave two thoughts about packing away an item in which she hadn't allowed herself to become emotionally invested in the first place.

Except, she had a suspicion this might reveal something sad about herself.

Instead, she blurted, "Fake trees don't stink." Natalie didn't actually have a problem with the natural scent of Christmas trees, but she committed to this line of argument and had no choice but to proceed full steam ahead. "If I wanted to feel like I was living inside of a forest, I would exchange my apartment for a tent."

"You don't like the smell of Christmas trees?" His face reflected utter confusion. Even Mia gave her an odd look.

Natalie had no choice but to stick with the opinion, no matter how ridiculous it was. "Nope."

Mason gave this one a bit of thought, appearing stumped as he scratched along his jawline. "Gee, you might have me there."

Natalie almost threw her arms in the air in sweet victo-ry—

"Except…"

What? *No*! There was no exception. The man wasn't allowed to win when she had her heart set on gloating about the superiority of fake trees, ones that didn't slowly die on her, and never let her down because she knew what to expect, which was *nothing*.

"You might like having a white fir," Mason replied.

"White fur?" Natalie, confused, exchanged a glance with Mia. "What does white fur have to do with Christmas trees? Are those similar to designer trees owned by rich people, holding 14k gold ornaments?"

He offered a patient smile. "No. White fir. It's like a Douglas fir or a noble fir. In fact, we're actually standing in the middle of them because, if I was to pick a tree for you, this is the one I would go with. You seem like a white fir kinda gal to me."

"Oh." Natalie didn't know how else to respond, and she was in danger of melting a little, except she caught Mia bringing a hand to her chest as if she was on the verge of swooning. *Stop it.* It was a silly tree. Natalie strengthened her resolve.

"They don't look like anything special," she said. Although, the white firs did look healthy…and also round and lush and full, if Natalie was pushed into saying something more about them. Okay, fine, they were better-looking than any of the typical Christmas trees she was used to seeing in the pop-up tree stand in the Rite-Aid parking lot. It looked like the type of tree that would be nice to hug, kind of like Mason himself.

He shook his head, coming nearer, too near, until she was sure she'd be engulfed by both a large tree and an equally large man. He reached for a nearby branch beside her face, crushing it in his palm. "Smell."

She tentatively took a breath, expecting the usual pine scent, before taking a deeper one, letting the sweet, bright notes of something citrus-like fill her lungs. It took her by complete surprise. Her gaze lifted to him. "Is it oranges?"

"Something like that." A smile lit his face.

"How did you do that?"

"Do what?"

"Get it to smell like that?" It was intoxicating, wonderful, like being surrounded by a spicy citrus on a sunshiny winter day, one where the sky was the brightest shade of blue and the snow sparkled like jewels. She wanted to crush the whole tree to her chest.

"Do you think we're out here spritzing our trees with perfume or something?"

"Or something? You are a part of Big Christmas after all."

"But I must be better than those other Christmas tree lobbyists. I can tell that I've won you over to Team Real Christmas Tree with the white fir."

"I don't know if I'd go that far." All this was proving was that Mason had some gumption in him, which had the potential to be trouble for her, considering she might be working within the same vicinity of the guy for several weekends in a row.

"You want one of the other trees then? We can keep looking. I'm perfectly happy spending the day with you ladies as you decide."

To maintain the pretense that she was considering other types of trees would be a waste of time for everyone. Her heart had already chosen and, once her heart was set, it was pretty much a done deal. "All right, fine. I want a white fir."

"You just need to pick out which one you want. You guys brought a good vehicle for transporting your tree, right? Otherwise, I don't mind bringing it to the coffee shop."

"Mia brought—"

"Actually, no," Mia said. "Sorry. I forgot to tell you, Natalie. I…can't bring your tree back."

"What?" she said. "Why not?"

"Uh, because I…just got the truck washed for Ross and I don't want to get sap all over it."

"Mia—"

"Sorry, I should have told you earlier. It totally slipped my mind." She flashed a dimpled smile at Mason before pointing to the exact spot where her brain was supposed to be located. "You know how it is, when you have a hundred things running around in your mind all the time? It's easy for things to just slip through. I really hate to put the extra burden on you, but would it be okay for you to deliver it to Pony Expresso yourself? And she doesn't have a boyfriend, or anyone, to help her carry a big tree in. Both Natalie and I would really appreciate it—and my husband too because then his truck won't get sappy."

Natalie glowered at her soon-to-be ex-best friend. Mia's weird powers of persuasion could be used for good or for evil and she clearly woke up today and chose straight violence.

Mason took Mia's fake excuses in stride. "Yeah, sure. Not a problem." He patted the pockets of his flannel shirt. "I, uh, don't have any ribbon on me but why don't you guys pick out a tree while I grab some. We can tie it around a branch to mark it, and I'll cut it right before bringing it over so it's fresh. This way you have time to get a water stand set up or rearrange the area you want the tree in. Does that work?"

Mia answered before Natalie could. "Yes! Great! That sounds great. Thank you so much."

He whistled for Bentley, who came sprinting from among the trees, before he went to retrieve the ribbon for their task.

"What the hell, Mia?" Natalie said as soon as they were alone. She loved Mia with all her heart but that didn't mean she wasn't going to rip her a new butthole, she'd just do so with love.

Her friend removed a random pine needle from the sleeve of her jacket, the picture of casual innocence. "What?"

"You know exactly what. Don't act like you aren't trying to manipulate things when you just happen to throw out I'm single and you're married and I happen to need a strong man to carry a *big tree* for me. I don't need anything carried for me and even if I do, there's Diego who can do it and—Did you have to be so obvious about it?"

"I'm not sure what you mean. You just got me thinking about what you said before, and I started to worry that maybe he did think I was flirting with him. All I was trying to do was make sure he knew I'm totally unavailable. And I would think you'd agree with me that leading a guy on, especially a nice guy like Mason, would be the wrong thing to do. So, the right thing would be for me to nip the whole thing in the bud. Therefore, there's nothing for you to be angry about and all I've done is proven myself to be a person of upstanding integrity. While I can see how you might perceive things differently, it certainly wasn't my intention as I've just now explained." She finished her speech by adjusting her glasses with a smug confidence.

Natalie stared at her flatly with her arms crossed because it wasn't worth the effort to respond to all that, not when there was a clear reason why Mia had been a star of her high school debate team back in the day. It was obvious her strategy was to do nothing more than to talk circles around Natalie until she was too dizzy to respond. Sometimes giving the right look proved to be a better tool against her fancy way with words.

It didn't take any time for her friend to break. "All right, all right, I'm sorry. But in my defense, you're not watching all of this unfold from my perspective."

"What are you talking about? I know what happened. I was standing right here the whole time."

"Yeah, but you were seeing it from your perspective, which isn't the same at all."

"Huh?"

Mia's face softened. "You know when you see a couple and you wonder, how in the world did they get together? Nothing about them makes any sense."

Of course, Natalie knew. She had this very same experience with her own parents. Regardless, she wasn't sure what any of this had to do with her or Mason, or anything at all. "Okay."

"You and the Christmas tree guy. It was like the opposite. You guys make total sense. I could see everything in my head." Her brown eyes even took on a dreamy quality as if she was ten seconds away from swooning again.

"Are you kidding me? I just met the guy." She laughed because this was nothing but an absurd theory from one delusional friend. "And he's not even my type."

Mia adjusted her glasses again. "Oh, okay. Well, the only thing I know about your type is *not local*." She copied Natalie's previous lazy style of finger bunny ears. But she stopped, seeming to change tact. "What if I wasn't doing it for you? What if I was doing it for Ross?"

Sometimes Mia said things that only made sense to her. "What the hell does your husband have to do with this?"

"I don't know. I like Mason. Ross needs some friends and I think they'd get along great. If you guys were hanging out, then they would probably become best friends. Don't you want Ross to have a new friend?"

"Are you serious right now?"

"No. I just like giving you things to think about."

"Whatever. I'm not going to date someone just to give Ross a friend. Because I don't want to have a boyfriend or a relationship or any of that, so stop trying to make something happen when nothing happened at all in the first place."

"Again, because you were seeing everything from over there and not over here where I happen to be standing."

Natalie glared at her. "I like it better when we have our discussions in Spanish."

"Only because I'm still learning and it's hard for me to make a nuanced, foolproof argument when I have a limited vocabulary. But I guess having an advantage is the only way you think you can win, chica."

Exactly. Having an advantage on things was the only way Natalie liked to play, one where she could predict the end results. If the house always won, then she wanted to be the house.

After wasting time arguing, they only had five minutes to pick a tree before Mason returned with some red ribbon. Natalie resisted the urge to press her nose into the tree one more time. She'd hold off until the tree was in her shop and she could do it when no one was around to make fun of her. What did Mason smell like? Being surrounded by Christmas trees all day made it easy to assume his scent could only be good, but then she realized she was watching him again. She tore her focus away.

The group took the small dirt path again, making their way to the farm entrance. Mia made sure to put herself on the outside of the group, forcing Natalie and Mason to walk side by side. He slid a glance at her. "There's a lot going on at the farm right now, preparing things for the upcoming opening weekend. So it might be a few days until I can cut the tree and bring it to you. Is it okay if I text you later to let you know when I might be able to bring it by?"

"Anytime is probably fine. You don't need to t—"

"That's a great idea. I would think Enrique would want the manager to be there for something like this," Mia inserted lightly, and Natalie threw another glare at her friend.

"Okay, you can text me. I'm usually there pretty early but you know how busy mornings can get in a coffee shop. Maybe Mia wouldn't mind helping me out."

"Ugh, no. I'm done with early mornings at the coffee shop. If I'm going to drink coffee early, it's going to be made by Ross and brought to me in bed with kisses. I'm sure this is something that you and Mason won't have any problems figuring out on your own. About the tree, of course. I would never presume to make assumptions about kissing, as some people need to do a lot more figuring out than others. Hypothetically speaking, of course."

She poked Mia's side in order to get her to shut up before attempting to change the subject away from Mia's marital bliss and weird ramblings. "So, do you guys actually get poinsettias at your Poinsettia Paradise?"

"We do," Mason replied, smiling. "When you come back

for opening day, you'll see. Do you need any for the coffee shop?"

She felt her cheeks heat at the implication that she may have been dropping a hint. "Oh, no, that's okay. I shouldn't be trusted with live plants. I-I was just wondering that's all."

Silence filled the air. She wondered if Mia had been right earlier and maybe she did purposely wear blinders. What if there was some kind of spark between her and Mason and she was falling into her normal habit of pretending there wasn't?

They had reached the parking lot with him escorting them the whole way, arriving at Ross's old truck which, most definitely, was not sparkly clean. She suspected the last time it had been touched by water was due to rainfall. Mason stood nearby, rubbing his big hands together as if to warm them from a chill, studying her.

"Thanks for your help," Mia said.

Her words snapped his focus to her. "Yeah, no problem. I guess I'll talk to you later, Natalie." That hazel gaze slowly slid back in her direction.

Natalie gripped her arms to her chest, her best attempt at holding herself together. "Okay. I hope I'm not pulling you away from your farm too much."

"It's fine. I just work on the farm. I actually live in Placerville. So it's not out of my way or anything."

She exchanged a glance with Mia who looked at her nervously. "Oh, so you're actually a local guy then? Good to know." She got into the truck and shut the door.

And, with that information, Mason became just another man Natalie intended to keep in a box labeled, *Business Acquaintance Only*.

Chapter Four

AFTER THE WOMEN departed, Mason tried to return to work but thoughts of Natalie made it difficult. He was happy when his dad's oldest employee, Charlie, interrupted with, "Your dad was looking for you."

Good. Any conversation with his dad was sure to bring his focus on to something other than the beautiful woman with the sparkling dark eyes and smoky voice, one that made it sound as if she'd recently woken up. She'd appeared on the farm wearing a white jacket with a bright red scarf, reminding him of Sierra snow flowers popping up through the snow in springtime. It was fire and ice, just like her. Both elements could be dangerous and, yet, he didn't want to avoid either one.

He entered the greenhouse, finding his father checking the soil of one of the many potted poinsettias. Bentley, the Labrador, was now snoring under one of the potting shelves.

"You wanted to see me?"

His father's aging brown eyes turned to him. "Ah, Mason. I heard you were helping Enrique's niece. How'd that go? She got everything she needed?"

He wished he could have done more than given her a Christmas tree but, at the moment, he was happy to be guaranteed future interactions with her. "Yeah, fine. I'm going to deliver the tree to her later this week."

"I think Charlie is going into town later today and can probably—"

"I think Natalie needs to make room or get a tree stand or something. Probably better if I just do it."

His father gave him an odd look, like he knew Mason was making excuses and possibly getting himself sucked in by a woman again. But he was being friendly and nice, and Natalie already knew him, so there was no reason to bring Charlie into the picture. And, okay, maybe he did like her but that didn't mean he wasn't about to make the same mistake he had made with Dakota. He cleared his throat and was determined to sound as mature as possible. "So, was there something in particular you wanted to talk about?"

Daniel sank onto a nearby stool, returning the poinsettia to the shelf. "How much are you expecting to inherit this business, Mase?"

"Uh, what?"

"The business. Is this what you really want? Are you expecting to take over for Mom and me after we're gone?"

Mason wasn't sure what he expected from this conversation, but it wasn't this. He woke up this morning with nothing but excitement at the prospect of seeing Natalie again and that was it. While he was trying hard to prove to his father that he could respect his father's business and take it seriously, he wasn't sure he was ready for this conversation yet. He wanted more time to prove himself, so when the business was put in his hands, he'd earned it.

The problem was that his parents had Mason late in their

lives. His mom had been forty-five and his dad had been ten years older than that when he'd been born. He'd grown up with his parents frequently mistaken for his grandparents. This wasn't necessarily a bad thing as he had always been loved by both of them, but he couldn't help thinking about how he wouldn't have as much time as his peers. The pressure of limited time left a weight in his stomach, like he had to hurry up before he squandered another opportunity.

It didn't help that his father frequently used the phrase *After I'm gone*. Whether this implied his parents' retirement from Motherlode Nursery and/or their move to Arizona to be closer to his mother's sister and/or his father's eventual earthly demise, it felt like Mason always had to be prepared even though there was nothing wrong with them.

At least nothing was wrong yet. This time felt different. His father didn't seem to be asking him about some hypothetical plan in the distant future. His heart panicked at all the horrible possibilities his father was trying to prepare him for. "Is something wrong?"

His father's gaze snapped to him. "What? No, I-I just thought it was time we talk seriously about it and I…" Daniel stopped, taking a moment to pause. "I think this is going to be our last season."

A million questions flooded Mason's mind. The first one being, was the business in financial trouble and was it somehow his fault? His past mistake of previously taking a few hundred dollars from the business no longer seemed insignificant and maybe his shortsightedness had caused a greater consequence than he originally thought. "Are things that bad we have to close?"

Daniel's face reflected surprise. "No, It's not that. You know your mom wants to move to Arizona and we both just feel it's time. We're ready to retire. And Charlie offered to buy the business."

He didn't hear anything after that because what the fuck? Charlie? Sure, the man had always been his dad's right-hand man but—He couldn't deny it. Mason had assumed he'd get the business.

Why not me?

Deep down he knew why.

"You don't want me to have the business," he said calmly to his father even though he didn't feel the emotion at all. He was trying not to feel betrayed or appear entitled.

His father pressed his lips together. "It's not that, it's just Charlie has a lot of experience and really knows the business—"

"I grew up in this business."

"But are you here because you want to be or because that's just where you ended up?"

He wasn't sure how to answer that question because it was possible for both of those things to be true at once.

His father must have taken his silence as confirmation of the latter option. "This isn't a punishment. And Charlie focuses one hundred percent on the nursery and tree farm. It's not a hobby for him. He takes this seriously."

Mason understood the implication. It always returned to the same thing. It's not that he didn't take his father's business seriously, it was more that his father always wanted things done in a particular way. Anything veering from this path meant it was being done wrong and not taken seriously.

Mason's detour from his father's path happened when he became interested in beekeeping a few years ago. What started as curiosity, became so much more to him.

"Neither Motherlode nor the bees are a hobby for me either. Besides, I would think someone who owns a nursery would understand the importance of bees, especially in terms of agriculture. Not only can they provide another source of revenue that fits in perfectly with our current business in providing honey, which may I remind you has been more successful every year since I've been selling it at the marketplace. But if I can expand, I can rent hives to some of the nearby farms that pay a lot for pollination services. With this extra revenue, it can make weathering the off-season a lot easier."

His father sighed in response because they'd had this same discussion many times before with neither side bending. "Maybe I need to see you master the core business first before you start gambling on something else. You didn't build this business. Your mother and I did. And it's not that I think you'd purposely make bad decisions, it's just that you're still quite young and have a lot to learn. Let's be honest, are you really ready for this kind of risk? Do you really want to have something like a business bankruptcy following you around the rest of your life? You need to understand that a business is bigger than you and your needs. You can't let something, like a crush on a girl, cloud your judgment."

And there it was. The same old argument popping up to bite him in the ass again. "Come on, Dad! Am I ever going to live that down? That was a while ago."

"Six months wasn't that long ago."

"Six months? Try two years!"

Six months. Two years. It didn't seem to matter. To his dad, the event was fresh enough to always feel like yesterday and Mason could never escape the shadow.

"I don't want to argue about this again," Daniel said. "What's done is done and I have to do what's best for your mother and me. And even though it doesn't feel like it, maybe this is the best for you too."

Mason threw up his arms in frustration. "Apparently, it will never be done because no matter how hard I try to make up for that, how much I apologize, it's always going to sit between us."

"All I'm trying to do is protect you."

He did his best not to explode. "Why does everyone act like I need to be protected from myself? Like I'm incapable of learning or improving. Is this really how you see me?" Having this revelation hurt. How could it not when it seemed like his own father didn't believe in him. The mistake he'd made two years ago cost him a lot more than whatever monetary amount he had borrowed.

Daniel studied him, his expression shuttering as he rubbed a hand across his face. "Mase." He sighed. "I'm sorry. I didn't—I didn't mean to say you're not capable. It's just that I worry that after I'm gone… You don't know what it's like to have a business all on your shoulders. To have employees who completely depend on all this to survive year after year. It's tough on me and I've been doing it since before you were even born." His father took a few moments to focus on him. "Do you really want this? You've decided this is what you want for your life? And don't bullshit me. It's fine if you don't. I won't be upset if you want something else. I just want you to be sure."

"Yes." Even though he tried to sound absolutely sure, a wave of fear went through him at the small seed of doubt planting itself inside him. Could he actually do this? Could he have all that pressure directly on him and do as well as his father had done? And what if he did his best and lost it all? How could he manage the guilt of being the one responsible for ruining his father's legacy? But, in spite of this, Mason decided he did want this.

"I want it," he said.

Daniel nodded slowly. "This thing with Charlie isn't set. We're just talking right now. But how about this? I'm going to give you this season of Poinsettia Paradise. It's all on you. You'll be the boss and run the show. And don't see this as a test, but rather as an opportunity for you to see if you really want this for yourself."

"Okay," Mason agreed.

But regardless of what his father said, he couldn't see it as anything but the biggest test of his life. He had to make it work, to finally prove his worth once and for all.

Chapter Five

WHEN NATALIE SLIPPED on her jacket, as she was leaving her apartment, she discovered a spool of red ribbon in one of the pockets. She'd forgotten Mason had handed it to her while he tied the ribbon around a tree branch. She had slipped it into her pocket, forgetting to return it.

She could bring it to Pony Expresso and give it to him whenever Mason delivered her white fir Christmas tree. Except, this was risky as she might forget. Or he could buy another spool. This was cheap gift wrapping ribbon, after all, and easily replaceable.

Regardless, she should tell him.

On her way to her car, she found their previous text exchange and typed,

Before you file a police report, your ribbon wasn't stolen. I put it in my pocket and forgot to give it back to you. Remind me to return it when you deliver the tree.

As Natalie drove to her parents', she thought about the text, wondering how quickly he'd respond. Was the text *too* friendly? Perhaps she should have stated, *Got your ribbon,* and left it at that. Did he really need a whole explanation about sticking the ribbon in her pocket, as if she was being cute or something? Which was absolutely not her intention at all.

Her parents' standard-tract home was a mere five-minute drive away. After parking in front of their house, she checked her cell.

No reply.

He was probably busy felling Christmas trees or whatever a person normally did on a tree farm. Serving eviction notices to owls and squirrels? He did say the farm was busy preparing for the season. Besides, it wasn't as if her text required a reply or anything. Only…he seemed like the kind of guy who'd give someone a response, even a small one.

Whatever.

She didn't care anyway.

Natalie entered her family home, finding her grandmother sitting in the gray-blue rocking recliner, watching some kind of reality-TV garden makeover show. "Ay, mi amor," the older woman said.

She went to her, pulling a wrapped gift from her bag and depositing it into the older woman's frail hands. She dropped a kiss into the center of her grandma's head. "Abuelita. Para tu cumpleaños."

Her grandma went through the usual spiel of telling her granddaughter that her love was enough, and she didn't need any gifts and to save her hard-earned money. All this was said as the woman eagerly ripped into the wrapping paper.

Natalie waved off her grandmother's words which she'd heard a hundred times before. "Lo sé . Just open it."

"Ay!" Abuelita said. "Mi amor, mi amor." She hugged the Chris Evans calendar to her chest as though Natalie had presented her grandmother with jewels.

"You love it?"

"Sí."

Natalie's sisters thought their grandmother's obsession with Chris Evans was hilarious, but she found it sweet and didn't mind indulging the woman. She hoped when she was her grandmother's age, she had her own Chris Evans items to get excited about. A Chris Evans calendar, like a fake tree, wouldn't disappoint her.

"Natalie?" her mother called .

She walked into the kitchen, checking her phone and, again, being confused at the lack of notifications. Were text services down? She should text Mia to be sure.

lol I accidentally stole Mason's xmas tree ribbon

Natalie's phone vibrated as she took a seat at the table and reached for a chip to dip into the guacamole her mom set out.

Mia responded, *You should definitely put that in a keepsake box. Maybe it's a sign.*

She replied with a laughing emoji and a rolling-eyes one, because they both knew she was the last person who'd ever have a keepsake box. But the exchange proved her phone still had the ability to receive text messages. The mystery of why she wasn't getting a response from Mason was still unsolved.

"Who are you talking to, mija?" her mother said, putting a glass of water in front of her. "Un hombre?"

She resisted another eye roll even though her mother's inquiry deserved it. "I'm just talking to Mia."

"You should have invited her. You know she's welcome to join, especially since it's Abuelita's party. There's plenty of food. Ask her and tell her to bring the family."

"She and Ross went out of town to visit her family in Sacramento."

"But she knows she's always welcome to join us?"

"Yeah. She knows." Natalie checked her phone again and there was only a response from Mia with a winking emoji blowing a kiss.

"Nat! Did you get Abuelita that calendar?" her youngest sister, Carla, yelled from the other room before flouncing into the room with all energy and no grace. "She's hugging that thing like it's her favorite grandchild. Thanks for making the rest of our gifts look like garbage in comparison. You know I'm not good at buying gifts."

"Yeah, because you buy exactly what you want."

Carla stuck out her tongue while being adorably cute, because out of all the sisters, she was the one who got everything she ever wanted. Her dark hair hung in glossy curls, and she wore a headband with rhinestone cat ears. "That's what you're supposed to do. Haven't you heard the saying?"

"I don't think Abuelita wants the newest glitter eye shadow palette. She doesn't even wear makeup." Unlike Carla who treated her face like a canvas and did perfect makeup almost every day.

The chip making its way to Carla's mouth stopped midflight. "Did Mari tell you that? Okay, but do you know what she bought? Slippers. Every year she buys Abuelita a pair of slippers."

"Yeah, because she actually wears them every day and they're worn out," Mariana, Natalie's other sister, said while entering the kitchen and running a hand through her partially shaved head of short dark locks. “Unlike your gift.”

“Abuelita!” Carla yelled through a mouthful of a half-eaten tortilla chip. “I’m going to do your makeup for the party, okay?”

Their grandmother responded but it was unintelligible. Although, to Natalie’s ears, it sounded like a prayer to one saint or another. Regardless, her sister wasn’t discouraged as she grabbed another chip before leaving.

Mariana took a seat beside Natalie. Between all sisters, they were the closest. Mariana, who was an EMT, was only a year younger than Natalie. They were almost equal in temperament and would work out and run summer marathons together. They kept each other steady both physically and emotionally.

Her sister leaned toward her and said, “Did you hear Luis was coming?”

“She’s taking him back?” Natalie pressed her face into her palm. Mariana lifted a hand as if to say *what can we possibly do*.

“Mijas, you need to talk to your sister about Luis. No one listens to me. What do I always tell you?” their mother said.

“Don’t make the same mistake I made?” Natalie replied.

This had been the absolute right advice because Carla also found herself the victim of what was turning out to be the family curse. At least in this case, she’d dated Luis for a whole six months before marrying him, but it still hadn’t mattered. It was later discovered that the man had been married twice already due to his habit of being unfaithful. The last Natalie heard, Carla had poured cooking oil all over his car. It might have been the most Natalie had ever admired her youngest sister. Hearing she was considering taking him back was disappointing. The couple had bounced from in love to out of love more times than she could remember. If this was love, Natalie didn't want it.

"That's right. You learn from my life. It is not all love and rainbows. Choose someone wisely," their mother said.

"I already chose not to choose anyone, so I don't think you have to worry about me." Scooting closer to her sister, Natalie asked in a low voice, "How's everything else going so far?"

"The same ol', same ol'," her sister responded with a shrug before digging in the bowl for a tortilla chip. "Dad's hunkering down in the garage. You know, the usual."

Natalie was lucky to have one sister she could vent and confide in, especially when it came to their parents' marriage. Mariana was willing to share the load with her when it came to keeping peace in the house. The situation didn't bother her as much as it did Natalie, as she was more willing to let it roll off her back and accept the mantra of their mother: *It is what it is.* But Mariana did whatever was necessary for Natalie's sake and always brought a calming presence.

It didn't take long for her mother to start muttering about their father while fiddling with the dishwasher.

"What's wrong?" Natalie asked.

"I swear that man is no good for anything. I ask and I ask for a new dishwasher, and do I get a new dishwasher? No. Will he fix it? Also, no. I'm just expected to do all this by hand. I cook all the food. He should at least do something around here. You girls, go talk to him. You tell him to buy a new dishwasher. He doesn't listen to me. This is what I mean when I say you need someone who is actually useful."

"I'll go talk to him," Mariana said, starting to rise, but Natalie stopped her.

"That's okay. I got this. I'm sure you've been playing referee too much already." She was the eldest, and therefore, it seemed only fair that she'd step in the middle as much as she could.

She made her way to her father's domain: the garage. Miguel was a mechanic by trade, but there were no cars in here. Instead, her father had it set up as his own personal man cave, complete with recliner, TV, and his own mini fridge. He'd spend all his time in the garage if there was less of a chance of dealing with her mother. Natalie suspected her father sometimes slept in the recliner. Today, Miguel was bundled beneath a large, ratty throw blanket.

"Hey, Dad," Natalie said, hopping her ass on top of the dryer.

"Ah, mija. Did you just get here?"

"Yup." If she admitted to spending the first ten minutes visiting her mother in the kitchen, it might cause hurt feelings on her father's part. Natalie learned early it was better to lie. "As I was coming through to visit you, I heard mom complaining about the dishwasher being broken. I wasn't sure if you knew or not?"

Her father muttered to himself before saying, "I already told her I'd fix it. She's the one who's using it wrong and broke it in the first place. If she wants a dishwasher, she needs to take care of it."

"Dad. That thing has got to be over twenty years old. It's

going to break eventually, and it did. It's not fair to Mom to not have a working dishwasher."

"Why are you always on her side?"

"This isn't a side. I'm just telling you the dishwasher is broken and the household itself could benefit from a new one."

Miguel didn't move from the recliner. If the dishwasher was going to be replaced or fixed, it wasn't happening today. Instead, he shook his head. "You don't know what she says to me. You don't know because you aren't here. Do you know the last time she let me share the bed with her? I bought that bed. I bought this house. I did that, and she won't let me sleep in the bed with her."

Natalie *did* know because this had been going on for years. She had more knowledge about what was going on (or not going on) in their bedroom than she ever wished to be privy to. It wasn't as simple as picking one single villain who was the root cause of the family's problems, because both her parents were equally disrespectful and rude to one another. Whatever started this war had never been clear to her. Both parents showed their love for each of their daughters, but they couldn't bring themselves to show anything resembling love to each other. Instead of talking to each other or a therapist or doing anything to change the situation, they'd rather complain about each other to whatever family member would listen to them.

"You're going to come out to the kitchen for Abuelita's party, right? The rest of the family is going to be here too and it's weird when you stay in the garage, Dad."

"I bought this house, and I don't even get to enjoy it.

Your mom is so mean to me. What did I do in life to deserve such a mean wife? You and your sisters are my only joy, and you won't come to visit me every day."

"You can come into the house. You're not stuck out here. If you guys can just not say anything mean to each other, then you won't fight."

Miguel plucked at the fibers of his blanket. "She wants me to be miserable."

"You just sit out here, and you don't fix the dishwasher. What are you good for?" her mother said as she entered the garage to grab a roll of paper towels from a shelf.

"Mom, stop."

"You don't know how to use the dishwasher."

"Oh, so I cook and I clean for you and my family all these years and I don't know how to use the things in my own home? You just want to punish me."

"If I can't use my bed, then you don't need to use a dishwasher. You've already taken everything else, including my soul."

"You've taken *my* soul! Do you think I want to be with you?" her mother yelled.

"I wish I never saw you at that party," her father spat out. "You're a mean, ugly woman, the worst wife."

Thankfully, Enrique appeared, helping Natalie separate her parents once again, her mother storming from the garage while spitting further insults. How her parents had gone from being in love to this was the biggest mystery of all.

"Miguel," Enrique said. "Come on. Everyone's here for the party. This is a celebration. Let us have peace for this afternoon. You can do that at least."

Her father stood, making his way toward the door. "Did you know, Rico, she doesn't even let me share the bed? I am so unhappy."

"We're going to have some good food and right now we'll try to be happy. Okay?" Enrique patted his brother on the shoulder before they all entered the kitchen. By keeping each parent occupied with other things and conversations, the party was able to proceed and was festive for the most part. Halfway through the party, her father shuffled back to the garage and disappeared again. They kept trying but for some reason he always chose to exclude himself.

"Natalie," Enrique said at one point. "I want to talk to you about the trailer."

"What trailer?" she responded while eating a slice of tres leches cake.

"For you to use at the Christmas farm. I got one for a really good price, but we need to tow it there."

At this point she was completely confused. "We're using a trailer? What kind of trailer? Why aren't we using a regular food truck or something?" If Natalie was going to do this, she hoped for something cute, not any old thing her uncle found for a good deal.

"It's one of those trailers they carry the horses in."

"What? We're using a damn horse trailer?" This whole plan was becoming worse and worse. She was going to be working on a Christmas tree farm in the cold with a man who was currently ignoring her. *And* she had to do it from a horse trailer? Natalie wasn't sure if a Pony Expresso partnership was worth this indignity.

"It's not what you think. It's been repurposed and outfitted inside so it's food-service ready. It's cute. You'll like it. And it was a lot cheaper than a food truck. Plus, you don't need all that room."

"Is it white and does it look like a horse trailer?"

"Why does that matter? If you want to be an owner, you'll make it work."

Natalie considered joining her father in garage purgatory because, apparently, that's where one went when they were unhappy with what life had dealt them. Instead, she strengthened her resolve. "Fine. I'll figure it out." She would because she had to.

After getting home, Natalie went to plug her phone into a charger but was surprised to discover a text from Mason. Her heart did a tiny leap within her chest.

Thank you for confessing to your crimes. We'll call off Bentley. He's a good dog but a bad detective. He's been falsely accusing birds. I'm not telling you so you feel bad, but this crime has ruined a lot of lives.

Instead of plugging her phone in, she carried it with her to the bathroom, sending a quick text in response. *That would certainly explain all the new bird shit on my windshield.*

She set her phone on the countertop before wrapping her hair in a loose bun and washing her face. She was halfway through brushing her teeth when her phone screen lit again. *That can't be good. Luckily, it's only been little birds but if they go to the blue jays, it's probably all over for you. Everyone knows blue jays are the mobsters of the bird world. I don't want to scare you but…I'm just glad I'm not you.*

Natalie almost choked on the toothbrush hanging from her mouth. *I'm not worried. I'm sure even mobster blue jays can be bribed with a little seed money.*

I…I'm pretty sure you're a woman after my own heart… It's

too bad you have a target on your back. I can't afford to get caught up in this bird nest.

Natalie rinsed her toothbrush, catching her reflection in the mirror. She had this ridiculous grin on her face, one that didn't belong there because she had no business having anything resembling a flirty-type conversation with a guy she'd already decided not to get involved with. She ripped the ponytail holder from her head, scraped her fingers through her hair as she did her best to school her features back to neutral.

He was too local. Too nice. Too much of a distraction she definitely didn't need. Her focus should be on making the coffee horse trailer a success. Get the Pony Expresso partnership. Plan her next trip to Tahoe because clearly missing this trip was affecting her brain more than she realized. It for sure explained her body's eagerness to release these weird bubbles of funny, flighty sensations streaming through her bloodstream, resulting in ridiculous grins on one's face. Next thing she'd expect was some absurd sigh while pressing her hand to her chest, like Mia when she got swoony.

She gave herself one more good look, pressing her lips together tightly, and flicked off the light.

Chapter Six

MASON SENT A text to Natalie a few days later regarding tree delivery. This time he made sure to keep it short and professional.

When he received her first text regarding the ribbon, he had been working and didn't want to fail under his dad's scrutiny this soon. Mason had slipped the phone into his pocket and tried to ignore it. He'd tried to ignore it as he created a work schedule for opening weekend. He'd also tried to ignore it when he made calls to vendors and verified Santa would be ready and that the photo area would be appropriately decorated. He'd definitely tried to ignore Natalie's text when his dad had stopped by with Charlie and they'd had a chat about what type of things were still on the to-do list and if they were going to move the parking area to another spot in the open field.

Mason became so focused on ignoring the text, his brain was exhausted by the time he got home in the evening. As he heated leftover spaghetti in the microwave, he read it again and arrived at the conclusion he'd proven he could stay focused at work, passing whatever test he'd set for himself. Being off the clock meant there was no harm in replying to her.

Mason loosened the reins on himself and proceeded to have the most delightful conversation in his life. He was used to feeling awkward and unsure around women but, with Natalie, he became clever and funny, like he'd finally discovered someone who got him and his weird sense of humor. Every message he got from her had him laughing in his usually lonely apartment, and, for a short period of time, it was less lonely. Until he ruined it.

He told Natalie she was a woman after his own heart, which had been a joke, but it didn't matter. She'd stopped responding.

This was why the Christmas-tree-related text was short and to the point. Mason mentioned work had been busy and asked if he could drop the tree off on his way home from the farm instead of early morning. She said okay and they set a time for after hours. There was nothing fun or flirty about the conversation, almost as if their text exchange about stolen ribbons and avenging birds never happened in the first place.

His truck sat parked in an alleyway spot behind Pony Expresso and he sent a quick text to inform her of his arrival.

Soon her head popped from the rear door and he did his best to keep his heart from reacting but failed. "Hey. I don't know if going through the back is the best way. This hallway is a little tight. Street parking is kind of a pain right now, but maybe I can help you carry the tree to the front. Is that okay?"

"Yeah, that's fine." He lowered the tailgate of his truck and pulled the tree out, setting it on the pavement trunk-first. The ribbon was still tied around the branch, reminding him of her red scarf. She wasn't wearing it today. Natalie wore a black, puffy parka, bundling herself in it and zipping it up as high as it would go to protect against the November chill.

She stood beside him on the other side of the tree as he held it upright with one hand. Her dark brown velvet gaze slid their way upward until they reached his eyes. "Hi," she said on a light breath, a wispy strand of hair playing across one cheekbone.

He was tempted to remove his own gloves and press the warmth into her cold cheeks with the palms of his hands, and then press the rest of her into him. Instead, he could only stare, mesmerized, in return. "Hi."

"Do I need to pat you down?"

"Sorry?" Her question caught him off guard. Was she reading his mind?

"Oh! I didn't…I didn't mean that," she stammered, covering part of her face with a palm. "I'm so sorry. I wasn't trying to make it weird. I was just referencing our last conversation. I swear."

He laughed. "You were? I might need a reminder of this conversation because it sounds intriguing."

"You know how gangsters hide their machine guns in a trombone case or something?"

"They still do that?" Mason had no idea where this conversation was going but he liked her turning all awkward and cute. She used a lot of hand gestures when she spoke, and, even when flustered, she was as graceful as someone conducting an invisible orchestra.

"They do in old movies, and I just imagined you were smuggling in a vengeful blue jay the same way. Except, instead of inside a trombone case, he might be in the tree or in your jacket. So I'd need to pat you down to make sure you're clean and not smuggling any blue jays—Okay, now that I've had to explain it, it's no longer funny and I look ridiculous about the whole thing. Forget it. God, I want to die. So if this is an ambush, just get it over with because my dignity has already been massacred."

Mason held up his free hand in a half surrender pose. "No ambushing birds here. Just an ally bringing you your tree. You can trust me."

"Can I?" she asked while he tipped the top of the tree toward her so she could carry the lighter end.

Mason lifted his side and they made their way through the alley. "I've never met someone so suspicious of things that would be innocuous to most people. Normal people."

"Excuse me? Like what?" She shifted the weight of the tree in her hand before continuing on the path.

"Birds. Big Christmas. Don't tell me that's all there is because I don't believe it."

"Okay, first of all, I take offense that my skepticism of these things somehow makes me abnormal. More generous people would say I'm a free thinker. Secondly, I have dreams of becoming a fairy-tale villain. Being the mortal enemy of Christmas trees, birds, and everything nice, has to put me on the right path toward reaching my goals."

"If you're a fairy-tale villain, what would that make me?"

She gave him a quick glance, as they adjusted their angle to make a turn and continue on the sidewalk. "You're more of a Prince Charming type and therefore you'll never be a true ally. I have every right to be suspicious and expect bird ambushes."

Most people would consider being compared to Prince Charming a compliment. Coming from her it didn't seem like it, as if she was drawing up lines and he'd already found himself on the other side of it. "Does a fairy-tale villain ever get a happy ending?"

"I think they make their own version. It just doesn't look like how you'd imagine."

"I'm imagining mass destruction and chaos."

"Okay, well, in that case, it's exactly how you'd imagine it." She stopped at the door entrance. "Wait a minute. Maybe you should go through the door first so the branches won't get caught. The shop's closed but the door isn't locked yet."

After a person passed them on the sidewalk, Mason moved his side of the tree past Natalie's end and pushed the door open with a hip. They were able to slide the tree inside with minimum needle loss. Some of the tables had been rearranged and there was a tree stand in the corner of the shop. He put the trunk into the stand on the ground, tightening the screws as she held the tree upright. "Can you bring some water in a pitcher or something? I might as well add it while I'm down here," he said.

She handed him a pitcher already filled.

"Just make sure to keep this full. That'll keep your tree fresher longer and you won't get as many dry needles falling off. If you let the stand go empty the water uptake of the tree stops, so even if you put in more water, the trunk won't take it in. That's when it starts to dry out."

With his task done, Mason stood, finding Natalie beside

the tree, her eyes closed and her expression completely serene. She didn't appear at all like a fairy-tale villain in the making.

"Everything okay?" he asked.

Those beautiful eyes opened with all the brilliance of a sunrise. He was instantly warmed by her gaze. "Yes. I-I was just smelling it."

With his job done, he should leave, but he didn't want to. "Do you want help decorating?"

"Oh, no, you don't have to do that. I can manage. You've already gone out of your way to deliver the thing and you probably want to get out of here. I'm not that much of a villain."

"I don't have anything going on right now and maybe if Prince Charmings offered their services to villains more often, there'd be a lot more friendships between them."

"Okay, well, it's actually not very much." She went behind the coffee counter and soon returned with a cardboard box, much smaller than one expected to hold Christmas ornaments. His own mother had two giant Tupperware storage containers that she made him lug down from the attic every year.

"Is there another one?" he asked.

Her gaze dropped to the box in her hand. "Uh, no, this is it. I haven't gone shopping for new ornaments since we had a small tree two years ago and even then I just grabbed a few generic boxes from Dollar Tree. I don't like to invest a lot of time in setting this stuff up, and I do it alone. I just want to get it over with so I can go home."

Natalie set the box on the table before removing her

jacket and pulling her hair tight into a ponytail. She took off the lid and removed two strings of basic white lights and a few boxes of solid red ball ornaments. She wasn't exaggerating about the basicness of her holiday decoration.

He decided not to say anything further about it. "You want to start with the lights?"

She untangled them before handing them over. "Do you have other vendors that are going to be on the farm?"

"Yup. We have a waffle vendor, a hot dog/fair food vendor. And, of course, your truck. This year we wanted to make it a whole family-destination thing. Plus, we have a craft vendor coming. Kids, or even adults, will be allowed to paint their own ornament to take home. That might be of interest to you. And, there's the Poinsettia Paradise Marketplace where we sell poinsettias, handmade local crafts, and some of my honey."

"You make honey?"

"I didn't make it. The bees do. It's called, 'It's the Motherlode, Honey!'" and he said this last part with the exaggerated accent of an old prospector discovering gold.

A smile flashed across her face while she handed him the next section of lights. It was like he caught sight of a shooting star. Her smile was large, and creases created soft brackets around her mouth, making him feel as if he'd hit a jackpot. He didn't mind appearing as ridiculous as possible if it meant experiencing her joy again.

"I've always wondered what happens to bees when the weather gets cold. Do they migrate like birds? And how do they remember which beehive to return to when they get back?"

"Those are supposed to be winter flowers or snowflakes or whatever. I don't know. I'm not very good at this stuff."

"So, as a villain, you're actually not very crafty?"

"No, I guess not. You're not really going to take the tree back, are you?"

He shook his head as if he hated delivering bad news. "I'm sorry but it is our standard farm policy. Napkin decorations won't be enough to save you." He removed the scarf garland like he was a repo man about to retake possession of the white fir.

"Nooooo," she said, her hand grasping onto his arm, her eyes sparking with humor. "What if I promise to pick up another box from Dollar Tree? Don't take my tree."

Mason began wrapping the scarf around her neck. "Please maintain some decorum, ma'am. Don't make this harder than it already is. You're going to make the little elf children cry."

She lifted her gaze, her full lower lip in a pout. As he let go of the end of her scarf, his hand grazed along her jawline. Her fingers, still gripping his sleeve, tightened. Until this point, they'd never touched before. This was barely anything and, yet, he felt the heat of it down to the marrow of his bones. Her teasing pout disappeared as his own emotions shifted from playfully serious to wanting. He took a chance, reaching for her again and brushing a strand of hair from her cheek. "You're so soft," he said in a low tone.

"Fairy-tale villains aren't supposed to be soft," she replied but made no move to escape his grasp.

"I don't care what you're supposed to be. You can just be what you are."

Her eyes grew large, her lips fell apart, and her chest began to visibly rise.

His desire to kiss her was reaching a fevered point.

The distance between his arm and her waist was mere inches and he tentatively closed it, her hand sliding across his forearm, as he found purchase on the small of her back. Fast or not, touching her, holding her, wanting to kiss her was the easiest thing in the world, like falling into bed after a long day.

"Mason," she said, her other hand clasping over his, stilling it on her cheek.

"Yeah?"

"Don't make the mistake of kissing a villain when you really want a princess."

This one tiny sentence had the ability to pop the bubble. His hands automatically dropped away from her. "What?"

Natalie turned toward the tree, grabbing the impromptu napkin flowers and packages of tea bags from the branches, and stuffing them into her box. "I-I'm just trying to—I'm not the woman for anyone in this town."

"What does that mean?" There was a spark of something here, of this he was certain. He didn't understand anyone who would prefer to ignore it.

She held the box to her chest, turning it into a shield between them. "I'm not looking to start anything with anyone. I'm a dead end. Get it?"

Mason set his hand on his hips as he considered this. He should drop it, leave her alone. He shouldn't be trying to start anything with anyone either, instead he should be focused on the farm, doing exactly what he told his father he would do. Except, he couldn't stop himself from wanting to understand. "A dead end by choice? Or because someone made you feel like one?"

"What difference does it make? I'm still not going to start anything with anyone, especially someone I'm going to be kinda working with in the next month. I've got enough on my plate. I don't need anything else."

"And if you feel something? What are you supposed to do with that?"

Natalie looked him dead in the eye. "Wait for the feeling to pass. It always does."

Chapter Seven

WHEN A PERSON considered themselves on the path to villainhood, it made it a lot easier to accept people's unhappiness or disappointment. If she did things that were met with displeasure, she could shrug and say, "What did you expect?" It's not as if she didn't warn them.

At least, this was how it was supposed to be in theory.

There were a limited number of places Natalie could just be and it was usually when she was alone. This could be why her Tahoe trips were so freeing. She didn't have to pretend to be anything because it didn't matter. Unfortunately, pretending was getting harder all the time. If she embraced the inner villain, a little at a time, maybe people would be less shocked at her final transformation.

Unfortunately, her heart wasn't chilled to arctic temperatures quite yet. When she did catch someone off guard, she felt bad. But it was better they discover it early before falling into the trap. Natalie was still learning how to avoid the trap herself.

After Mason departed the shop, she wanted to weep rather than celebrate her avoidance of getting stuck in a potentially sappy love story, one that would inevitably fade into unhappiness. Her sparsely decorated tree proved to be the perfect metaphor for it all. So much beautiful potential, but poor intentions and lackluster execution made it not worth cutting the tree in the first place.

No matter how much she wanted him to kiss her, how much she'd been drawn to him and his easygoing personality, she didn't want to hurt him. Mia's argument had been right all along. Better to nip things directly in the bud before anything had a chance to bloom with deeper feelings. If anything, she was doing him a favor and, in time, he'd realize this himself. They always did.

Even so, it probably would have been a nice kiss.

She couldn't remember the last time she had one full of sweetness, instead of a fast, sloppy make-out session with some Tahoe guy because she had to squeeze everything in before returning home. It could have been a kiss that had something behind it. One that was solid, grounded, and actually meant something, instead of being a single burst from a firecracker, burning itself out too quickly and leaving behind the same emptiness as before. It had been so long, she was beginning to doubt the existence of such kisses.

THE NEXT DAY she stopped by the mechanic shop where her father worked. "Mija! You're coming to visit me?" he asked while wiping his hands on a dirty blue rag.

"Hi, Dad." She kissed a weathered cheek smelling of transmission fluid and car parts. "And why are you acting like I never visit you? You know I saw you yesterday. Should I be worried about your memory?"

Her father shook his head. "No. You came to visit your mamá—"

Natalie groaned. "Stop. I'm so damn sick of this. I visit you both. I love you both. I'm not going to keep getting caught up in this damn game you and mom keep playing. Can you guys please get help? I'm begging you at this point."

Her father stared in shock, even if she'd given a similar speech at least twenty times. This wasn't anything she hadn't said before except with far fewer damns involved. Her frustration with the whole situation was reaching her breaking point and soon she'd react with more damns than non-swear words.

"Your mom always tells me to get help and now my own hija..." He acted as if he'd never been so betrayed.

"I'm telling you and mom to both get help. Why do you guys want to be so damn miserable all the time? Can we just have one conversation that doesn't devolve into this same thing over and over again? I can't take it. Pretty soon I'm not going to visit anyone anymore. Is that what you want?"

"So you'll visit with your mamá but not me?"

"Ugh!" She was about to start flinging ratchet wrenches against the wall. All she wanted was to be heard, for someone to actually listen to what she was saying. Perhaps it'd be better if she was more like her sisters who shrugged everything off. But Natalie couldn't. Her parents' behavior would never not bother her.

"Can I borrow your truck?" she asked, changing the subject rather than taking her frustration out at her dad's workplace.

"Why?"

"Tío bought a trailer for the coffee business and I need to take it to the Christmas farm."

"Enrique won't take it for you? Want me to call him?"

"No. I know he can. But this is sort of my thing and he already went through purchasing it so I want to take control and show him I can do this."

"I'll go with you after work. We can go together."

"It's not that far. I can do it. I just want to borrow your truck. So can we swap?"

"Of course. You know I would do anything for you."

"Yeah," Natalie said. Although, there were some things he wasn't willing to do, along with her mom. She wasn't going to put herself into the discussion once again. Instead, she kissed him on the cheek, assured him she loved him, and swapped keys with her father, driving away in the small gray pickup truck.

The next morning at work, she called her uncle and got the information regarding where to get the horse trailer. She then called the owner and set up a time for later that day to pick it up. Natalie was focused, putting her mind strictly into work mode.

She didn't even think about Mason…much.

Of course, she couldn't help it when she departed her office. The white fir was a big presence inside the small shop. Its appearance hadn't changed from when Mason had departed a few days earlier. Although she did add fabric at the bottom of the tree for a makeshift tree skirt. Other than this, the tree decoration was as pitiful as ever.

Natalie cleared garbage from a table nearby, and she couldn't resist touching a branch, releasing the light spicy scent of citrus in the air. This was getting to be a bad habit. How was she supposed to work without the white fir? January depression was already setting in.

That's when she saw it.

Tucked between branches was a small blue jay glass ornament. It glinted from the nearby string of lights when she touched it, the wings covered in a dusting of glitter. She turned, searching the faces of the coffee patrons around her and, though she recognized many regular customers, none of them were him.

"Did Mason come in this morning?" Natalie asked Diego.

"Who?" her cousin replied, not raising his head and paying more attention to the drink he was making.

"Big, tall guy with brown hair, beard, has a dimple in his chin."

Her cousin glanced in her direction, confusion spreading across his face. "I don't know. I hardly look at anyone. And what the hell is a chin dimple?"

"It was the Nutella latte guy. I think his name was Mason," Crystal, their coworker, interrupted.

"Oh, yeah," Diego said once his memory had been jogged. "I think that was forty minutes ago or so. I don't know. You were in your office. He didn't ask for you or anything. Just took his drink and left."

Natalie's gaze drifted back to the tree. Now that she knew the blue jay was there, she couldn't see anything else.

Chapter Eight

"DID YOU GET them to set out the extra cones to help direct traffic?"

Mason took a breath, willing calmness, but this had been going on for the last few days. "Dad, stop. It's been taken care of. You're stressing me out."

"I just want to make sure—"

"I know. Trust me. If you want to see if I can handle the season, then you need to let me handle it. Why don't you go see if Mom needs help with anything? Last I saw, she was doing some last-minute decorating in the marketplace."

Daniel frowned. "I already tried that and she said I was bugging her and to go see if you needed help."

Mason attempted to keep from smiling. It seems he and his mom were experiencing a similar problem. It was clear, no matter what Daniel had promised, he was having trouble letting things go and hadn't stopped pointing out when Mason chose to do something a slightly different way than him.

"Maybe you can go check on my bees then."

His father huffed. "What's there to check?"

"It was really windy last night. Just make sure the winterization I put up hasn't been blown away." He had put up a wall on the west side of the hives to block out the worst of the bad weather a few weeks earlier. The wall was temporary for now but he wasn't too concerned about it. It was more that his father taking a long walk would do them both a lot of good.

His father grumbled about how Mason should be focused on the Poinsettia Paradise and not the bees but he, at least, went away.

Mason returned to his work but his attention was captured when a gray pickup truck pulled through the gates with a small, white horse trailer. Worried that the farm's regular Christmas Santa was up to something, he made his way toward it. He wouldn't put it past Stan to transport live reindeers without telling anyone.

Except, when the driver door opened, Natalie stepped out. His step faltered. There he was, being thrown off guard again even when he knew she was coming.

"Hi," she said, her breath light. "I'm not sure where I'm supposed to set up."

"Natalie. Hi. I can help you."

She got into the vehicle and he helped direct her to a spot beside another vendor, Placerville Waffle Company. When rotated, the horse trailer had the word *COFFEE* painted in a military font at the top. While it was enclosed with solid walls, he worried she wouldn't stay warm enough while working and was calculating which heating lamp he could sacrifice to sit between her truck and the waffle vendor. At least it would be something.

"Do you need help unhitching the—"

"I got it," she said, going to work by unhitching the trailer and setting down the jack to level it.

As much as Mason wanted to help her get situated, he hadn't offered to help the other vendors and couldn't do so now without people, like his dad, taking notice. As much as he hated to, he sauntered away and returned to his previous task.

When it got close to opening, he, with Bentley, walked through the vendor area to check on things. While the horse trailer didn't appear to be anything special on the outside, he could see it had been converted. No one would describe it as sparkling top-of-the-line, but an order window had been cut out of the side. Inside there were coffee machines and supplies on shelving. Natalie, still wearing her parka, was outside the truck, writing a menu on a chalkboard hanging beside the order window.

"Everything good?" he asked.

She glanced at him over her shoulder. "Yup."

"I brought you this." He held out a bright red potted poinsettia, offering it to her.

She looked at the flower, frowning, before meeting his eyes. Her shoulders locked into a line. "Look, Mason, I don't really need you to be giving me flowers—"

He stopped her before she made the situation more awkward. "Oh, no, I… All the vendors have them. We like to spread the holiday decorations throughout the farm. It's my mom's idea. Gives patrons a real experience. You're the last one on my list who doesn't have one in your, uh, truck window."

She took the poinsettia from him. "Oh. Okay. Thanks." She looked at the plant, a worried expression flashing across her face as she chewed on her lower lip. "You're not expecting this plant to be returned to you alive are you? I don't exactly have a green thumb. I'm a plant killer."

He gave her an assuring smile because he found every part of her adorable, even the parts considered deadly. "You don't have to do anything. I'll make sure to keep an eye on it, like a plant wellness check." Mason noticed her shiver from the cold. "You know, I think I have an extra heat lamp. I was going to put it between you and the waffle truck, if that's all right. It might not give a lot of heat, but it might help a little."

Her face softened. "Really? Yeah, th-that'd be nice. Thank you."

He opened his mouth to reply but was interrupted with the noise of a car horn going off to the tune of "Jingle Bells," making the vehicle heard before it was spotted barreling through the gate. Beside him, Bentley barked his displeasure, adding to the sudden chaos.

Shit.

Stan Anderson had arrived.

The red two-door beater car, decorated with about twenty bumper stickers including *Rudolph is my co-pilot* and *My other ride is a sleigh*, came to an abrupt stop beside Natalie's truck, sending a dust plume into the vendor area. Complaints and coughing were barely heard above the blast of Christmas tunes from the car's speakers.

She gave Mason a questioning glance but there was no point in explaining anything when it would be difficult for her to hear anyway. Instead, he shook his head, rolling his eyes.

The music cut mid-song when the car shut off. Out stepped Santa, dressed in a red velvet costume, snow-white wig, and beard. The one thing not fitting with this stereotypical picture were the designer sunglasses and Santa texting on his phone. Bentley ran to greet the guy, continuing to bark.

"Yo, Mase, I didn't see my VIP parking spot. I thought we added that to my contract." Santa tossed Mason his keys as though he was the valet. "It's all right. I'm sure you'll figure it out."

"Bentley, hush." He tossed the keys back. "We took that out, along with your request for a personal nap trailer. Remember?"

"How many times do I have to reiterate? It's not a nap trailer. It would be a holiday meditation room. It takes a lot of energy to be *on* all the time. You know who doesn't holiday meditate? Dick Kline. And it shows. That old man is sleeping in half the photos he takes. The elves that run that pony show use a special app to apply open eyes and rosy cheeks, so parents don't have to explain why their kids are sitting on the lap of what looks to be Weekend at Bernie's: Santa Edition. I keep telling you, Mase, being Santa is not an old man's game. It's a way of life and you paid for Kriss Kringlegold, so your families are going to get the Kriss Kringlegold experience. Just make sure that check is made out to Stan Anderson. For some reason, the bank won't let me open an account under the name Kriss Kringlegold even when I showed them the article featuring me in the *El Dorado Times*. This is a page-five Santa you got working here. Don't ever forget it."

Diva Santa took the gig seriously and also had the bona

fide middle-aged white guy confidence to go along with it, making for a barely tolerable personality during the season. But the man was liked by children and parents alike, and his seriousness meant he was good at the job. He just allowed the obnoxiousness to fester over his whole life from October to January.

Natalie scoffed, catching Stan's attention. He turned, his mouth open as though he was ready to unleash fury on her, only to find himself faced with a beautiful woman. The open mouth switched to a page-five-Santa smile. Mason, the VIP parking spot, and the nap trailer were forgotten at this point. Stan reached one pristine, white-gloved hand in her direction. "Hello there, young lady," he said, claiming a handshake before speaking again to Mason. "You know, Mase, it wouldn't be a bad idea to finally get Santa a Mrs. Claus this year. No one likes a lonely Santa."

"Nope," he replied, not appreciating how Stan was still grasping her hand.

"Well, Kriss Kringlegold is used to carrying the show." He rubbed a thumb across Natalie's knuckles while keeping his eyes locked on her. "I'm Kriss, that's kiss with an R. You probably recognize me from the Cameo app. I get a lot of personal requests there. If you ever get tired and need a rest, my lap is yours. It even comes with a big candy cane." He wiggled his eyebrows and tipped her hand nearer as though he was about to kiss it even though she was making a not-so-subtle attempt to pull away.

"I'm pretty sure someone told me I was paying for the Kriss Kringlegold experience, not for you to creep on the other vendors," Mason said while prying Stan away. "People are going to show up soon and you need to get to your area." Thankfully, the Santa photo booth was on the opposite end of the food vendors.

While Stan allowed himself to be escorted away, he walked backwards, still talking to Natalie. "Hey, baby, I'm also going to need a hot chocolate brought to my booth. None of that packet shit. I want grade-A real hot chocolate served at 160 degrees and exactly three marshmallows." He held up three fingers to confirm his exact order.

She crossed her arms, not appearing at all amused. "Yeah, I'll get right on that, Santa. You have cows on this farm, Mason? Apparently, I need to go milk one to make sure the ingredients are fresh enough for his jolly holiness."

"I'll have someone bring that extra heater over to you as soon as I get this one situated," he replied, yanking Stan toward his end of the vendor section.

"I might need some heating up too. Santa get cold, baby." Stan was walking with Mason willingly now instead of fighting him. "Hey, hey, careful manhandling the suit. I got this custom-made with velvet brought all the way in from Carson City, the Paris of Nevada. This ain't no velour shit. This is hundred percent silk rayon velvet here. Do you think Dick Kline is walking around in silk velvet? No, he's polyester from top to bottom. The only thing real about him is the hair...and the beard. But I special-ordered my wig with real hair so I think we can agree it's pretty much the real thing."

"All right, Stan, you can tone it down now."

"It's Kriss. K-R-I-S-S. So, who's the lady? Do you know if she's available?" He broke out his phone again and started scrolling through his Instagram feed.

"She's not available to you. And I don't want to hear about you bothering her."

"Who said anything about bothering? I just want to, I don't know, get to know her a little better. What's her handle?"

"Stan. No."

He slid his sunglasses down the bridge of his nose, his blue eyes studying Mason closely. "Is there something going on between you guys? Are you dating?"

He didn't think, responding quickly. "Uh-huh. Yup. There, uh, might be…something going on between us. Leave her alone." He knew this lie had the potential to get him into trouble but if he explained everything to Natalie, she might understand. Plus, he was actually doing her a favor because Stan could be extremely buggy, especially when he considered himself the biggest catch outside the North Pole.

The man clapped him on the shoulder. "Good for you, Mase. You got yourself a sweet little candy cane there."

"Yeah, don't say that. And don't tell anyone. This is a business, not a high school text group. No gossiping." Mason was already sounding more like his dad.

He pushed the sunglasses up his nose again. "Yeah, I hear you, big guy. I hear you. So…can I get that heater then?"

"Fine. I'll bring an extra heater. Are we good?"

Stan tapped his phone against his fake-bearded chin, the wheels clearly turning in his head. "What about that V.I.P. parking spot?"

The muscles along his jaw tightened as he realized Stan was attempting to take advantage of his inside information. He didn't see what could be gained by admitting the blackmail material Diva Santa thought he possessed was in reality a lie to keep him in line. It was probably better to push ahead and make Stan happy. "You have to park in the same area as everyone else. But if I put up an orange cone in the corner of the lot and tape a piece of paper with your name on it, will that work?"

"Will you put Kriss Kringlegold?"

He sighed. "Whatever you want."

"What about my trailer?"

Mason threw his arms up in frustration. "Come on, Stan. Be reasonable. We're not going to rent a trailer."

"People trust Santa with all kinds of secrets, Mase. What they want for Christmas. Who they might be shacking up with in order to get free coffee. The question is how do you want to play this? Naughty or nice?"

"I'll set up a spot in the barn where you can do your holiday meditation or whatever. But you can only go in there during breaks. Understood?"

"We're cool, we're cool. I knew we could work it out. I've always liked you. You're like a brother to me."

"You blackmail all your siblings?"

Stan touched a hand to his chest as if his heart hurt. "It's only 'cause I care, baby. You know that."

"Yeah, sure, whatever."

A young woman with a pixie haircut and wearing a green elf costume strode past them with a black camera bag and a tripod, drawing Stan's attention. "Hey, Candy. Guess who's getting his own V.I.P. parking spot?"

"Is it up your ass? Otherwise, no one cares, Stan," the woman said, continuing her walk to the Santa photo booth, which consisted of a raised wooden platform covered in red carpeting, an ornate velvet throne, and surrounded by decorated trees and poinsettias.

"Oh, yeah? Well, I bet you…dream about my ass," he replied, getting flustered in his retort. "I don't know why you keep bringing Candy back," he said to Mason. "You know she can't stand me. How am I supposed to remain jolly in the pictures when she's staring death daggers at me from behind the camera the whole time? Santa shouldn't have to work in such a toxic environment."

Mason found the feud between Stan and Candy amusing. Even though they didn't get along, it didn't stop either one from returning to the farm year after year. It was almost as if they enjoyed getting on each other's nerves.

He smacked Stan on the shoulder. "You're Kriss Kringlegold, baby. A page-five Santa. I'm sure you can handle it."

Chapter Nine

BESIDES THE OVERABUNDANCE of cheerful families, the Christmas music playing on speakers, and the distant sound of saws, Natalie's day wasn't so different from her usual time spent working in the coffee shop. Well, there was also the fact that she was freezing her ass off working in a converted horse trailer, but, other than that, yeah, it kind of was the same thing.

It was still early in the season with Thanksgiving being a week away, and the farm wasn't too busy, but she'd had a steady stream of customers buying hot beverages from her. She liked it when it was busy because the day went by faster. She couldn't wait to scratch a tally mark on the inside wall of her horse trailer as though she was ticking off the days of a prison sentence.

Ironically, Natalie had spent her last few nights with Mason on her mind before falling asleep. She thought about that damn blue jay ornament more times than she'd care to admit. The reason for her straying thoughts wasn't for any reason Mia would have supposed. It wasn't as if she had a crush on the guy or anything. She didn't. Although, she may have let her imagination entertain what could have happened if she'd leaned into him, let him kiss her. Once or twice, she even considered it a good idea. He was the type of person who would be so easy to sink into and—

But, again, she didn't allow herself to go there often. It was more along the lines of, *Well, I hope our paths don't cross too often at Poinsettia Paradise.*

Their last interaction at Pony Expresso had ended clumsily and she wasn't eager to repeat it. Too bad she'd already failed when he innocently handed her a poinsettia and she assumed it meant something more. The whole situation made her want to dig a hole next to the horse trailer, fling herself into it, and bury her body from head to toe. Her family could get a tombstone to mark the spot, reading, *Here lies Natalie. She died of avoidable embarrassment.*

It appeared all her worry about him had been unfounded because, besides this morning, she'd hardly seen the guy. Another employee had been by to bring the extra heat lamp. She'd actually been hit with a ping of disappointment. In fact, she'd seen Bentley roaming around the yard more than she'd caught sight of Mason. Not that she'd been searching for him.

Luckily, day one was coming to an end, and she'd soon make her escape. Natalie couldn't wait to go home, order a pizza, toss the eggplant-shaped bath bomb (also a joke gift from Carla) into the tub and relax. She was in the middle of cleaning when she noticed Stan strolling toward her truck.

He gave a couple carrying a tree across the yard a pair of finger guns. "Nice. You guys went with a Dougie. That's a good tree."

Oh God, she thought, taking a deep breath, and preparing herself for incoming annoyance.

"And how's your day going, baby?" Stan asked, leaning against the trailer, but somehow making it not at all casual or cool.

She pretended to be involved with deep cleaning. "Busy. Did you need something?" She wasn't optimistic but perhaps he'd order a drink, take it, and leave her alone. She could always dream.

"You know, I never got that hot chocolate. I bet you make a good one."

"Yeah, well, like I said, I've been really busy. I can't just stop everything and run a hot chocolate over to you. Maybe Santa should consider hiring an elf assistant."

He laughed but it wasn't the big, gusto type of laugh Mason had, one that expressed his enthusiasm with his whole body. She found Stan's laugh to be grating, the same as the rest of him. He acted as if she was a teasing friend instead of a person who was setting boundaries and not interested in befriending him.

"I like you," he replied, emphasizing this by pointing a white-gloved finger in her direction. "You're feisty. And I also happen to know something about you. I know your…" he paused dramatically before whispering, "…*secret*."

The way he emphasized the word made Natalie freeze with a cleaning rag in her hand, her gaze slowly returning to him. She didn't consider herself to be a secretive person but there was one big secret. How would he know anything about her Tahoe trips? It didn't seem possible, except…

"Do you spend a lot of time in Tahoe?" Natalie tried to decipher the exact physical specifications of his face, but it wasn't easy through the Santa disguise. All she could tell was that he was a white guy with pale blue eyes and wasn't very old.

His face lit at her question. "Not as much as I would like. Of course, it's much better when you're with the right friend, who can, you know, help you have a good time."

Oh God.

Had she met Stan before?

Maybe he went by a different name. Like Kriss. She may have met a Chris or two on her vacations. She may have even made out with a Chris. Her stomach twisted into a knot. Had she done something with Stan, a guy who was now a photo-booth Santa, and he had found her in real, everyday life, serving coffee in a converted horse trailer? The thought made her want to vomit the protein bar she scarfed for lunch in between customers.

One thing was certain. Either she needed to stop these fun trips to Tahoe or the place wasn't far enough away to prevent these types of run-ins. Perhaps her next vacation would be a ticket to Atlantic City, someplace on the other side of the country.

Her eyes stayed glued to him. What was he wanting from her now? Did he expect she'd be as flirty and free as she was at the state line? He was smiling at her again, all confident and smug.

"Do you recognize me? I get that a lot," he said.

"You do?" Maybe because Kiss-with-an-R also did regular trips to Tahoe. Oh God, what a nightmare this day was turning into. She took it all back. This wasn't like a regular day at all. It was her worst shift at Pony Expresso times ten. At least there she could hide in her office if necessary.

He nodded. "*The Santa Heist.*"

"What?" She couldn't be more confused.

"I was one of the Santa extras in *The Santa Heist.* Well, the second one. *The Santa Heist 2: Wreck the Halls.* It wasn't in theaters, went straight to streaming, which was too bad because it was good. Some even say it was better than the original *Santa Heist,* at least according to a reviewer on IMDb. I was one of the Santas in the elevator scene. I pushed the button. Well, not really, but I stood next to the guy who pushed the button. You can tell it's me because my Santa suit is a slightly deeper red than the other Santas. It's the silk rayon velvet. Even the set costumer was impressed with the quality of my suit. It was filmed in Tahoe, you know. Right at Harveys. I got a hundred bucks and a comp ticket to their buffet from the production team. Do you have Tubi? Because if not, I'm totally willing to let you borrow my account information." He stopped, seeming to remember something. "I mean, I might be willing to do that if I can get that delicious hot chocolate and then secrets can stay secrets." One of those blue eyes winked at her.

"What?" she repeated. What was even happening here? Was he bargaining with her? Blackmailing her? Or flirting?

"Is everything okay here?" Mason appeared, his gaze shifting between Stan and herself, as though he was somewhat nervous about the situation. Regardless, she was never more glad to be bothered by the man.

"Mase! Hey! I was just making friendly conversation. I'm a friendly guy."

"Was he bothering you?" he asked her. "There may be a meditation spot and V.I.P. parking at risk here."

Stan's eyes widened. "No, I was not bothering her. I just wanted a hot chocolate and her window wasn't closed yet, so I assumed she was still open. Oh, and I was telling her about my Santa extra work. She didn't know I was in *Santa Heist 2*. Besides, it's not like I'm telling the secret to anyone who doesn't already know the secret."

She shot a look at Mason the same time he looked at her, his own features tensing. When Stan's mouth opened again, she scrunched an eye, anticipating him blurting the news about how she and Stan had a Tahoe fling. She never expected this secret to be revealed between a horse trailer and a waffle truck.

"I mean, you guys already know you're dating."

Her eyes popped open. What the hell was Stan saying? "Wait—Who's dating?"

"Look, we agreed to drop it in exchange for the things you wanted and you're not keeping your word, *buddy*," Mason said through a strained jawline. He turned to her, lifting his arms in a helpless pose. "Sorry, honey. I tried to keep it a secret because I know you love your privacy, but Santa Romeo here can be *very* persistent." He gave her a sly wink.

She stared at Mason, then Stan, before shifting back to the first man again. The pieces were starting to come together. "Soooo, we don't know each other?" she asked Stan. "I mean, before today, we've never met?"

He gave a confused glance to Mason. "Have we? I don't remember and I have a pretty good memory. Have you also done extra work in holiday blockbusters?"

She leaned against the counter, placing her head into her

palms, relief flooding through her as ridiculous, out-of-control laughter burst forth.

The two men, unsure how to react to her strange outburst, exchanged uncomfortable looks with each other.

After she was able to catch her breath, she addressed Mason. "And you told him we—you and I—are dating?"

He appeared stricken, his face flushing, the only thing coming out was a series of stammers.

"Yeah, you should feel bad," Natalie said, interrupting him and putting a hand on her hip. "After we had the whole conversation about keeping this news quiet until after the holidays. You had to tell the one guy working the farm who's pretty much talking to everyone. Do you know how gossipy kids are? Why not just take out a billboard, Mason? I'm sure at this rate, half of El Dorado county knows by now."

It took a second for him to recover and respond. "I said I was sorry. But, I mean, look at you. You're, like, the most beautiful woman I've ever known, and I'm just supposed to stay quiet when all I want to do is shout to the world." Mason dropped to his knees as though begging for forgiveness. "Please don't be mad. You know you're the strong one. I'm nothing but the weak, pitiful man who adores you." It was all pretend, but this didn't stop Natalie's heart from doing a tiny dance in her chest because how exciting would it be to have someone who meant those words.

"God, Mase. Now you're just embarrassing yourself. It's not really that big of a deal," Stan said.

"And you." She turned her attention to Stan, and she could have sworn he did a hard swallow behind the Santa beard. "I really hope you're not going to get in the habit of trying to blackmail me into giving you hot chocolate." She did a slow full-body lean against the counter, making her gaze as steely as possible. "If you want to address me, you'll call me Natalie. I will not answer to anything else. I am not your hot chocolate girl. If you want something, you can come here and stand in line like everyone else. And you get whatever number of marshmallows I feel like giving you, if any. Got it?"

Stan gave a sheepish grin. "Yeah, yeah, of course. And all that before, about the hot chocolate and stuff, I was just joking. Mase will tell you. I just like joking around." He then looked at his phone. "Well, I better get going. I'll see you guys tomorrow then." He took off toward his red car in the parking lot.

Mason slowly got on his feet and patted the dust from his knees while Natalie finished her task of putting things away for the night.

"Are you going to tell me how I ended up inside a sit-com?" she asked. "You're welcome by the way."

"I kept meaning to come over here earlier and tell you about it. Sorry about that. The lie kind of sprang out of nowhere and it was the only way I could think of to get him to back off so he wouldn't come around here and bug you all the time. So you're also welcome by the way."

"Do I seem like the type of person who can't take care of that myself? You should save your rescuing for someone else, Prince." It was true. She didn't need to be rescued. Natalie was more than capable of shutting someone down when she didn't want the attention. Sometimes it was as easy as being herself. Although, once she got over the shock of the situation, and the relief she didn't ever have a secret rendezvous with Stan, she found the situation kind of funny. Despite his weird way of going about the whole thing, what Mason did could be considered sweet.

He didn't respond to her, becoming quiet as she finished locking the horse trailer for the night.

"You're right," he finally said. "I'm sorry. I shouldn't have put you in that position. I wasn't thinking."

His apology surprised her, and she felt bad for getting snappy at him. "It's okay," Natalie replied as she pulled her knit hat over her head and zipped her coat. "I'm just tired and hungry. I haven't had much to eat today and the whole thing was a little unexpected, as I'm sure you can believe."

Mason grinned. "You didn't imagine you'd end up with such an amazing boyfriend on your first day on the farm?"

"Certainly not one who appears to worship the ground I walk on. I'm a little surprised at how much I like it."

"I find it hard to believe this was your first time experiencing that."

"Believe it." Natalie dug through her bag, searching for her keys. She had tossed them in this morning, and they'd disappeared somewhere in the void.

"Here. You can have this." From his pocket, he pulled out a burrito-shaped item wrapped in paper foil. "The waffle truck gave it to me before I walked over here. It's one of their fried chicken waffle wraps. It might not be super-hot anymore but they're still good even when cold."

"I don't want to take your food," her mouth said even while her stomach protested with a loud grumble. She'd been hit with the smells from the waffle truck all day, and taking his food was getting more tempting with each passing second.

"Take it. You're hungry. It's the least I could do after saddling you with a boyfriend," Mason replied.

He didn't have to tell her twice. She snatched it, ripped off the wrapping, and took the biggest bite. "Oh my God," she moaned with her mouth full and her eyes fluttering upwards. "This is the best thing I've ever had in my life."

"I'm glad you like it. Luckily, for you, I have another one." He pulled out a similar package from the other pocket of his jacket, offering it to her.

She snatched this one from him as well as though she was a chipmunk building a nest egg of fried chicken waffle wraps. "I take back everything I've ever said. All is forgiven."

He laughed, and it was one of those hearty ones that she couldn't help but compare again to Stan's. His laugh was so much richer and lovely.

"So, do we really have to keep up this charade or do you think Stan's gotten the message?"

"As much as I'd like to keep up the pretense of fake dating you, I don't think it's really going to be a problem. Stan might even be too afraid to walk past your coffee truck at this point."

She released a laugh. "I admit fake dating was more fun than I'd expected."

"Five out of five stars even though there was a brief moment of panic on my side. But I would definitely fake date you again."

Mason escorted her all the way to her vehicle. As much as she had been eager to get home to her bathtub and eggplant-shaped bath bomb before, she was now strangely disappointed she'd have to leave. She liked talking with Mason and didn't want it to end, not when he made her laugh and fed her delicious food. The cynical side of Natalie wanted to roll her eyes at how easily she could be won over by a man who did nothing more than produce comfort food from his jacket pocket as if he knew she needed it. But that's exactly what it was. Comfort.

Her cynical side was strong though, and she couldn't help wondering if her father had brought a drink or snack to her mother at that fateful party where they'd met. Maybe that was all it took for her mother to fall head over heels. Natalie couldn't allow herself to fall into the same trap. People should set their sights higher than pocket food.

Regardless, she didn't move further or get into her dad's truck. She merely stood beside it, eating the last of the fried chicken waffle wrap and stared at the sky. "You need to be careful, Prince. You might find yourself on the villain side."

He put out his hand, palm side up, as though requesting her hand. Instead of submitting to something so ridiculously corny, (because why would he want to hold her hand), she discarded her balled-up food wrapper there. Mason laughed, placing her trash into his pocket. The laughter soon faded, and he gazed at her, his face becoming serious. Almost too serious, as if he was thinking about kissing her again. She was considering it. As he bent his frame, his face coming nearer, her breath hitched in her chest and no words came. Nor did she try to push him away. She simply allowed him to proceed.

Except he didn't kiss her. Instead, his mouth bypassed

hers, going straight to her ear. His breath was warm and sent tingles along her skin. “I don’t think you realize how weak and pitiful this prince actually is. He’d all but leap over to the villain side if he thought he’d be welcomed. Goodnight, Natalie.”

With that, Mason strolled away, leaving her a bit breathless.

Chapter Ten

DAY ONE OF Poinsettia Paradise had gone pretty well for Mason. Better than well. In spite of first-day chaos, it had ended on the sweetest of notes with Natalie gazing up at him over her waffle wrap, those big dark eyes softening towards him. When she looked at him like that, he could forget about a lot of things. He could forget worrying about whether his dad would ever trust him again. He could forget about whether the first day of business matched what they did last year. He could even forget his stomach rumbling because he'd given his dinner away. But, as long as he was alive, he'd never forget how she had looked at him at that last moment, as though she'd wanted him to reach out to her. It took everything in him not to. He tried that once already and he wasn't ready to get knocked down again so soon.

"Mason?"

"Hmm. What?" He turned and found Charlie there. The older man came into the office, removing his gloves.

"One of the power strips got unplugged yesterday and half the Sawzall batteries didn't get charged."

Shit. Just when he thought things were going fine, something had to come along and remind him that he didn't have everything together. "Does my dad know?"

"Nope. I just found out and you're the first one I told."

He took a moment. He could do this. "It's Sunday. People will probably take their time coming in today. Let's start charging them now and we'll use the Sawzalls we have. The rest will probably be charged in about four hours. If anyone complains about the wait, maybe we can offer them a complimentary coffee or something from the truck." He snuck a glance at Charlie. "What do you think?"

"Yeah, I think it's fine. What else can we do?"

"It'll be fine," he reassured himself.

Having an excuse, he went to Natalie soon after she appeared at the farm that morning. "I need to ask for a huge favor."

"You're not going to ask me to be your fake girlfriend at a high school reunion or something, are you?" Her eyes reflected more of an amused glint than a suspicious one.

He smiled, feeling similarly amused himself. "If that's what you consider to be a huge favor, then I need to rephrase myself. I need to ask for a very small favor."

"How small are we talking about?"

"Compared to fake dating, it'll be hardly any effort on your part."

She finished unlocking the horse trailer and went inside but not before saying, "What a shame. I like a good scheme."

When she put it that way, he wouldn't mind a good scheme himself. He was about to tell her that when he noticed his dad approaching and rushed through an explanation. "We might have a problem with a limited number of Sawzalls for cutting trees today. If anyone comes to you saying we promised them a complimentary drink while they wait, can you do it? Just keep track of it and I'll make sure your truck is compensated later."

She looked at him oddly, as though trying to figure out what everything meant, but he ran out of time because Daniel was here. "Dad, hi."

"Mason. I went to the office to talk with you and you weren't there. What are you doing over here?"

"Oh, I was…" He tried to think of a reasonable excuse to offer on why he appeared to be randomly hanging out at Natalie's truck as though he was more interested in a crush than handling business. He was hit with a moment of panic because this was exactly what it looked like and he was stuck.

"Sorry," she interrupted. "I wanted to pay Mason back for the food yesterday. He was nice enough to spring for me when I was starving. Here you go." She shoved a ten-dollar bill at him.

"You don't have to—"

"It's fine," she said, smiling sweetly. "I'm returning the *favor*. It's not a problem."

He took the bill, mumbling his thanks, as he turned his attention to his dad. "So, did you need something?"

Luckily, his dad simply wanted to chat about normal business things and hadn't suspected any panicking on Mason's side.

Throughout the day, Mason pushed himself as far away from the coffee horse trailer as he could by helping people load their trees and getting the saw situation worked out. If he was out among the trees, he could almost pretend he didn't smell the fresh roast of coffee beans in the air. In reality, he probably couldn't but his mind played tricks on him all the time and he imagined the scent teased him everywhere.

Toward the end of the day, he returned to her truck fully intending to return her ten dollars and to thank her for helping out with the earlier situation, even though it ended up not being necessary. Also, he was worried this was another day where she went without eating a proper meal. He stopped at the waffle truck before making his way to Natalie's. She was finishing with a customer, her last of the day since everything was shutting down.

"Hey," she said with a smile. Soft creases bracketed her mouth as though she was pleased to see him.

"Hey, yourself. Thanks for covering for me today," he replied, sliding the ten dollars across to the counter. "How's your day been? You haven't been bothered by any Santas lately?"

Her face scrunched adorably as if in thought. "He did come by for a hot chocolate, but he stood in line, did not blackmail me, and was, in fact, very well behaved. I guess you're one intimidating guy."

Mason laughed, leaning against the window. "I don't think I was the intimidating one."

She feigned shock, pressing a hand to her chest. "I can't imagine you mean me."

"That a villain can be scary? Why would I ever imply that?"

"You don't seem to be scared."

"Nah," he said. "I like it."

This might have been the wrong thing to say, because

her gaze dropped and she scratched a spot on the counter with her nail, turning the conversation awkward. He was trying to think of a way to turn his comment into more of a joke, when she glanced at him and said, "Can I get you something to drink?"

"Oh, uh..." He glanced at the menu, which was shorter than the one at Pony Expresso and he still had trouble deciding.

"You really don't like being put on the spot at the register, do you?" she asked.

"It's like I suddenly forget how letters are supposed to work. What's Mexican hot chocolate?"

"Ah," she responded. "Chocolate caliente mexicano. ¿Tú quieres?"

"Uh, sí," Mason responded even if he wasn't sure what he was getting himself into. "What makes it different from the American version?"

"Well," she started while pouring milk into a metal container and warming it. "It has a little extra kick to it. That's the cinnamon and sometimes there's a little chili in it. It warms your body and your tastebuds." She roughly chopped up a bar of what appeared to be dark chocolate, putting it into the milk.

"So it's less boring."

"You said it. I didn't." Lastly, she brought out a wooden whisk-looking tool. The wood was aged as if she'd made countless hot chocolates with it. The ball end of it went into the milk and chocolate mixture, and she twirled the handle part by rolling it between her palms. "The molinillo froths up the milk," she explained.

Mason was fascinated, as though he was watching a witch concocting a special spell. She was so graceful and competent.

Finally, she poured it into a paper cup for him. "A cinnamon stick," she said while dropping a small one into the cup. "Marshmallows?"

He nodded.

"Do you have a specific number you require?" Her eyes glittered at the question.

"Making marshmallow demands is probably risky."

"Smart man." She tossed in a few and handed him the drink.

Mason was excited to try it, especially considering it took more effort than opening a packet of instant. He took as generous of a sip as the hot liquid would allow. It was… Well, it wasn't what he expected. He supposed even with her explanation, he still expected traditional hot chocolate, and this was definitely not it. "It's, uh, it's good," he said, forcing himself to take another sip.

She laughed while cleaning her workspace. "Are you lying to me, Mason?"

"No. I, uh, it's just different."

"You know I can see your face, right? You're not fooling me. Do you want me to make you something different?"

"No, I'll drink it."

Natalie shook her head, laughing again. "Maybe close your eyes when drinking it. Then your brain won't be telling you it's American hot chocolate. It's completely different."

Mason closed his eyes, taking another slow sip, this time noticing the hints of cinnamon. "Mmm."

"You don't like it."

"Maybe I just need to get used to it." After a few sips and the shock wearing off, he was already adjusting to the flavor. He still didn't love it, but it wasn't bad.

She eyed him. "You think it'll be worth it?"

"Yeah, I think it will be," he replied, holding her gaze, meaning so much more than whether or not he'd like the drink in his hand. "Oh, I also brought you this. Wanted to make sure you weren't starving again." He pulled the waffle wrap from his pocket, setting it on the counter.

Her face lit. "You know how to spoil a person, Prince. Thank you."

"Are you doing anything after you close up?"

She stopped unwrapping the food and frowned at it, as though she was suspicious of what was contained inside the wrapper, like there was something attached to her acceptance of it. He jumped in before she could say anything.

"I just thought you might like to see my beehives. I can show you them while you eat. That's all. I did offer before, remember?"

The softness returned to her face. "Oh, okay. I just need to clean up a little and lock up."

"Fine. I'm going to finish this delicious Mexican hot chocolate while I wait."

She shook her head and laughed.

After she finished cleaning, she zipped herself into her coat, slipped on her knit beanie and locked the trailer. She pulled out the waffle wrap and Mason pulled another from his pocket.

"Oh good, you got one for yourself this time," she said

while peeling the paper from hers.

"Unless you're so hungry you need two of them again." He offered it to her.

She froze. "Oh God. Did I eat your dinner yesterday? How rude of me."

"It was fine. I wasn't even that hungry. This one's different. It's a falafel waffle wrap." He enjoyed sharing his dinner with her.

Natalie took a bite from hers, moaning like she had the day before, as though it was the only way she could appreciate anything she put in her mouth. He bit back a grin. He loved the moans of pleasure she made. It made his heart beat a touch faster.

He unwrapped his own food. "Thanks for, you know, covering for me earlier today. My dad is great but I've made some mistakes in my life and, for once, I'd like to not be under that shadow."

She glanced at him. "I get it. Family may love you but that doesn't mean they always understand you."

"Yeah."

It was quiet for a few moments before she said, "Do I need to put on one of those beehive outfits?"

"No, they're pretty much inside the hive full-time at this point." Although, he wouldn't mind seeing her in a beekeeper suit. Mason pictured Natalie being with him during the warm summer months as he tended his hives and then tackling her in the nearby field and peeling the suit off. It was a new fantasy he never expected to have before.

"Oh, yes, vibrating together to generate heat."

He almost choked on his food at the thought she'd read

his mind before remembering they were talking about bees. He did his best to recover, keeping his words light. "Yup. That's right. The bees. Vibrating."

"Speaking of vibrating. Stan. More specifically how and what and why?"

"Are you asking for Diva Santa's origin story?"

Laughter crackled from her. He imagined it was the same sound shooting stars made as they flickered across the dark sky, like a melody. "That's what you call him?"

"It fits, don't you think?"

"Like a glove," she replied.

"Stan Anderson's story isn't too different from Superman's."

"He comes from another planet? That makes so much sense." She touched his arm excitedly and it reached his soul. He wasn't sure how it was possible to be both at ease with her, but also have all this energy within him ready to burst out.

"Non-holiday season he's a roofer but, during the winter months, there isn't as much work going on. One year, my dad hired him to be one of the parking attendants, so he could earn a little extra cash until business picked up again. He was a good guy, quiet, kind of unassuming, not that you need a ton of charisma when directing people where to park. This same year, our regular Santa got in trouble for tax fraud or something. I don't know. He just disappeared because of some kind of legal trouble he was in. So, I was going to do it until we could hire someone else but my dad's really old cheap Santa suit from storage was too small for me, like comically too small. The sleeves went up to here." Mason demonstrated by making a chopping motion halfway up his forearm.

"Like Santa went through a growth spurt?"

He laughed. "Yeah, exactly. So my dad thought we could probably lose a parking attendant and still be okay, and we asked Stan if he would do it because he looked about the right size for the suit. And, this will be hard to believe, but he actually said no."

Natalie feigned a gasp. "You're right. I don't believe it."

"He was a reluctant hero until my dad offered him more money and said he'd just have to sit there. And, at the beginning, that's exactly what he did. He was more like a Santa statue, afraid if he moved or said the wrong thing, he'd be carted off to jail or something. It was hilarious. But then something happened. Candy, our photographer, said something to him—I have no idea what—and he changed. He came out of his Santa shell. And, yes, now he's completely obnoxious, but the kids really love him, even the ones who are scared and cry at first. So, yes, we put up with Diva Santa because, and don't ever tell him this, he's really the best guy for the job."

"Hmm. Actually, now that I know his origin story, it makes him a bit more bearable. I'll still have to keep him in line though."

"Of course. Blackmailing for VIP parking spots and hot chocolate is a line too far to let him cross, so boundaries are good for him. But, at the end of the day, he may be a Diva Santa, but he's *our* Diva Santa."

They'd arrived at their destination. "Actually," he said, rubbing his neck, "now that we're here, I'm realizing how utterly unimpressive showing you my bee boxes are. I feel a little like Stan trying to impress you with his extra work in *Santa Heist*."

"You're trying to impress me?"

"I guess I can't help it any more than Stan can." He snuck a look at her, and she was staring at the boxes rather than making eye contact with him.

"Why would you care what I think?"

The question felt like a trap. For him to show all his cards only for her to push him away again wasn't something he was eager to repeat. He forced an easy smile on his lips, putting up his hands as though he had nothing to hide, no ulterior motive. "You just seem like a person with very strong opinions, like you're someone worth impressing. You can't blame that on me. That's entirely on you."

"I do?"

"Yup. Natalie… What's your last name?"

"Gonzalez-Torres."

"You have two last names?"

"In Mexican culture we use both our mother and father's surname."

"Oh. Got it. Natalie Gonzalez-Torres, you get these little creases right here between your eyebrows when you look like you have some very strong opinions in your brain." He gently touched a finger to the soft spot above the bridge of her nose.

She scoffed, batting his finger away before rubbing the exact spot. "No, I don't.

"Yup, you do. It's happening right now. My beehives have a very delicate ecosystem going on inside them and bees can be notoriously sensitive. I just don't want anything to happen because they sense you're passing strong judgments about them."

"Do you only use them for honey?"

"For now, but I want to do more with them. A lot more. They're so important to agriculture and the environment. I'd like to rent out hives to assist in pollination but it's hard to convince my dad of anything that's different from what he's been doing for forty years already. He doesn't quite see the need to try something different."

"Ah, one of those. I'm quite familiar with that predicament."

"Your uncle?"

She nodded before changing tone. "Well, Mason... What's your last name?"

"Lavigne."

"Well, Mason Lavigne, we've been standing next to these hives for about five minutes now, and I have yet to see one bee. How do I even know there are bees inside the boxes and you haven't brought me into the middle of the field for nothing."

"That's easy. If you press your ear to the box and tap it, you'll hear them buzzing."

Her expression shifted to suspicion, the tiny creases appearing between her brows again. "Yeah, right. I'm not doing that. I tap and suddenly a swarm of angry bees are going to shoot out and mob me."

He laughed. "Why would they be angry?"

"Because I'm interrupting their vibrations or something. Don't you get mad when unexpected visitors just show up to your house?"

"I'm not sure that's ever happened to me before."

"In my family, it happens all the time. No one waits for an invitation."

"I'm inviting you." He took one of her gloved hands in his and pulled her to the side of the box. Both of his knees dropped to the ground, but she stayed standing, watching him with large eyes. Mason tugged on her hand. "Come on. Nothing is going to happen." The promise related only to a potential bee attack but not to anything else.

She did a glance around as if checking to see if anyone was watching, but the farm was quiet at this point, then she released a long breath and slowly sank to her knees, facing him. Natalie used her fingers to swipe across her forehead as if to smooth away any trace of judgment from her face. "Okay, I'm ready."

As he had instructed before, he pressed his ear against the side of the box.

"You're seriously putting your face against that?"

"It's okay. Come on. You don't seem like the nervous type."

With some visible reluctance, Natalie pressed her ear to the box and tapped lightly on the side. From inside the box came the sound of buzzing.

"They're vibrating," she said with amazement.

While Mason's bees were always a sense of pride for him, he was stuck on how lovely she was. The side of the beehive was under twenty inches. They weren't necessarily pressed against each other, but it was close enough. Those warm brown eyes of hers lit with delight at something as simple as hearing bees buzz inside a box, and he understood the feeling. Some of the dark strands of her hair had escaped the edges of her beanie and were lightly sweeping her cheek. The lines of her full lips were perfect curves and they slightly parted. When his eyes returned to hers, she was watching him with equal intensity.

Mason took a chance, brushing his thumb softly along her chin and heard a light breath in response. His heart wanted it so badly his mind began playing tricks on him, imagining she tilted closer. He continued believing this until he felt the soft brush of her lips against his, as soft as a sigh.

And then he was floating.

Chapter Eleven

CURIOSITY KILLED THE kissing cat.

Okay, not killed.

How about curiosity nearly made the kissing cat stop breathing so there was danger of damn asphyxiation?

Yeah, something like that.

Shit.

Natalie jerked away, fumbling with the phone in her hand. Had it vibrated? Whether it had or not, she pretended checking it was the most important thing in the world. "It's Mia. I was supposed to stop by later today." She scrambled to her feet.

Shit. Shit. Shit.

What the hell was wrong with her?

It hadn't been a full kiss, not a real one, merely a brush of lips, but she couldn't bluff her way into making him believe it was anything other than what it looked like. She couldn't say, *Oh, sorry. I thought I saw some delicious crumbs on your face and decided to wipe them away with my lips.*

Again, what *the hell* was wrong with her?

It was just waffles and bees and…and nothing. There wasn't one particular thing about the moment that screamed romance. She only had her ear pressed against a box, listening for damn bee vibrations. Why would this warrant kissing Mason?

Curiosity. It was curiosity. Plain and simple. Done.

But why was she curious?

Natalie wanted to scream because she didn't know.

UGH!

A nervousness settled in her gut. She considered racing away and never returning. How could she do this without giving the impression she was running away?

"Sorry I—Are you okay?" Mason asked behind her as he stood, his voice soft.

She noticed the concern etched in his brow, which she supposed wasn't fair because he hadn't done this, she had. It wasn't Mason's problem, it was hers. She was the one who'd put herself on a strict romance diet, one where she was only allowed cheat days at specific times of the year and a single location on the map. And crushing hearts of nice guys wasn't the type of villainy she wanted.

"No…I… M-my leg fell asleep. And I forgot about Mia. I shouldn't have forgotten. The sun is going to set soon." Her rambling gave the impression she was a complete mess. She walked with purpose toward the parking lot.

He stuffed his hands in his pockets as he followed her. "Yeah. Okay." For most of the way, they walked in silence; each seemed to be lost in their own thoughts. "Sorry, if I did something to—"

"No," Natalie heard herself say, even if this was the perfect opportunity to reiterate her decision to not start anything with anyone but, for some reason, she didn't. "It's fine. You're fine. I-I think I'm just tired from the weekend.

I'm not used to working at a coffee stand by myself and… I don't know. Sorry." Oh, okay, so now she was going to give the impression she had a habit of kissing guys when she was tired. *Wow, Natalie.* Why didn't she admit the truth?

Mason was someone she thought would be nice to kiss.

He brought her dinner, made sure she had a heat lamp, showed her his beehives, and escorted her to her car. She wasn't sure how to express appreciation without making it weird. Saying thank you didn't seem to be enough. Touching him again was too risky. Instead, she did this odd arm pat on his bicep and said, "Okay. Thanks. I guess I'll see you next weekend then. Your bees were nice."

"The bees you never saw."

"I suppose you could have stuck a recording in a box simply to lure me out there."

A small smile crept along his lips. He had a nice one. It wasn't large but it was soft like the rest of him. "I suppose you're also suspicious of the Big Bee lobby."

She couldn't help but laugh. The awkwardness never lasted with him. He had a way about him, making her at ease again. "Yes, now you're getting it."

He'd stepped nearer until she had to tip her head to make eye contact. "They're only a seasonal lobby. As soon as it gets cold, they just vibrate in a box and eat honey." Mason tucked the end of her scarf into the front of her jacket.

"Uh-huh." Her reply was somewhat breathless and also automatic. She didn't process his words and would have given the same response regardless of what he said.

"Goodnight, Natalie Gonzalez-Torres," he said. "Drive safely and I hope you get some rest."

"Uh, yeah, thanks. You, too."

Too bad she couldn't drive away from trouble so easily.

A COUPLE DAYS later, Natalie sat in her office, staring at the order form on her computer screen while crunching on a hard cinnamon candy. After fifteen minutes of trying to focus, she gave up. She spent a few days inside Pony Expresso during the week to give Enrique a break from managing but, seeing as how he wasn't used to the position, it created more work for her. At this point, it was as if she had two jobs: working the horse trailer and spending a couple days in the coffee shop cleaning up whatever mess her uncle left for her. The current problem: they'd run out of paper towels for the bathroom because the weekly supply order hadn't been done. Natalie had to run to the store to get enough to hold them over.

She pulled another hard candy from her desk drawer and left her office. The morning rush was nearly finished but she looked for some busy work, something to keep her mind occupied. Unfortunately, there wasn't much. She was too nervous, like she was waiting for something to spring on her. Natalie unwrapped the candy, popping it in her mouth.

"¿Estás bien?" Diego asked her.

"Yeah, everything's fine." Then she saw it. A new ornament had been added to the tree. Near the top was a smiling marshmallow sitting in a mug of cocoa. She looked at it while running a finger across her lips.

"Natalie?"

"What?" She jumped, finding Mia beside her. "God, M! Where'd you come from?"

Her best friend tilted her head, appearing concerned. "Is everything okay?"

"Yeah, of course. Why wouldn't things be okay?" Everyone was being ridiculous, as though she was acting differently than normal. They were wrong—she was still the same old Natalie.

"Well, I've been talking to you for a few minutes, and you haven't even noticed me. Oh, did you get a new ornament? Cute! I like it."

"Your friend dropped that off for you yesterday morning," Crystal said as she wiped a nearby tabletop.

Mia's attention homed in on her. "You have a friend decorating your tree? Was I supposed to bring an ornament? Am I failing my best friend duties?"

"No, it's not—It's nothing. Crystal doesn't know what she's saying."

"Okay," she said slowly. "But the ornament came from somewhere. Are you going to make me guess or are you telling me? I can guess, but it's probably going to be more fun for me than for you."

This was all getting out of hand. "It's nothing. They came from Mason."

"Mason? The Christmas tree guy?" Her mouth fell open in happy astonishment. "And what do you mean, *they*? Did he also bring the blue jay ornament? Good Lord! Is he wooing you? Are you being Christmas wooed right now? I knew it! I'm telling you, Natalie, I saw something at that tree farm. He likes you."

She grabbed Mia's arm, dragging her from the Christmas tree to a more private corner in the rear of the shop. "Okay, stop. You're making too much out of this, especially considering you know that nothing is ever going to happen between us." At least nothing more than the brush of his lips that happened at his beehive. Nothing more was going to happen—an important distinction.

Her friend flicked a hand in her direction as though to brush her words away.

"What? You don't think I can maintain my boundaries with the guy?"

"No. I know you can. What I'm saying is why would you want to?"

She huffed out a frustrated breath and crossed her arms. "I'm not going to have a fling with the Christmas tree guy."

"Well, when you put it like that, it sounds incredibly snobbish."

"Why are you pushing this so hard? I don't need to be in a relationship or to have a fling with this guy. I'm fine. I have work and this partnership to worry about. And I'm happy with how things are. I don't need to be wooed."

Mia adjusted her glasses. "Nat. You're one of the most resilient women I know. And you're right, you don't need a guy. I don't get excited about things like this because I feel like you're incomplete or you need to get laid or whatever. It's more of a case that I think you deserve to be wooed. I get excited when I see someone who looks at you like you're special, because you are."

She wasn't sure how to respond. While she knew this was Mia being Mia, it was hard maintaining a level of annoyance toward her. Her friend had a way of saying things that made her look at everything differently. Still, she had trouble accepting it. "Mason doesn't look at me that way."

"It's okay. I know you have blinders on. And I know people see me as a people pleaser, but I hope you see me as your friend and, when I say something is true, you believe me. Because he does look at you that way."

As much as Natalie wanted to continue pleading ignorance, in her gut she knew Mia was right. She closed her eyes, leaning against the wall behind her. "God, Mia, what am I going to do?"

"What do you want?"

She could face the most disgruntled customer in the world. Or take vacations by herself and make out with virtual strangers. But the thought of facing Mason again was anxiety-inducing. "I want everything to go back to normal, to how it was when I was just doing my work here at Pony Expresso and didn't have to deal with any of this."

"So you like him too." Her best friend stated this as though it were a fact.

She opened her eyes to glare at her. "How did you get that from me saying I just want everything to go back to normal?"

"As if I haven't gotten a good idea of your M.O. If you really had no interest in the guy, you'd have no problems telling him to leave you alone. But you're not doing that. You'd rather avoid him instead. That's different."

"Don't psychoanalyze me. I'm putting you on bathroom-cleaning duties. I don't care if you don't work here anymore."

Mia snorted a laugh. "Yeah, nice try."

She pushed from the wall, returning to standing. "I just got an idea. What are you doing this weekend?"

"You mean, Thanksgiving weekend? Eating leftovers and hanging out with Ross."

"So, like every weekend?"

Mia stuck her tongue at her. "Better than working."

"Oh, come on. Don't you want to make a little extra money? It's just for a few days and I could really use the help." Having a buddy around might prevent the situation from getting worse and keep her from giving in to temptation.

Mia studied her. "You're asking me to be your buffer, aren't you?"

"No! I just… It's probably going to be the busiest weekend for people getting a Christmas tree and I'm there all by myself, and it was hard enough last weekend when I barely had a chance to go to the bathroom or scarf some food down. Please." Natalie interlaced her hands together, bringing them to her chin as if this was a desperate plea.

Her friend groaned. "All right, fine. I'm doing it because I care about your bladder. And after I convince Ross that we need a fancy tree this year, you have to give me a break to go pick one out with him."

"You mean you haven't convinced him yet. That doesn't sound like you."

She adjusted her glasses while smiling smugly. "That's because I haven't even begun to try yet."

Natalie was so grateful she wrapped her in an excited hug. "Thank you! It's going to be like old times with us working together. We'll have fun. I just have to warn you about Diva Santa."

"Wait. Who?"

Chapter Twelve

On Black Friday, Natalie returned to the horse trailer, but this time with Mia. She commended herself on a brilliant idea because, as she had predicted, the farm was busier than the previous week. Having another pair of hands made everything run smoother. It was also colder, evident by the foot of fresh powder that had fallen over the last week, giving the Christmas tree farm more of a winter holiday appearance. While normally having an extra body inside the small coffee truck would be stifling, Natalie was happy to have another person producing body heat. The heating lamp was still there but another had been added to the opposite side of the truck, plus all the snow around the area had been shoveled.

Having Mia was nice, even if she appeared in her corny Christmas sweater with the decorated reindeer antlers. Her friend grinned while pulling a wrapped package from her bag, handing it to Natalie.

"What is this?" she asked.

"I came across it while scrolling through the Internet and thought it was perfect for you."

She undid the wrapping and found a blue Christmas sweater. She was about to protest until the front was revealed. It had typical holiday sweater motifs like snowflakes but in the center was a skeleton wearing a Santa hat and drinking from a mug with the words *Chilled to the Bone*. "I love it."

"Quick. Put it on. I'll finish setting up."

As busy as the day was, Natalie was pleased with how smooth it all went. The one time Mason stopped by, she made sure to mention his beehives to Mia. As her friend took an authentic interest in most things, she asked him a ton of questions. In the end, Natalie's interaction with him was minimal. She hardly had to do anything besides making him another Mexican hot chocolate because he insisted on trying the drink again. Mia proved to be the perfect buffer.

Natalie hoped Saturday would go as smoothly as Friday and, at first, it did.

"Oh, Ross is here!" Mia said excitedly, as if she didn't see her tall, dark, and handsome husband every day. She pushed her way past Natalie in order to escape the horse trailer. Acting as though it were the last reel of a romance movie, she flung herself into Ross's arms and kissed him.

"Hey, Natalie," Ross said over his wife's shoulder as he continued holding his wife close.

"Hi. How's it going?" Okay, it was cute how much Ross and Mia were clearly still into each other. If anyone was going to make her second-guess her whole opinion on the existence of love, it would be them. Their relationship was somewhere between being utterly content with each other while still being excited to spend their days together. Natalie tried to imagine her parents at that stage, but she couldn't see anything past their mutual contempt. How long would it take Mia and Ross to get to that point? The thought made her sad.

"Are you okay if we go pick out our tree now? It's not too busy. Plus, I need to take some pictures for Poinsettia Paradise's Facebook page." Mia was two birds, one stoning it again. Natalie didn't know how she'd convinced Mason to pay her to take pictures for him, but it worked like a charm.

"I see she was able to convince you about this whole Christmas tree thing," Natalie said to Mia's husband. Ross B.M. (Before Mia) never would have been the type to care about things like holiday decorations. At the time, Natalie didn't realize the jewelry store owner next to Pony Expresso had a personality. She and the rest of the coffee shop employees simply thought of him as the jewelry guy with the dog because that was all they knew about him. In fact, his three-legged dog ambled into the coffee shop more than Ross did in those days, begging for muffin scraps.

He shrugged, tucking Mia's hair behind her ear with care. "You know how persuasive she can be."

"I don't need to be persuasive when I'm right. I haven't had a Christmas tree in a few years. And you probably don't even remember the last time you had—"

"All right, Russo. All right. You've already convinced me. You don't have to keep trying," he replied.

Regardless of how Ross pretended he was being forced into this, the truth was clear enough. Mia simply had to ask and he would pretty much say yes to anything.

She watched the couple put their dog, Hermes, on a leash, who was greeted by Bentley. Mia pulled her husband toward the path where the trees grew, still chatting away. She was probably sharing everything she'd learned about bees. Natalie caught herself smiling. She jumped when she noticed Mason stood at the order window. "Oh, hi. You scared me," she said, pressing a hand to her chest.

"Sorry. Was that Mia with her husband?"

"Yeah, they're going to pick out a tree." She hoped by mentioning this, he might excuse himself to help the couple personally, but he didn't move from where he leaned against the counter. Nervous energy returned to her stomach. She didn't like to be here without her buffer. Damn Mia for being married and wanting things like Christmas trees.

"Did you want a drink?" she asked, making minimum eye contact.

"Sure. I'll take the Mexican hot chocolate."

At this, a smile lifted the edges of her mouth. "You know, you can order something else. I'm not going to judge you or anything."

"I'm actually starting to like it. It has a warm kick to it. I think you were right that you need to appreciate it as its own drink and not compare it to American hot chocolate."

She proceeded to make the drink for him. Maybe this could still be normal, even with Mia gone.

He cleared his throat. "So…" he started, his hands rubbing the back of his neck. She got a sinking feeling. "Are you, uh, doing anything after you close up today?"

Was he actually asking her out? If she wasn't dealing with anxiety, she'd be impressed with his guts. Her mind scrambled to come up with a convenient excuse. Natalie could say she and Mia were already doing something after work, so she could avoid him without making it sound like a rejection.

"I just thought that—I really enjoyed hanging out with you after closing and sharing waffle wraps. Also, now that we have snow, we have this really great hill just on the other side of the barn and it might be fun to go tubing."

"Oh." It was a sweet invitation. Natalie couldn't remember the last time she went sledding or snow tubing. Some of her older cousins had kids and it was enjoyable to watch them have fun. These days, she was beginning to feel too much of an adult to participate in such activities herself.

"I could do it alone but for some reason people think it's weird if you go snow tubing by yourself. A guy has to be careful with his reputation."

"Look, Mason," she started, and his face instantly lost some of its jovialness. Mia had been right. How she'd been behaving around him wasn't her normal M.O. If she wanted things to return to how they were before, she'd have to revert to her old self, the cynical barista who gave no shits about finding love and whose heart was untouchable, unhurtable. Except this time, the words were harder to get out. "I-I'm here to work. That's all."

She almost added the word *sorry* because the rejection gave her an uneasiness in her gut, as though she'd made the wrong choice even if her brain was convinced it was correct. Some guys didn't get the hint if she wasn't blunt; therefore, the apology remained missing. She focused her attention on finishing his drink, rolling the molinillo between her palms.

"It's okay," Mason said, which raised her head in surprise. She was used to expecting either silence or contempt, both of which she could handle. While his eyes reflected sadness, his lips tipped in a slight smile. He took his drink from her. "I'll leave you to your work then. Thanks for the drink." Mason slid his money across the counter before departing.

She continued to watch him, expecting the nervousness to leave her, to be replaced with a sense of relief. The anxiety remained, as though it was too late to return to the way it was before.

"I'm back!" Mia said, bounding into the horse trailer later, glowing with joy.

"What took you so long?" Natalie asked, irritation flaring through her. For the first time, she experienced annoyance at perfect Mia with her happy marriage and getting to live a blissful life, where she got to partake in things such as skipping through family farms to pick out a Christmas tree with the love of her life. What she felt wasn't logical, but she felt it all the same, even while realizing how unfair it was to her best friend.

Mia flinched. "I've only been gone for twenty minutes, and you knew I had to also take pictures."

"I asked you here to help me." For some inexplicable reason, Natalie wanted to cry but she could only allow anger through. Tears didn't make sense but being mad at the situation somehow did.

"Sorry. Was it really that busy?"

"No. It's just… Mason stopped by while you were gone."

"Okay," she said, appearing not to understand the implication.

"He wanted…" As much as Natalie didn't want to prove Mia right once again, she had to confide in someone. "He wanted to see if I'd hang out with him after closing."

Surprisingly, her friend didn't throw confetti in the air. "He asked you out?"

She picked at the edge of the countertop. "Yeah. Wanted to take me sledding near the barn."

While Mia's expression didn't change, she did touch a hand to her chest.

"Stop it. You know I can't."

"Come on. I mean, I understand, but also I don't understand. You're really going to deny yourself sledding because you're that worried about becoming your parents. It's just a fun evening of sledding. He didn't ask you to move in with him."

"It's not just—" Natalie stopped herself. She had told her a lot, but she hadn't confided everything. "I almost had a quick marriage myself."

"What?" The word vibrated off the walls. "When was this?"

She released a frustrated groan, fighting the urge to cry again. "You're not going to judge me are you? It's not something I'm proud of."

Mia's shocked expression softened. "No. We've all done something we're not proud of. That's just a normal part of life." She rubbed a reassuring hand along Natalie's arm. "You can tell me."

She shrugged her hands. "I was nineteen. I'd just started working for my uncle. Some guy came into the coffee shop, started flirting with me. He was cute and I was flattered so I agreed to go out with him. I was instantly in love. Every day, after work, I'd hang out with him and I was so sure he was the one. And after a week of us being obsessed with each other, he asked me to marry him and I said yes. We were going to run off to the state line."

Mia handed the drink she made to a customer while paying attention to Natalie. "Wait, so you've been married?"

"No, thank God. He was pressuring me to get married as soon as possible because his job was transferring him to the East Coast, and wouldn't it be great to start our lives together as soon as possible? And I thought, yes, this is it. I can do this because I loved him. But I started thinking about what that really meant, leaving my whole life, my family, everything I know. It suddenly hit me that maybe it might be a good idea to stop and slow things down.

"I decided maybe we should wait for a little bit, not rush into it. Then he was different. Stephen went from someone who was charming to someone cruel. He insulted my family, my job, saying he thought I was someone who was special, someone who was stronger, but apparently, he was wrong about me, that I didn't care about him at all. I was just a carefree flirt who didn't care what I did to people's hearts. And I started to think that maybe he was right."

"Are you kidding? Of course, he wasn't right."

She nodded. "He said dealing with someone like me wasn't worth it. *I* wasn't worth it. I was making him feel nothing toward me. And it killed me because if I truly loved him, I'd be able to do this for him. And if he had loved me, he'd understand that I wasn't ready. If I can almost make a huge mistake while *thinking* I was in love, what kind of trouble can I get into if it's actually the real thing? And the funny thing is that there never was any job. He'd lied to me.

He was unemployed, couch surfing at a friend's house and was about to get kicked out. But I'd been so charmed by him, I didn't see anything. I'd probably be miserable if I had married him. And why be stuck and miserable when I can work in a horse trailer on a Christmas farm with you?" She did her best to lighten things with a smile at the end, like none of this bothered her anymore.

"Okay, that guy was clearly a douchebag, but Mason isn't him. So, you got whatever you needed from that experience, and you learned. You can do better."

"Yeah, well, now I'm looking out for myself. So now you understand."

"I get that it's sometimes scary to throw yourself out there. God, if anyone knows, it's me. But I don't think you should cut yourself out of things completely, not allow any risks."

"I take risks. What do you think my Tahoe trips are about?"

She rolled her eyes. "I'm talking about risks of the heart, and you know it."

"I'm going to do what's best for everyone and going out with Mason is not it."

"Sure," Mia replied, but then her tone switched to a more chipper one. "Well, no one is going to force you, least of all me."

Natalie was surprised. She wasn't sure if she expected more of a fight, but she seemed to accept her reasoning easily enough. She was grateful to have such a supportive friend.

Business was surprisingly quiet. Mia leaned against the counter to people-watch. Natalie took out her phone to scroll through social media.

"I really like that woman's coat," her friend said, staring across the farmyard with her chin propped on a hand.

"What woman?"

"The one talking to Mason. That coat is gorgeous. Do you think it would be weird if I went over to ask her where she got it or at least take a picture of it? I definitely don't think it's too early to start dropping Ross some hints on what I want for Christmas."

She became curious about this coat. Sure enough, standing beside Mason was a beautiful blonde woman wearing an elegant long wool coat in an attractive shade of magenta. She stood out in an environment of white and green, both her and the coat were eye-catching.

"Maybe I should ask Mason," Mia mused to herself.

"You really think he's going to have information about a coat?"

"No, but they seem *really* friendly. Maybe they know each other, and he can introduce us so it's less weird. He'd vouch that I'm not a coat creep, right?"

Were they being friendly? She studied him and the woman with a new eye. Although they were too far away to hear any conversation, it was clear they were conversing easily. He stood beside her, propping up a wrapped tree in one hand. A friendly smile lit his face while the woman happily conversed with him. It seemed more than a strictly business transaction.

"Wow, she's really pretty," Mia said. "She could probably pull off any coat. It's really not very fair. Well, good for Mason. He's a nice guy. It's great to see he can get right back on the sled again."

She narrowed her gaze at her friend before returning her attention to the couple, trying to see if this assumption was due to a wild imagination or there was actually something there. The blonde touched his forearm, tossing her head back in laughter. Oh, they were *definitely* flirting. Natalie twisted the rag in her hand in annoyance. "Or he's just helping her," she said, trying to sound as though she couldn't care one way or the other.

"You're probably right," Mia replied with a shrug. "Except he just pointed to the barn, and it looks like his lips said the word *sledding*."

"You really think I'm going to believe he's asking someone else to go sledding a mere hour after asking me?" Although, maybe he would because, as Mia had stated, he had pointed to the barn area.

"I guess it doesn't really matter what we believe. I mean, the truth of the matter is that nothing has really happened between you two so it's not like he's doing anything wrong if he connects with someone else. When you make a connection, you make a connection. It's not like you can always control the timing of it. I have to say, they make a really cute couple. He's definitely found someone who has great taste in coats."

The blonde woman touched Mason's arm again and Natalie tossed the cleaning rag, grabbing her own five-year-old, not-gorgeous coat as she stomped past Mia and out of the horse trailer.

"What are you doing?" Mia yelled after her.

"I don't know." And she truly didn't know what she was doing. She was irritated at Mia, Mason, whoever that blonde woman was, at the whole damn world. All she wanted was one day of peace.

She didn't expect him to pine over her forever, but it didn't seem right for him to get over her in the span of an hour. All this did was prove his affection didn't run deep. Typical. Just like Stephen. She hated men like that, guys who flitted from woman to woman as if one was the same as any other. He shouldn't be able to do that to anyone, let alone to her. Someone needed to tell the man off and it might as well be her.

"Mason!" she said, striding toward him, powered on some weird sense of vengeance. Finally, her anger had a proper direction to focus on instead of poor Mia. This was for all the women he'd suckered by making sure they were warm and fed and didn't have Diva Santas bothering them.

His gaze snapped to hers, along with the pretty blonde woman's, both sets of eyes wide as though not sure what to expect from some wild woman stomping across the yard with revenge on her mind. Mason may have even looked around nervously because he knew he'd been caught.

Her mouth opened to unleash her fury when Stan, sucking on a candy cane stick, stopped as if an internal sensor had alerted him to impending drama and possible gossip. This gave her a moment of pause because, as far as she was aware, Stan, and whoever else he told, thought she and Mason were dating. While Mason most likely deserved a good verbal lashing, she wasn't sure she wanted to be in the center of what would appear to be a messy fake breakup.

Except, after interrupting everyone's conversation, they were staring at her, waiting. What blurted from her mouth was: "I'll do the damn sledding with you."

This was sure to let Mason know she was on to him and save the woman grief if he'd also offered her the same invitation. She'd take one for the team, even if, up close, she didn't think the woman's coat was so spectacular.

His face broke into a grin.

It was then she realized she'd soon be in the market for a new best friend because she was going to kill Mia.

Chapter Thirteen

NURSING A HEART after a rejection was never easy for Mason. It was as though the universe was once again telling him, *Nope, you're not meant for anyone. You're going to die alone in the field next to your bees, and they will use your rotting corpse for their next hive.* It was the beekeeper's equivalent of a cat lady's face being eaten off by her beloved pets. Considering how much joy his bees had brought him, it wouldn't be the worst way to go.

He'd been wrong, once again, about there being a real connection with someone, and maybe he was feeling somewhat foolish thinking Natalie was a possibility. As soon as he asked her to go sledding, he'd seen the answer written all over her face.

It sucked, but there wasn't much he could do about it. He returned to his job, trying to push her from his mind. Except, Natalie was always there, even when Lana stopped by. A local event planner, Lana was someone he had become familiar with since she'd approached the farm about holding special events, most of them being weddings. In fact, Lana had been entertaining him with a story about a chipmunk that had crawled up a bridesmaid's leg during a wedding reception inside the barn and mass chaos had ensued.

He forgot about the conversation as soon as Natalie appeared, fire sparking from those beautiful brown eyes of hers.

No one was more surprised than him when she blurted, she'd *do the damn sledding* with him. He wasn't quite sure why she sounded angry about it, but he wasn't about to ask. While he would have preferred her to accept his invitation with more glee, the point was she'd agreed and that was enough for him.

He couldn't stop a smile from spreading across his face. "Okay. Great. Sounds good. Oh, this is Lana, she's a local event planner. Lana, this is Natalie. She runs the coffee truck here. Great coffee. If you ever need one at your events, I highly recommend her." The two women shook hands although Lana appeared way more enthusiastic about it than Natalie. When an SUV pulled up, Lana's husband stepped from the driver's seat.

"Is loading here okay?" he asked.

"Yeah, it's fine," Mason replied, bringing the Christmas tree closer so he could help tie the tree to the vehicle's roof.

"You picked a great tree, honey," the man said to Lana. "The kids are going to love it."

Natalie backed away as if she was attempting to escape unnoticed while everyone was busy. "I'll come see you at closing, Natalie," Mason said before she could disappear completely.

She lifted her hand in acknowledgment as she walked away. He did hear her say, "Dammit, Mia! You are the worst."

Through the coffee trailer window, Mia appeared to be cleaning furiously with a rag, only glancing at him to offer a tiny wave. He wasn't sure exactly what had happened, but he was coming to like her more and more.

He caught Lana studying him with a funny little smile playing on her lips. "Maybe someday you'll need my services for yourself, Mase. I'd love that."

He dropped eye contact, focusing on tightening the tree's ties. "Oh, uh, probably not anytime soon."

The rest of the workday was uneventful. As the day started to wind down, he asked Charlie to keep an eye on things so he could slip into the barn to find the old snow tubes and fill them with air, making sure they weren't duds. He obviously hadn't thought far enough ahead to consider maybe they had sprung leaks or were unusable. Luckily, they were in good shape.

As the day's end drew closer, he made his way to the Placerville Waffle Company truck. "Hey, Marco. How's it going?" Mason said to the young guy working the window.

"Mase, hey. You want the special?" Marco brushed his long, unruly locks from his forehead.

"Yeah, I'll take two."

"Ma, I need two of the Philly wraps." He leaned on the counter. "Sounds like two is getting to be a regular thing with you. I heard from Santa's little helper that you have a thing going on with the coffee girl. That true?" The man pumped his eyebrows suggestively.

"Is that Mason?" Marco's mom asked, pushing her way to the counter with his food in hand. "Is it true about you and the coffee girl? She's a pretty one. I told Marco he better get a move on it, but you know…" His mom gave her son a playful smack on the head. "You snooze, you lose, buddy."

Mason wasn't sure how to approach this situation he had created. As much as he wanted to trust Stan not to be a blabbermouth, this was Stan. The chance of maintaining any kind of secrecy was low at best. He attempted to appear casual. "Yup, I have a thing for her." This was technically correct even if it wasn't exactly what they'd asked.

"Good for you, Mase. She seems like a nice girl," she responded while handing the food to him and refusing to take his money no matter how many times he offered.

"She definitely keeps me on my toes," which was also true considering how the day had been a roller coaster of emotions but, so far, he was coming out on top. Mason hoped it stayed that way.

He made his way to the coffee trailer, and Natalie was locking the doors as Mia stood nearby, zipping her coat. Mia gave him a bright smile and a tiny wave.

"Are you sure you don't want to go sledding with us?" Natalie asked, unaware Mason was already there.

"I want to get home to Ross so we can decorate our tree. Hi, Mason. I think Natalie might be a little nervous going tubing with you. She told me that she hasn't done it in a while. You better stick close to make sure she doesn't wipe out or something."

"I'm not nervous. It's tubing, not skiing. I don't think it's possible to get hurt," she said, not appearing any less irritated with her friend.

Mia leaned closer to him, whispering loud enough for anyone to hear. "Don't believe her. She's definitely nervous."

"Ugh! Mia, I swear to God." She shoved her beanie on her head and jammed on her gloves, turning to address him.

"Do you have any customer bathrooms, outhouses, port-o-potties that need cleaning? Because I might have someone I can volunteer for the job."

Mia stepped to Natalie, throwing her arms around her in a huge hug. "You know you love me no matter what. Have fun and text me later. Bye," she said before wandering away, arms swinging in a carefree manner.

With Mia gone, it became quiet between them. He considered maybe she hadn't been looking forward to hanging out with him. She didn't look happy as she glared after Mia.

As much as he didn't want the evening to be cut short, he also wasn't trying to drag someone against their will. Dakota had taught him that being present wasn't enough. He wanted someone who actually wanted to be around him. "Look, Natalie, I don't know what happened between the time I asked you and you agreeing, but if you really don't want to, I'm not going to pressure you into it."

"So if I want to go home, you'd be okay with that?" she asked, eyeing him.

"Yeah, of course." Although he couldn't hide his disappointment.

She took a moment to ponder this and it was pure torture on his end. Natalie took the steps necessary to stand close, tilting her face up to him. She carefully reached into his jacket pocket, removing today's waffle wrap. "I think I'll stick around."

The tension dissipated and he smiled, half happy, half relieved. "Really?"

Her gaze dropped as she peeled the paper from her food. "I'm sorry about earlier. I was unfairly rude. When you're used to being a villain, it's a hard habit to break."

Her position remained fixed; she hadn't shifted away. It would be the most natural thing in the world for Mason to slip his arms around her and settle them at her waist. It took all his willpower to keep his hands to himself. "Rough day?"

If the reason was Stan, he may resort to taking away all his negotiated perks. The temptation was there, especially considering the man didn't know how to keep his mouth shut even after bribery.

"It certainly wasn't the best but it's my own fault. I should warn you that I'm not the most normal person in the world, as I'm sure you're more than aware."

He laughed. "God, if you want to hear about *not normal*… I like this woman, see, and I visit her truck to order Mexican hot chocolate. I want to expand my taste buds so she doesn't think I'm boring but I'm also starting to like it. And I bring her offerings of food and ask her to go snow tubing on my family's farm instead of taking her out to a fancy restaurant because apparently I'm still ten years old and super awkward."

Her brown eyes took on a mischievous glint. "It sounds like the only thing you haven't done is pull her hair."

"That's probably pretty risky."

Those eyes grew glittering and dangerous. "Some villains actually like it.

This time he didn't resist, giving a loose strand a playful tug. Her lips parted in a gasp and—God, he wanted to kiss her so badly, just to press every part of her against every part of him. If a small tug could elicit this kind of response, he couldn't wait to see what else he could draw from her.

She gave him a light smack on his stomach, and he released a small grunt in surprise.

"I wasn't ready! And I never said that *I* was that kind of villain." Natalie focused again on her waffle wrap. "What kind is it this time?"

"I think it's a Philly cheesesteak waffle wrap." He pulled his own food from his other pocket and they made their way toward the barn.

"So that woman from earlier today, she does events here at the farm?"

Mason took a bite from his food, nodding in response.

"How long has that been going on?"

"About five years or so. Do you want me to give you her contact information?" He was happy to do anything he could to help Natalie.

"Oh, I was just thinking about your bee situation and your father. Have you ever created a full business proposal? In my situation, it felt like my uncle never listened to me either, and I realized, even though I'm thirty and have been working with him forever, he still sees me as a kid most of the time. It wasn't until I started approaching him as a businessperson that I could make some leeway. It wasn't just me bothering him to ask for something. I put in the work to give him actual numbers. I show him that if we do this, this is what we can expect and this is how I can back it up. And, as reluctant as I was to do this coffee truck thing at Poinsettia Paradise, I can understand why he wanted me to do it. It was from one of my proposals and now he wants to see me prove it. I'm sure it was the same thing with the event planner. Her proposal got your father to listen, and maybe that's the only way he's able to see past the person."

He had never thought about it before but what she said made perfect sense. Mason almost laughed at having his mind blown away at this different perspective. "Yeah. Maybe you're right."

They had arrived at the barn, and he opened the door in order to usher her inside. They would be able to finish their dinner while being somewhat protected from the cold.

She took a seat on a haystack. Natalie removed her gloves, but her jacket and beanie remained in place. He wondered what it would take to see her hair in its full glory, thick and cascading with those dark, glossy locks tangled around his fingers. It was hard to focus on anything else.

"Wow," she said, taking in the barn's interior. "It's actually pretty nice in here. I don't know why I expected the barn to be full of cows and cobwebs."

"It used to be. But since Lana started using it for weddings and receptions, we thought we should at least sweep out some of the cobwebs and get rid of the cow shit."

She laughed, her head tilting backwards. Getting her to laugh felt the same as discovering he could perform magic. "You're telling me that no one's wedding theme is cobwebs and cow shit? Better adjust those dream wedding Pinterest boards."

Her eyes continued to survey the area as she ate her wrap and pulled a water bottle from her bag, offering it to him before getting one for herself. "I take it that's the infamous holiday meditation spot," she said, pointing her bottle toward one particular stall with a red curtain around it.

He nodded. "Yup, that's it. You should take a look."

"I'm not going to be weirded out, am I?"

"Not unless he's changed it since I looked in earlier today."

"Okay, well, now I'm curious." She jumped from her seat, stuffing her empty food wrapper in her pocket. He followed behind her, watching as she pulled the curtain back to reveal the inside of the stall.

"You did this?" she asked.

He wished he could tell her yes because she appeared impressed. "No. All I did was nail up the fabric around the stall."

"My God." Natalie plopped onto a small red chaise, running her fingers along the edge. "He brought this in?"

When Stan had asked Mason for help in dragging the velvet chaise into the barn, he had agreed but not without rolling his eyes because, as usual, Diva Santa was being ridiculous. But seeing Natalie upon it did funny things to his imagination, things that Stan had never intended for his chaise, and they got Mason's heart beating. He leaned casually against one of the stall's posts because, if he didn't, he might take advantage of the couch. In addition to the chaise, there was a small table with a mirror propped up and a candy dish full of peppermint balls. He leaned to flick on the battery-operated twinkle lights so she could get the full effect. Pinned on the wall was a copy of the *El Dorado Times* article, a small photo of a tan and white guinea pig wearing tiny antlers, and a selfie picture of Stan and Candy the Elf.

"Yup," Mason answered. "He said the couch was something he had lying around at his place."

She leaned to grab a peppermint candy from Stan's dish,

unwrapping it before popping it into her mouth. "We might have to fake break up. Stan is starting to win me over with his style."

He put his hands in a surrender pose. "Fair. Maybe you understand now why I was so eager to keep you guys apart."

"It's too bad he's obsessed with Christmas. I'd probably only make it until November before wanting to stab myself in the eye. Christmas guys and I are probably a recipe for not only disaster but also severe food poisoning and vomiting."

"Yikes. I hope it won't be that bad." Did she also see a relationship between them as that same recipe? He brushed the thought aside, reaching an open hand to her. "All right, food's gone. You're getting too comfortable. It's time to go tubing."

She put her hand in his, allowing him to pull her up. "I don't suppose I can request a coffee meditation stall."

"I'm going to have to start charging stall rental fees. Do you think I should add that to my future business plan portfolio?"

She laughed.

They left the barn, each with one of the tubes Mason had filled earlier, venturing to a nearby hill. The area was one he'd snow tubed many times with his mom when he'd been a kid.

The sun was already setting, making the day shift into dusk, but there were still a few rays of light, plus Mason had made sure to turn on the lights on the side of the barn so it wouldn't be too dark. They trudged up the hill in at least a foot of snow, Natalie dragging her tube behind her.

"Do you want me to carry that?"

"I got it," she replied, even if she was breathing heavily as they continued up the hill. "God, I run marathons in the summer. I feel like if I go down the hill, I'm not going to want to come back up again."

"Come on," he said, feeling somewhat winded himself. "We're almost there."

After reaching the top, she set her tube on the snow and gingerly sat inside it with her legs dangling over the edge. "Can you just push me? It's been a while since I've done this and I'm tired from being on my feet all day."

Putting his hands on her shoulders, he leaned closer and said in a low voice, "I think you are exactly the type of villain who likes getting her hair pulled."

"What?" She turned her head, but it was too late because he gave her a good shove and she went over the edge. A gleeful shriek transitioning into laughter followed her.

Mason couldn't wait and grabbed his own tube before tipping himself over the edge as well. As much as going up the hill was a pain, doing it with her was nothing. He might be able to float up.

"Maybe we should go at the same time, make it a race, and see who gets to the bottom first," she suggested.

"Okay." It wasn't a fair race considering he weighed a lot more than she did. This had to give him an advantage but perhaps he could use one. "Does the winner get to pick their prize?"

"Hmm, maybe." She tapped a finger to her chin, her eyes drifting upwards as she pondered the proposition. "Okay, if I get down the hill first, I get my own meditation stall in the barn."

"All right, and if I get down the bottom of the hill first..." which Mason definitely would because, again, he had the advantage here "...I get a kiss."

Natalie's gaze snapped to his but the glint soon shifted into something he didn't recognize, as though maybe the wheels were turning in her head. "Fine," she said. "But, first, rules. You have to hold the tube in your hands until the count of three. At the bottom of the hill, the winner is the first person to stand up."

She was being crafty. While he got a lot of momentum going down the hill, he wasn't the most graceful person trying to get out of the tube once it stopped. On this front, she had the advantage, and this race was becoming more interesting. Although, if he wanted the kiss, he had to win.

"Ready?" she asked, putting her body in a runner's position with her tube clutched to her side. With a grin, he put himself in a similar stance and nodded. He didn't care if she ran marathons, she was going to lose this race.

"Okay, good luck. One, two—" She smacked his tube hard, sending it bouncing to the ground. "Three!" She sprinted off, jumping on her tube and flying down the hill. A wicked cackle followed in her wake.

"What the fu—" Mason barely had time to react as he scrambled for his tube and then made his own dash to the hill's edge. Natalie got to the bottom of the hill first, pushing herself to stand. She was in the process of raising her arms in victory, when Mason realized he was on a trajectory straight for her. He was only able to get the word "Watch—" from his mouth before his tube knocked hers out of the way and crashed into the back of her legs, sending her flying into his lap. Instinctively, his arms wrapped around her, as she grabbed his jacket, her initial shocked gasp turning into peals of laughter as his tube glided to a slow stop.

"You bumped into me on purpose!"

"You cheated!"

She threw back her head with laughter, eyes sparkling, as she raised an arm to point toward herself. "Villain, remember? Don't ever forget."

"Oh, I won't ever forget. I have a feeling that's what makes it fun."

Her giggles tapered off as she seemed to realize their position, how close they were to each other, the atmosphere growing heavy around them. Though they were stopped at this point, she didn't make a move to scramble off his lap and his arms remained around her. Her teeth scraped along her bottom lip as one of her gloved fingers traced along his jawline.

"Do you grow a beard because it's hard to shave here?" she asked, her finger touching the center of his chin.

"No." He was finding it hard to breathe evenly. "I grow a beard because it's an easy way to keep my face warm when it's cold."

"Oh." She continued stroking a finger along his jaw.

The tension was getting to be too much, but Mason hadn't won the race. He'd take whatever this consolation prize was. "I suppose that even though you're a cheat, you're still expecting me to deliver your winnings."

"Yup," she said, her focus dipping to his lips. "Too bad for you."

It would have been too bad, except she pressed her lips to

his, and torturous villain that she was, her kiss was sweet and tender. He let her lead, only too happy to follow her into this blissful activity. His arms tightened around her as she adjusted the angle, pushing the kiss deeper, a slow slide of their lips in lazy play as if Natalie had all the time in the world to kiss him. This ranked as the best kiss he'd ever had in his life, like experiencing the fiery burst of rock candy on his tongue, one that tasted of peppermint.

To his regret, she stopped, her brown velvet gaze slowly lifting to his. "Still feel like a sore loser?" she asked.

"No," because this was the only thing his brain could manage to say. Her kiss had stolen every clever and non-clever remark from him, leaving nothing but the sensation of her behind.

"Good," she replied, brushing another soft kiss on his lips, before pulling herself from his lap.

Mason simply lay in the tube for a moment, trying to recover from the absolute shattering of his world.

"I better get going. It's getting late," Natalie said after a minute.

His moment of elation broke in sobering reality. "I have to say that was the best way to end a snow-tubing race."

She smiled but looked away as though she'd grown shy. He found it adorable.

They each grabbed their snow tube and walked in silence to the barn where they both were lost in their own thoughts. They stopped by the barn to drop off their tubes, and for Natalie to grab her bag. Mason escorted her to her vehicle.

She turned to him while removing her keys, her eyes glancing at him from beneath her eyelashes as though her impulsiveness to kiss him had fully settled into her mind and she wasn't sure how to treat him anymore. "Goodnight," was all she said.

He didn't have the same problem. Mason stepped nearer, one hand sliding along her waist while the other went to her chin, tilting it to a more pleasing angle. His hand and mind were in complete synchronization with each other. He took a moment to breathe in her space before pressing a kiss on her lips, giving it to her as tenderly as she had given it to him, his mouth moving over hers leisurely as though she was something to appreciate and revel in.

He wanted to torture her a bit, same as she had done. But he could feel himself getting caught in his own trap as his cravings for her became stronger. He stepped away in time, his hand coasting from her nape down the side of her body.

"Goodnight," he said.

Those deep brown eyes were glassy with a hint of bewilderment, and she fumbled to get into her car before driving away without a further glance.

On his side, Mason was in a dream. After he was alone in the parking field, he considered allowing his body to flop into the snow, resulting in snowflakes bursting around him in a puff of magical swirls in the shape of hearts. Instead, he approached his own vehicle, pulling out his phone in the process.

She kissed me.

Gemma:

WHAT?! Invite her to game night!

Isaac:

Was this before or after you promised her a free tree?

Gemma:

I need to see what this woman looks like.

Can you send a pic?

No.

That's weird.

Isaac:

Say you need a photo for your farm's social media page or something.

Gemma:

Oooo. I like this idea. Good thinking.

That wouldn't make you suspicious, Gemma?

Gemma:

No, it would. I'm not falling for one of your harebrained schemes.

God. You guys are useless.

I'm not getting tricked into taking a photo for you.

But he felt so good, he didn't care about anything other than replaying the memory of that night again.

Chapter Fourteen

NATALIE SHOULDN'T HAVE been surprised when Tío Enrique showed up the following day to check in on things.

"Is everything going okay?" her uncle said, while leaning against the side of the trailer, smoothing his fingers over his mustache.

"Yeah. Great." She tapped a nervous finger on the counter. There was no reason for her to be anxious. A visit from Enrique at the Pony Expresso location wasn't unusual and she was doing fine; things were under control. Maybe it was the way he was eyeing Mia, her presence a surprise to him.

Her friend was oblivious to his scrutiny, giving him her usual bright, dimpled greeting and treating him like an adopted uncle as she asked about his wife and family.

When Mia left to use the restroom, Enrique gave Natalie a serious look. "You brought Mia to help you?"

She decided to evoke confidence because that's what an owner should be. "Yes. It's Thanksgiving weekend, probably one of the busiest times, and I made the decision that it would be helpful to have someone else so we can continue to provide quick service. And Mia was willing to do it for a little extra holiday cash."

He made it a point to peruse the yard currently around the truck and, of course, it wasn't busy at that moment, making her confidence falter.

"I see," he said. "That doesn't sound like a risky *gamble* to you? We'll see if you pull in more money than you spend just because you want to help a friend."

This irked her. "I'm not—She's helping me. And it's just for this weekend. Yesterday *was* busy and it's still early so it will be busy again. You'll see. Plus, I'm making contacts for new opportunities. In fact, yesterday I met an events coordinator who might be interested in having a mobile coffee truck available to add to their services."

"Hmph," was all her uncle replied, not sounding convinced.

As much as she loved him, she was happy when he departed. It was annoying to keep having to prove herself. She knew exactly how Mason felt.

Soon after, her sisters stopped by to visit. With her family and Mia as a distraction, one would think this would be enough to quell her thoughts about the previous night's activity of snow tubing (and kissing). As much as her family interrupting her at work could be irritating, it at least kept Mason at bay. Except when he had stopped by for his regular Mexican hot chocolate. She was torn between wanting to see him, and also *not* wanting to see him. It was all very confusing.

"Hey, there," her newly-single-again sister, Carla, said to Mason when he happened to walk by while carrying a Christmas tree over his shoulder.

"All right, everyone, just calm down and let me think!"

The wide eyes of her sisters and Mia turned at her sudden outburst. While Natalie was happy that Carla didn't end up taking Luis back, she also didn't want her near Mason either. She'd explore the reason later. All she knew was that her youngest sister was cute with big doe eyes and had a more bubbly personality than she did. Perhaps Mason might like this version of Gonzalez-Torres better. Even Mariana would be a better option than her. And there wasn't anything Natalie could do about it.

Not that she cared.

She didn't care. Not in the least.

Okay, fine. She did care. For once in her life she wanted to be the one who was liked best from the trio of sisters, even if it was silly and didn't matter.

"We can stay and help if you need it," Mariana said even though Natalie knew her sister had pulled a double shift the day before.

"Yes! I'd be great at pulling in traffic." Carla demonstrated this by swinging her arms in tandem with her hips, like she was part of an airline ground crew directing a plane towards the horse trailer. This was exactly what Natalie didn't need.

"I think Mia and I can handle it." She didn't need her tío dropping by and seeing even more help had been added.

Mariana shrugged. "Anyway, we were thinking about pooling our money together to buy Mom a new dishwasher for Christmas. What do you think? Do you want to go in on it with us?"

"Nat? Hello? Natalie? Do you want to help us buy a new dishwasher?" Carla said, clapping her hands for her attention.

She snapped out of her daydream again, which had been happening a lot lately. "Huh? Yes. Fine. Just let me know what you guys decide."

Mia leaned nearer to ask, "Is everything okay?" She had already asked an iteration of this question several times throughout the day, but Natalie blew her off, along with her inquiries into how the evening with Mason went.

"Yeah, great." Everything was fine. Except she had allowed the Christmas tree guy to get under her skin. Even worse, she wanted more of it. More touching and kissing and everything else. Being on his lap, within his embrace, was exactly how she imagined it would be, all warm arms and comfort. And she really liked kissing him.

She was still thinking about the kiss on Tuesday, while organizing the supply closet at Pony Expresso. Natalie entertained the possibility of making an exception for Mason. The holiday season was already out of whack for her. She wasn't able to go to Tahoe. Therefore, having meaningless fun along the way was something she deserved. Plus, he spent most of his time working in Apple Hill, so there'd be a good chance they may never run into each other after the holidays. Maybe he'd be up for a little holiday fling. She had yet to meet a guy who wouldn't be game.

Yes, she was becoming more confident about the whole idea. The thought was putting an extra spring in her step and she couldn't wait for the weekend to arrive. Too bad it was only Tuesday. She had to get through the whole week when all she was thinking about was Mason's big—

He stood at the Pony Expresso Christmas tree, drinking

from a to-go cup, and fiddling with one of the branches. Natalie set her box of napkins on the counter and approached, because maybe they could talk about her idea now.

"Hey," she said.

He choked on his drink, but recovered quickly, a grin already spreading on his face. "Hi."

"I see the ornament bandit is up to his old tricks."

His head tilted. "Would he really be a bandit if he's bringing a gift and not taking anything?"

"I'm not sure what the opposite of a bandit is. This still feels sneaky."

"A holiday philanthropist? It's only because I feel sorry for this tree not being shown to its full potential."

She wouldn't dare tell anyone, let alone Mason, she'd already spent an enormous amount of time with the tree in the morning, checking the water levels in the stand, and spending a few blissful moments with her face pressed into the branches to smell it. Putting on a bunch of ornaments would simply get in the way of Natalie's face-pressing time. She didn't know how to explain becoming obsessed with a Christmas tree and the man connected with it.

"So, Mason, I was thinking..." and that's when she saw the newest ornament. It was an inner tube with a reindeer reclining in the center. On the side of the tube, it read, *Snow Fun at Lake Tahoe.*

While Placerville was a city many people traveled through on their way to Lake Tahoe, it was still an hour and a half away with good traffic and clear roads. Any local shops selling ornaments could possibly have souvenir-type ornaments, but they would read Placerville or, if they were more tacky and played into the town's infamous history, Old Hangtown. Finding one specific to Lake Tahoe had to be less likely.

"You were thinking what?" Mason said.

"Where did you get that ornament?"

"Just from a small shop."

"In Tahoe?"

His smile had disappeared and he appeared perplexed. "Yeah."

She realized all of her earlier justifications were a ridiculous exercise, because the man she imagined for a fling wasn't him. It would never be Mason because he wasn't like the typical guys she usually had flings with. There was no way she could start something with a man who'd drive all the way to Lake Tahoe in order to buy her a silly sentimental ornament like a reindeer in an inner tube. All she could think about was how charming Stephen had been until he deemed her unworthy of any effort, and she had gone a lot further with him than she ever intended to go with Mason. The whole thing had gone too far and it was her fault for not making her line with Mason clear from the beginning and sticking with it.

She grabbed the newest ornament, pushing it into his chest until he claimed it. "Don't bring any more ornaments. I don't want them. You're wasting your time driving all the way to Tahoe. Nothing will ever happen between us."

His brows knitted together. He was clearly taken aback at her abrupt reaction. "What?"

She wasn't going to wait for him to accept her explanation because it would be pointless. At the end of the day,

Mason would always be Prince Charming and Natalie would be the fairy-tale villain breaking hearts. But at least that heart wasn't hers. She strode away from him.

"Natalie, wait," he said, following.

"No! I have work to do and this has gone too far." Natalie would rather be angry than depressed, and she was well on her way.

Much to her dismay, this didn't discourage the guy even when she tried to escape into her office. He entered with her, shutting the door behind him. The office wasn't larger than a closet but, with Mason inside, the walls were closing in on her, like a booby-trapped room.

She pushed her hair from her face, lifting her chin in defiance, ready to be the strong one. "I don't think continuing to work around each other is a good idea. I'm going to ask my uncle to get someone else to run the truck. It's only for a couple more weekends so it's not a big deal."

She realized this would put her partnership at risk, but she'd rather try begging her uncle for some other way to prove her abilities. At the moment, she didn't care. It was better this than to keep torturing herself with something that could never be.

Mason's stance was loose with his hands on his hips, but his eyes held onto hers with a glint of something she couldn't read. "Do you want to tell me why you don't want to come back? Because it seems like a pretty big reaction to something like an ornament."

"I don't owe you anything, let alone an explanation. I'm not your employee. I don't answer to Poinsettia Paradise. I'm only telling you that I'm not coming back because…it's common courtesy."

"Common courtesy?" He laughed but it wasn't his usual good-humored one. "Is this about the way you kissed me?"

Her mouth jarred apart at his bluntness. "The way…I kissed you?" It wasn't about that. It wasn't about anything except how she didn't want to work at that damn Christmas tree lot and have to stare at his goddamn kissable lips…like she caught herself doing at this moment, but only because she had trouble maintaining eye contact.

She made a concentrated effort to raise her gaze. "No, it isn't and, excuse me for getting caught up in some goddamn winter wonderland moment. I'm not a damn robot, you know. And I was just…cold. Dammit." Her control was held together by the barest of threads.

Much to her surprise, one side of his mouth lifted as though he found her tantrum amusing, which she hated. If she was going to be mad, why should he get off so easily? She considered stomping his foot and shoving him from her office. She didn't want to see his eyes soften as though he was truly attempting to figure her out. "I noticed you like to use the word 'damn' a lot whenever you're feeling frustrated."

Natalie's hands went into fists, jerking them downward in agitation. "Stop noticing things about me! I have work and family and stuff. I don't need anything else right now." She pushed a finger into his chest as the final period to this whole topic, but he covered it with his big, warm hand, pressing it to his chest and the rest of her train of thought flew off the track.

He dipped his head nearer, his voice becoming softer. "Do you not need anything right now or do you not *want* to need anything right now?"

"What difference does it make?"

"Maybe it doesn't make a difference to you, but what if it makes one to me?"

"You're a sweet guy, Mase. You are. It's just...all this isn't going to make me different. Trust me, I'm not worth all this effort. I'm not going to turn around and suddenly discover the magical spirit of Christmas because of a few ornaments or be the bubbly person who wears frilly aprons and bakes sugar cookies that are actual shapes instead of whatever premade cookie dough I picked up at the grocery store." She wasn't sure any of this made a lick of sense in the existing conversation, but she got it off her chest anyway.

"I'm okay with that," he replied with soothing patience. "I do the ornaments because it's something I enjoy. And I'm fine being the one who wears the apron and bakes the cookies or decorates a tree because you hate Christmas."

When did this become a negotiation? Did he not understand that their relationship would never reach that stage? "I don't hate Christmas. I just don't get swept away with all the tradition and shit. When you really think about it, Christmas is literally one day in the whole calendar and yet people somehow got it in their heads that it needs a whole damn season. You don't think that's weird? When you're a kid, you get all excited and spend so long ticking down the days and number of sleeps and setting up all your expectations on Christmas dreams, and you completely forget that there's the time after Christmas."

"The time after?"

"After the sparkle of New Year fizzles, there's just January. Cold, drab January where all you have are dried-out pine needles and that pristine snow has turned dirty and hard. The magic of the season is gone, and regular life is just the same as it always was, only now you don't have something to count down to. So, there's no point in putting in all the effort because the end result will be the same. The magic never lasts. We'll throw out our Christmas trees, and—"

"And the nursery turns its eyes toward getting things ready for spring, a whole new kind of magic."

"Mason," she sighed with exasperation. Why didn't he understand that this had nothing to do with Christmas? It was everything else that was hopeless.

"I'm not being facetious. I get what you're saying. And I don't see you as a person who needs to be changed. In fact, it's quite the opposite. I just really like you, the person who's obviously a little bit cynical and a glass-half-empty type of woman, but I like that. Most of all, I just really like how I feel when I'm around you. When I do get a smile, it's like that momentary burst of sunlight between the winter clouds. I've become addicted to that. I also can't help the way that I am, and I don't think that needs to change either. Do you agree?"

Natalie considered his question. Would she want him to be more like her? She didn't. To wish for him to be something different made her sad. "I guess. But it doesn't change the fact that I'm not going to do any of this with you anymore. It's just too much for me and not what I want."

"Okay," he replied, making it sound as if he accepted her decision, but he didn't move or let go of her hand or stop looking at her as if the thing he craved most was her lips.

"Okay," she echoed, because she didn't have another move either and was depending on him to turn his back and depart her office (and life) immediately. Natalie didn't have it in her to push him away, mainly because of all those nice things he had said, like her smile being a sunburst. She couldn't remember anyone saying something so authentically sweet to her before, certainly never any of the men she'd met in Lake Tahoe. Her hand on his chest tightened its grasp on his shirt.

He sensed her movement because his gaze dropped for a moment before rising to hers again. Suddenly, the thought of being abandoned in a room, less bright than it was before Mason entered, became unbearable. Like opposite magnets, their mouths crashed together. If she thought all he could do was the slow, tender type of kisses, she was quickly proven wrong. This kiss was different from the snow tube one. It was desperate and hungry and needy. With their bodies colliding, Natalie was pushed to her desk. With one hand, she swept her keyboard and paperwork aside. His grip on her thighs lifted her onto the desk, her head bumping against the closed shelf doors above her workstation. She couldn't stop herself from wrapping her limbs around him, hugging him closer.

"See?" she said between breaths. "This is all way too much."

His hands were trailing across her body. "You seem to be handling it okay."

"Sure, now, but what about later?"

"I plan on being there," he murmured against her lips.

The kiss deepened, his tongue sweeping into her mouth

before he bit gently on her lip. Maybe there was a bit of villainy in Mason after all, some spice along with the sweetness.

"Mmm. You taste like peppermint," he said.

Everything was melting inside Natalie, like one of the hard candies she'd eaten earlier. Her grip on him became necessary to keep herself from sliding off her desk into a heap. She moaned while scraping her fingers along the short hairs at the nape of his neck before they trailed to his bearded jawline. The prickling beneath the sensitive pads of her fingertips was delicious. The thought of the same sensation all over her skin had the potential to undo her.

Her prayers were answered when his kisses moved to her neck, his fingers tugging on her work T-shirt, untucking the hem. "Your office door locks, right?" he asked.

"Uh-huh, just…turn the…the thing." Words were becoming difficult to recall.

He stretched to lock the door before resuming his attention on her. "I just want to touch you."

"Yes." She tugged him, encouraging him closer. Whatever he was giving she needed more. Natalie was a stick of dynamite ready to go off as warmth flushed across her skin. She'd never so much as had a heated conversation in the tiny office before, let alone tried to manage something this physical. The logical side of her brain had vacated her head and the part wanting pleasure took over. She allowed him to pull the T-shirt off.

"You're so soft," he said. The prickling sensation mixed with gentle open-mouth kisses dragged across one shoulder before moving to the other one. She shivered in response.

"You're right. This is almost too much." It was almost hard to believe that this mountain of a man could be gentle, but he was. As he continued kissing her, one hand slid to palm one bra-clad breast. It probably felt like a molehill in his large hand but he didn't seem to care and neither did she. Her own hands had been busy undoing the top buttons of his flannel shirt, her fingers slipping inside to brush along heated skin and the soft strands of chest hair. Her desire ramped up. Natalie loved chest hair.

He pushed closer, and she wrapped her legs around him, his hardness pressing into her. She pressed right back. Her only thought was to drive him wild, wanting to see him go off.

"You have no idea how hard this is."

She laughed. "I have some idea."

He gave her a wicked smile before kissing her lips once again. Never before had a kiss felt as easy to slip into, as though she'd been kissing him all her life and yet the newness of it was there to thrill her. It felt so good she couldn't help but moan into it, wondering how far she could push this at work.

"Yeah, I'm going to see her." Mia's voice reached her ears and it was close. Too close. Like she was just on the other side of the wall, a wall Natalie shared with Mia's husband's office.

Oh God. What was she doing?

Chapter Fifteen

SHE HAD ALLOWED herself to get swept away again.

"Wait. Stop. Stop," Natalie said to Mason.

He paused, looking concerned. "Did I hurt you?"

She didn't hear Mia anymore. Ross's jewelry store butted beside Pony Expresso, and sound traveled easily through the shared wall. Natalie never paid attention to what was said on the other side, but she'd notice if Ross was on the phone, or if his small dog barked, or if Mia was visiting. Most of the time, there wasn't anything interesting to hear, including anything that could be construed as clandestine activities. (Although, she did have her suspicions about Ross and Mia one time.) If they were over there with their own suspicions at this moment, they'd be one hundred percent right because neither she nor Mason were trying to be quiet. In fact, she may have moaned once or twice.

"Natalie?" Mason said. He brushed a hand across her cheek lightly.

She grabbed her T-shirt and roughly pulled it on. "I'm fine. I—We can't do this here. My uncle stops by the shop all the time to check on things and he's a really conservative guy. I'm trying to prove to him that I can be a business partner, and not just a manager." She was rambling again, feeling flustered and wanting to get him out of her office as soon as possible. Mia could already be on her way over.

"Yeah. Okay. Sorry. I guess we did get a little carried away there," he replied while buttoning his shirt, taking away the vision of his chest hair.

She tore her gaze away, running a hand across her hair before jumping from the desk. She placed a hand on a nearby cabinet for support, her legs a touch wobbly from being swept away. "It's okay," she said, unlocking the office door. "You better leave though."

"Wait a minute." Mason put a hand on the doorframe, giving him one last hold on her office. "You're coming back to the farm this weekend, right?"

"I don't know. I have to think about it."

"I promise not to sneak into the coffee trailer while you're working no matter how much I want to."

"That's good because that'll probably be a good way to get yourself burned," she said while pushing against his chest.

Before letting go of the door completely, he leaned close, pressing a kiss beneath her ear. "Come back," he whispered.

"Stop driving to Tahoe for silly ornaments," she replied, shutting the door on him. She leaned against it, pressing a hand to her mouth. She was in deep shit.

Natalie retrieved the paperwork that had scattered to the floor, setting it on the desk, and put the keyboard back in its normal position as if nothing had happened. Too bad she couldn't say the same about her emotions. Putting her clothes and hair right wouldn't change the fact she was still thinking about—

"Hi!" Mia said, eyes bright and glittering, standing in the

doorway as soon as Natalie opened it.

She jumped. "What the hell, Mia?"

Her friend's gaze swept the small office as though her detective eyes might spot something different. She suspected something. "I just finished a photography job at the quilt shop and was visiting Ross. I thought I'd pop over and say hello."

Natalie crossed her arms because this had become a game of friendship chicken, to see who could pretend the longest that nothing weird was going on. "Oh, you thought you'd just pop over when you know I'm working?"

Mia didn't appear the least bit flustered, as she calmly adjusted her glasses. "I might feel bad if I actually thought I was interrupting work…instead of a man visit."

"God, Mia! I knew it! You and Ross were listening against the wall. You sickos."

"Wait, what? What are you talking about?"

Natalie gave an exasperated huff then tried to recover. "Nothing. What are *you* talking about?"

She jerked a thumb toward the hallway. "I just saw Mason leaving the coffee shop. I thought maybe he came to see you."

"He just brought another ornament for the tree, that's all," she replied, brushing a hair from her sleeve. If she told Mia some of the truth, maybe she'd be cool.

"So, you did see him?"

Shit.

"I was…guessing that's what he was doing here."

"Yeah, right. How would you know there was an ornament and—Why were you worried I heard something through the wall?" Mia gasped, before smacking Natalie on the arm. "I knew it!" She pushed her into the office, slamming the door.

"Why is everyone pushing their way into my office today? I'm seriously trying to get some work done around here."

"Does *everyone* include a certain Christmas tree farmer? And what were you guys doing in this office?"

"Do you really want me to tell you or do you want to use your imagination?"

Mia's eyes grew large behind her glasses as though she was imagining something and, whatever it was, it was good.

"Stop it. We just kissed once…or twice. I don't remember."

Her best friend released an embarrassing squeak, covering her mouth with her hands.

She rolled her eyes. "M, come on. You act like I just told you I was getting married or something. This isn't a big deal. I'm not a romantic like you."

"Okay, wait. Let me think this through." She put a hand up for Natalie to stop talking. "He brought you another ornament. It's a reindeer snow tubing and you guys went snow tubing so he's obviously picking these ornaments with purpose. Plus, he came to see you in your office and you were worried someone could hear you through the wall so either you were exchanging secrets in regards to espionage or this was the type of kissing that went beyond a friendly peck. Oh yeah, it's all coming together for me."

Natalie stared at her flatly. "Is there any way we can go with the secret spy theory? Otherwise I might hate you."

"Come on. You know you can talk to me."

She did know this. In spite of Mia's ridiculous excitement over office kisses, she did trust her. But as soon as she told Mia the truth, her friend would also know she'd been right again because the woman was always right. Natalie held a warning finger toward her. "I'll tell you, if you promise to get that funny grin off your face like you're falling in love all over again."

"Did I have this same expression when I was falling in love with Ross?"

"Yup. Exactly. But this situation is not like that one at all."

Mia took a breath, running a graceful hand across her face as if to calm herself, schooling her features into something more neutral. "Okay. Fine," she said. "Wait, let me sit down. And start at the snow tubing because you never told me anything."

"All right. Are you ready? He took me snowtubing. It was fun. We kissed. And then he brought an ornament today and we kissed again. The end."

Her friend frowned. "Wow. That was the worst story you've ever told. Even when you're telling me about a disgruntled customer, your story has more flair than that."

"Yeah, because I'm trying to convince you you're being ridiculous. Mason wants me to continue working at Poinsettia Paradise, but I might talk to my uncle about sending someone else because this whole thing has gone too far."

Mia leaned back in the office chair, pushing her glasses along her nose. "And *I'm* the ridiculous one who's overreacting? How has it gone too far?"

The question threw Natalie. She expected some argument about how Enrique wasn't going to let her off the assignment, a crush wasn't worth blowing off a chance at a partnership, and this reaction might prove she didn't deserve the title. She stuttered through an answer, but Mia stopped her.

"It's only gone too far *for you* because *you* don't want it to go anywhere at all. At least that's what you keep telling yourself. But you like him—you know you do. If you didn't, you wouldn't kiss him at all. The only one who's standing in your way right now is you."

She covered her eyes with a palm. "I hate you."

"I'm giving you the permission you won't give yourself. It's okay to get out of your own way, Natalie."

Chapter Sixteen

"MOM? DAD SAID you were looking for me," Mason said, entering his parents' home.

"Hey, sweetie, I'm in here," his mother called from the kitchen. He entered, finding his petite mother, filling a box with old cookbooks. There were other boxes littering the kitchen and Mason's heart stuttered.

"What's going on?"

His mother's hazel eyes met his. "I thought I'd donate some of these old cookbooks I never use anymore."

Mason released a breath of relief. His mother talked a lot about the move, but he wasn't quite ready for the reality of it. When his mom attempted to lift a box, he jumped in to help. "Those boxes are going to be heavy. Let me carry them. Are you already packing up for the move?"

"Not yet, but I thought it would be smart to start downsizing so that when it is time to pack, it'll be less overwhelming. Whatever place we do move into doesn't need to be as big as this farmhouse. Oh, that reminds me, honey, there's some boxes with your old art projects and collectibles in the garage. Can you finally decide if you want to take it or trash it? I'm not dragging all that to Arizona with me."

Mason was dismayed to discover his mother didn't consider his childhood stuff as a valuable treasure to hold on to forever. "You don't want it?"

His mother leveled a look at him over her glasses. "Come on, Mase, be serious. I can't hold on to everything. If you want it, you should take it home with you."

"Fine. I'll take a look," he replied. Although, he could think of other more important things he'd rather be doing, like planning something special for Natalie. She had mentioned she wasn't worth a lot of effort, and he wanted to prove just how very wrong she was.

"I also wanted to see if you needed some new frying pans. I have two sets of these and will probably only take one. They're a really nice non-stick and probably better than whatever cheap garbage you're using now." She showed him a pair of pans and they did look better than his current set.

He suspected his mom purposely bought two sets of everything for the purpose of eventually giving one to him. This was happening more frequently. His father had already offered to give him most of his good winter coats because he wasn't going to need them in Arizona. Mason felt as though he was running out of time. He didn't know what was at the end of that time, and, as much as he wanted his parents to trust him to do things his way, there was a side of him that was scared of such a major change in his life. "Do we have to do all this right now? I'm kind of in the middle of something."

"Are you doing something for your dad?"

"No, I'm, uh, putting together a small surprise for one of the women who works in the vendor area." Hopefully, if she did return to the farm that weekend, she'd be impressed with gestures like coffee meditation stalls.

His mom stopped, her eyes glittering. "Oh? Who is she?"

"She works the coffee truck. Her name is Natalie."

"Wait, is this the reason you went all the way to Tahoe?" His dad had given him a hard time about the trip, and it was clear he'd mentioned something to his mother. For some reason, he wasn't surprised.

"I don't know why everyone is treating that as a big deal. It's not that far and I'm a grown man who can drive where he wants."

"I don't care how old you are. As your mother, I'm allowed to be nervous about you driving over the pass with winter road conditions. Did she ask you to do that? Is she nice to you?"

He knew his mother was thinking about the Dakota situation. If he hadn't lived that down in two years, he might not ever live it down. "Natalie didn't know anything about it. And she also gave me a hard time about it when she found out. Besides, the highway was plowed the whole way, and I went early so there was hardly any traffic."

"I just want you to be with someone who's nice and treats you well. You give your whole heart, Mase, and you deserve someone who will appreciate that."

He wanted that as well, but he also wanted someone who'd challenge him and had fire in her veins, someone who'd make whatever he got from her feel well earned. If he stuck it out, fought for it, it might be all worth it. And once she knew she didn't need her stinger around him, things could be different between them, something so much sweeter. He had plenty of patience.

HE SENT A text asking if Natalie was coming back that weekend.

She responded with the word, *Yup*, and it put him in good spirits again.

Will you hang out with me after closing?

Maybe, she responded.

At least it wasn't a no. He could work with that. While the Christmas tree business was constant that Saturday, it wasn't as busy as the previous one. She was working the truck alone this time.

"Mia isn't helping you?" he asked when stopping by for his regular Mexican hot chocolate.

"Nope, not this weekend." She kept her focus on the task, not meeting his eyes.

"You know, if you ever need a bathroom break or need anything to eat, you can text me and I'll see what I can do to help. That's my job as the boss this year, making sure everything is running okay for everyone, including our vendors."

"You have experience in coffee making?"

Heat spread across his cheeks because his offer must have appeared ridiculous. "Do you have one of those pod coffee machines? I can work one of those."

She laughed and the tension between them melted.

He decided to take a chance. "Hang out with me after work today. I have something to show you."

"I bet you do," she said before her own cheeks darkened. "I mean…what I meant to say…" She covered her face as though embarrassed, and he found it adorable.

He smiled, touching her arm. "Come on, Natalie."

"All right. Fine," she said, her face still covered but she slowly pulled her hands away. "I said, okay. You can put away the goofy grin and leave now."

It was debatable on how goofy his grin actually was, but it wasn't going anywhere. "Aren't you forgetting something?"

Her eyes bugged. "I'm not going to kiss you right now!"

He laughed. "No. My drink."

Her fluster returned. "Ugh. Here. Leave me alone." She pushed his finished drink across the counter to him.

Mason claimed it, drinking a healthy sip even though it was too hot. "Mmm. I think this might be your best one yet." He started to move away but before he got too far, he turned, walking backwards. She was watching him. "I'm definitely going to kiss you later, Natalie Gonzalez-Torres. Just wanted to give you time to prepare yourself."

She may have rolled her eyes at this but he didn't care. He was no longer walking on hard compacted snow but rather crystalized water that sparkled like diamonds.

At the end of the day, he returned to her truck. She'd already locked up, her arms crossed tightly over her chest. "Have you brought me my waffle wrap?" she asked.

"Nope, sorry."

Her face fell. "What? Really?" She stepped close, reaching into his jacket pockets as if he was holding out on her.

"Wow. You're getting really comfortable getting into my clothes."

She tilted her beautiful face to him. "Like you don't love it." She had him there. He dropped his head to brush a kiss over her lips, but she dodged him at the last moment. "Nope, sorry. You really don't have any? I wish I would have known about this before I agreed to hang out with you."

"Oh, so you're only hanging out with me because of waffle wraps?"

"Uh, yeah. Some women want jewels. I want waffle wraps. I'd say you're getting off fairly easy."

"What if I have plans to offer you something better?"

"I'd say you're lying because I don't consider anything better than waffle wraps."

"I don't think you'll be disappointed."

"I'll be disappointed if it's not some kind of food. I'm so hungry, I want to start eating you. I'm going to start with your arm."

"Okay, so you're vicious when you're hungry. Good to know."

"I changed my mind. I'm going to start with eating your face because you're talking too much and not feeding me."

He laughed, putting his arm around her shoulders. "All right, come on. Food awaits you in a private dining room in the barn." This must have been the way to her heart because she let him lead her without any further argument. She may have even leaned into him, or she'd gone weak from hunger and was using him for support. Mason preferred to believe the former.

He let go to pull the barn door open for her and swept a hand forward, allowing her to enter first. He kept his eyes on her as she stepped through the threshold and took in the full scene. It was the inside of a barn, but haystacks had been shifted in order to circle a table he'd set up in the middle. On the top of the haystacks were most of the surplus of potted poinsettias, giving the inside of the barn a burst of color in varying shades of red. Strings of large bare-bulbed lights, usually reserved for special events, were strung across the area.

Her reaction didn't disappoint him. Her eyes grew large, her mouth dropping open with a small gasp. She jerked to a halt.

"I take it you're not disappointed then," he said, smiling.

"What?"

"Come on. I know you're hungry." He took her hand, leading her to the table and pulling out a folding chair for her.

"What is all this?" she asked, still in shock.

"It's dinner. I thought you were hungry."

"Dinner?"

"Yeah. Food. Well, actually, I think this might be considered breakfast." Mason took off the aluminum foil from the plate the waffle truck had left for him and slid it to her. It was a plate of cinnamon waffles, bacon, and strawberries. They also left tiny containers of Nutella and maple syrup. He passed her a napkin and fork before unveiling his own plate with a similar spread. "Oh, and I also have…" He leaned down to retrieve the bottle from beneath the table. "Wine or, if you prefer, I also have water."

She raised an eyebrow, removing her coat and beanie, her hair coming loose from the sloppy bun. Mason had plugged in a few heaters, so this area wasn't frigid.

"I'm not sure I've ever had wine with breakfast before." She slid the wine glass across the table, encouraging him to pour. She took a bite of her food. The relief hitting her taste buds must have been heaven because she closed her eyes, looking in absolute bliss.

"Good? Has to be way better than gnawing on my arm," he replied, removing his own coat.

"Yes. Thank you. I'm sorry I almost mauled you." She took a generous bite from a strawberry, those gorgeous full lips wrapping around the red fruit. It was mesmerizing.

He focused on his food. "If I had to get mauled by anyone, I'd hope it's by you."

She slid an amused glance at him, wiping Nutella from the corner of her lip.

"What?" He took a casual sip of wine.

"Why are you so nice to me?"

He almost choked on his drink. As much as he liked Natalie, the truth was he didn't know much about her. She had a strong personality, but there had to be a reason for it. He didn't like the idea that she had to be guarded against niceness and wondered if it was connected to why she sometimes felt unworthy of any attention. Mason set his glass on the table. "How do you expect me to treat you?"

She thought about it for a moment before shrugging her shoulders. "Your mom stopped by the truck today. She's also nice. Probably where you get it from."

Natalie was avoiding his original question, and he decided to ignore it for now. "And what do you get from your parents?"

"My love of eating. Do you ever plan on feeding me

something besides waffles? Not that I don't love this."

"So you've already accepted that there's going to be other meals? Good. And I thought you said there wasn't anything better than waffle wraps. Unfortunately, my options here have been limited. It's difficult to leave the farm for a food run when it's busy, especially when I'm the one running things around here. So that leaves the waffle truck or the funnel cake truck. Or I can get something from your truck, but I didn't know if serving you your own product would be considered tacky."

She laughed. "Also, my truck has limited options and none of them are food."

He studied her for a moment. "How do you feel about things like Shoestring hot dogs or picnics?" Shoestring was a hole-in-the-wall food shack that had been a Placerville staple. It would definitely qualify as a cheap date. It's not that he was looking to test her, but his talk with his mother was a good reminder that he deserved someone who liked him for more than what he could offer financially. And maybe he wasn't sure if his only appeal to her was being a provider of waffle wraps on days she was stuck on the farm.

She took another strawberry from her plate and ate it. "I like Shoestring. And this kind of feels like a picnic already so I guess that's your answer right there."

He couldn't keep the smile from his lips. "Maybe we can go sometime after the season, eat something other than waffles for a change of pace. Although, I'm not opposed to feeding you waffles again, but at a more appropriate time…like breakfast."

Her dark eyes glinted. "I'm certainly not showing up anywhere on my day off at the butt crack of dawn for breakfast, which means I'd have to already be with you. You really think you could keep me all night?"

"I wouldn't mind trying."

"Don't think I'm going to spend the whole night snow tubing with you."

"I'm sure we could come up with something more fun and a lot warmer."

"More fun than snow tubing? Now you're setting expectations."

He pointed to her plate with his fork. "You doubted I could satisfy you earlier and now you're eating your words. Out of the two of us, who's earned the right to be cocky?"

Natalie laughed, which was the best reaction outside of kissing. As much as he tried to hold himself back, it was no use. Mason liked her. He liked talking with her and making her laugh. She made him feel as though a beam of light flicked on in his chest around her, which had to be as obvious as if there were a lighthouse inside of him. He didn't care.

"When you're finished eating, I'll show you your surprise."

She paused. "There's another surprise? I thought this dinner was surprising enough, especially when I'm used to eating food from your pocket."

"I don't know if it's a surprise as much as it's fulfilling my end of the bargain, which, may I remind you, I shouldn't have to do since you cheated."

Her face lit, and she turned her focus to the rest of the barn as if she could get a preview of the surprise now. "I have a coffee meditation stall? Is it weird that I'm excited? I'm not even offended that I'm basically living my day as a farm animal, going from a trailer to a stall."

She moved to stand but he shook his head. "It's not going anywhere. You can finish eating. And I don't want to get your expectations too high, because I didn't really do very much. It's still an old cow stall."

"If it makes you feel better, my expectation is a horse blanket on the ground." She tilted her head, pressing a finger to her delicate chin in thought. "Yeah, that's all my imagination is allowing."

He faked a cringe. "In that case, yeah, I guess it's not going to be much of a surprise. You pretty much called it."

"Sorry. I've had people surprise me before and I set my expectations accordingly." She took the last sip from her wine glass before setting her glass down with purpose. "Okay, I've finished. Let's get this over with."

Chapter Seventeen

MASON SCRAMBLED TO his feet, leading her to the same side of the barn as Santa's meditation stall. "I didn't put you right next to Stan because I imagine you'd want a little privacy if you both happen to be nap—uh, meditating at the same time."

Stalls, in general, weren't very big. There wasn't a whole lot a person could do with one. The normal dimensions were about four feet wide by nine feet long. Stan squeezing a small chaise and end table meant he was pushing the limits of a stall's capabilities. But if tiny homes could be a thing, why not tiny meditation stalls? The only thing missing was a glowing endorsement from Gwyneth Paltrow.

He really liked Natalie though, so he assigned her the largest stall they had, which had been used for a mothering cow and calf. It still wasn't very big, and Mason didn't have many resources to improve it, but he tried to get creative. Like Stan's stall, a makeshift curtain had been tacked around it.

He stopped her before she could peek inside. "Wait here a moment. I have to check on something." He slipped in, careful to hide the surprise until he was ready.

"Are you making sure there's no cow shit lying around?"

she called from the other side of the curtain.

"Yup, just hiding it under a pile of some old moldy straw." He finished his setup. "Okay, close your eyes. Are they closed?"

"Yes."

Through the curtain, he grabbed her hand, guiding her inside. "Okay, you can open them."

She opened one eye first, taking a test peek, before opening both of them. "Oh my God."

On the floor was an old horse blanket being used as a makeshift rug. He'd also stacked hay and tucked a couple large sheets over them, making it appear like a haystack sofa. With permission (because he knew better) the couch was decorated with one of his mom's knitted blankets and a couple handmade throw pillows. An upside-down half wine barrel was used as a makeshift coffee table. On top, he'd decorated with potted poinsettias, a dish of peppermint candies, and battery-operated candles that he turned on before she entered. He also took Stan's idea and strung more twinkle lights. Mason didn't consider himself to be an interior decorator, but he'd seen what Lana had done for previous events held in the barn and used it for inspiration. In the end, he was quite proud of what he'd accomplished.

Natalie sank onto the haystack couch, one hand running a finger along the blanket draped over the back with the other hand pressed to her mouth. There was no way to know if she was happy or sad. Instead, she appeared dazed.

"Do you like it?" he asked. "I know it's a little colder back here, but I can move one of the small heaters to this area if you want. In fact, let me go get—"

The hand across her mouth finally moved as she latched on to his arm. "No, wait. You don't… You don't have to do that. It's not very cold. This is already way too much for what was actually just a joke. I didn't expect—You know that I don't really get much of a break when I work the truck, right? It's not like I can actually come in here and take a nap. My five-minute break is definitely not worth all this."

Mason took a seat on the hay-couch beside her. She watched him with wide eyes, her hand once again covering her mouth almost as if she was nervous. Of him? He knew his size could sometimes intimidate people simply by doing nothing more than existing. He scooted back so as not to encroach on her space. He leaned his elbows against his knees, rubbing his hands together before glancing at her. "You're really concerned about my amount of effort in things."

"It's just that this is a lot of work and I know you're busy and I'm certainly not worth all—"

"Natalie, I just want to make one thing very clear: you don't get to dictate how much effort I'm willing to put into something. Only I get to determine that. And I don't know who convinced you that you're not worth a lot of effort." He lifted his head, looking her dead in the eye. "They were wrong."

"Well," she said. "Shit."

And then she was closing the space between them, grabbing his face, and pressing a kiss to his lips. His own hands slid along her back and, in spite of what she was doing, there was a slight tremble along her spine. That's when he got it. She wasn't scared of him but more of what all of this implied. She was scared of relationships.

She was making more sense to him. And after his own experiences, he understood it. Being vulnerable with someone wasn't easy when they could use it against you. He should have been terrified at this moment, but he wasn't. All that existed was this aching need for her and a desire to do whatever he could to make her feel good.

"I'm starting to think the bees might be on to something with all that vibrating they do," she said low, on a breath, pushing her way to straddling his lap.

"While I'm all for it," Mason replied, amazed he was able to get any words in a coherent sentence. "I just want to put it out there that I'm not expecting anything. We don't have to do anything you don't want to."

"God, Mase, stop. You've already done enough to make me want you."

Unrequited love sucks, but he was quickly discovering how amazing it was to have someone who yearned for him as much as he did for them. All his previous relationships now appeared to be nothing more than him wasting time, trying to force a fire to light when this one had ignited easily.

Her fingers were already in the process of unbuttoning his shirt. She tilted her head to press kisses on his neck before moving to his chest as more of it was being revealed. His brain was rushing to catch up as everything was moving at light speed. He struggled to come up with something clever but all that he could manage was, "I like your sweater." This had to be the dorkiest compliment he'd ever given a person, but he actually did like the sweater with the skeleton wearing a Santa hat. It was all Natalie and, therefore, he couldn't help but like it.

"It's very versatile," she responded. "It can also be worn like this." In a single graceful swoop, she pulled the sweater over her head, depositing it on the hay-couch. The moment froze between them. Natalie nervously adjusted the strap of her purple bra. It wasn't lacy or in any way fancy. I n fact it was very simple in design, but she was beautiful in it all the same. She reached behind her as if to unclasp it, but he stopped her.

"Can I?" His voice was gruff as though he was parched, and perhaps he was.

She nodded, but her gaze dropped. His hands glided slowly along her skin until his fingers found the clasp. He brought them together to undo the hooks. With it released, his hands traveled to her shoulders and slid the bra away. His eyes had something new to focus on. Her breasts were small and pert, and he covered one with his hand, massaging it as he pressed his face against her collarbone, breathing her in and pressing his mouth there. Everything about her was lovely.

She released a soft sigh, her fingers gently scraping through his hair. "No one is suddenly going to appear in the barn, are they? Stan isn't going to pull a late meditation session or something?"

Mason chuckled. "No."

"I can't give you everything you want, you know. I'm telling you this up-front because I don't want you to be disappointed."

He tilted his face toward her. "You know what I want?"

She shook her head, continuing to scrape her fingers

through his hair. "Maybe not everything but I'm pretty sure people don't fill a barn full of poinsettias for a fling."

"Are you telling me you're not a barn-full-of-poinsettias type of woman?"

Her gaze darted away as she bit the corner of her bottom lip. "No, I'm not."

"Why?" His heart froze. He'd been hoping for something more substantial than crumbs, something more real than he got from Dakota.

"Does it matter?"

"Your reasons always matter. Is it because…" He wasn't sure how to ask this without being vulnerable himself. "Is it because I'm not enough for you?"

Her eyes widened. "No. It's not that. I'm just not sure I can give more to anyone."

"Okay," he said, not knowing what else he could say without pushing. He brushed a strand of hair from her cheek. "But I just want you to know, regardless, I've got you, okay? If you want it, I've got you."

He didn't feel hate very often, not even toward Dakota, but he hated, with every fiber of his being, whoever made Natalie feel this way. He would do whatever he could to wipe that stain of memory from her mind by filling it with something else, even if it took all the effort he had.

Natalie didn't say anything. She studied him while her fingers traced his bearded jawline before kissing his lips again, so sweet it almost hurt. If this is the only place the evening took him, he couldn't be mad about it, even if he wanted a lot more. She was, at least, being honest, and he appreciated that.

She began to impatiently pull on his shirt, trying to tug the garment off him. He helped her even though he had no six-pack abs or other impressive muscles to show off. It was clear Natalie didn't care and soon neither did he.

As soon as his shirt was discarded, her hands went straight for the tops of his pants, undoing the fasteners. She was clearly a woman on a mission and his heart was about to beat right out of his chest. He really shouldn't have eaten so many waffles beforehand and should have drunk a lot more water. Mason could tell this thing with Natalie was something he should have prepared for.

"Wait. Fuck. I don't have any protection or anything," he said while his dick cursed him out.

To his great surprise and luck, she plucked a condom from her back pocket. "Ta-da," she said as though she had performed magic.

"Do you always carry that in your pocket, or did you somehow know that you were going to need one?"

"It was in my purse, and I slipped it into my pocket before we walked over here."

"Even though you were expecting nothing but a horse blanket on the ground?"

"Yeah. I like you."

While the sentiment made him feel good, he said, "You deserve more than just a horse blanket. You're allowed to hold out for something better."

A lovely smile slid across her face. "Then it's a good thing I got something better." She placed the condom in his hand. "Put this on."

She didn't have to tell him twice. He pushed his pants

and boxers down his legs, ripping the condom package before sliding it on. Mason glanced over to find her watching him, she'd already removed her boots and was slipping from the rest of her clothes and—*Holy Shit.* His gaze swept across every curve and dip. How in the world did he get this lucky?

He blushed, and noticed he was still gripping himself, his hold tightening. "You're making me self-conscious."

"You're making *me* self-conscious. I feel like your gaze is so intense you can see right through to my bones."

"Sorry. You just look…good." *Dammit.* That was the best descriptive phrase he could come up with? He couldn't say *amazing* or *loveliness itself* or something equally poetic. His brain had settled on *good.* At least it was better than *greanks*, a word he continued having nightmares about.

Natalie returned, straddling him again. "You look good too."

"Can you take down your hair?"

She pulled out the hair tie, dark locks tumbling across her bare shoulders. It was slightly wavy and just as beautiful as he'd hoped. He took a moment to touch it, running his fingers through the soft strands that had a light scent of jasmine, until she rose up, adjusting him and sank down, leaving him engulfed in her heat and unable to focus on anything else.

"Oh, God, yes." His hands found purchase on her hips as he breathed through this in order not to lose control too quickly. "Are you okay?"

Her own eyes were dark but had an almost dreamy quality to them. "Yeah."

He kissed her again, starting slow with his tongue sliding

along hers until the kiss grew hungrier and then her hips began to move against him and all he could do was hold on. The air between them became hot and humid as she continued to ride him and all he could manage were words of encouragement, telling her how good she felt and what she was doing to him. He was unraveling quicker all the time.

Mason reached into her hair, wrapping the silken strands in his fist. "Are you ready this time?" he asked. When she nodded, he tightened his hold and pulled. Her body arched to him, her nails digging into his shoulder as she swore.

"So, you do like that?" He panted against the damp skin of her chest.

"Yes. God, Mason."

He gripped her hair tighter against her scalp and she cried out, jerking within his arms, and he suddenly lost his own control. The air filled with their heavy breathing as they returned to their senses. He didn't want to let go, for fear she would sprint away. He held her to him, feeling her muscles go lax while their hearts returned to their normal beating patterns. He brushed his lips across her shoulder.

"I've got you," Mason said in a low voice. "And I want to learn everything you like."

He meant it.

Chapter Eighteen

I WANT TO learn everything you like.

God, Natalie was in so much trouble.

No sentence had devastated her more.

This was probably why she wasn't actively looking to escape trouble, almost as if she didn't want to, even though she knew she should. This was one more thing Mia might be right about.

After they got dressed, Mason walked her to her car. She didn't resist being pulled into his arms again, allowing him to press soft, tender kisses to her lips, her body molding to his as if they were interlocking puzzle pieces finally being matched. She also didn't reply with anything but a good-night when he said, "I'll see you tomorrow," as if it was a given she'd show again on Sunday and not regret everything.

She needed her buffer back and considered messaging Mia to beg her to please help with the coffee truck again. Her uncle had been wrong. Natalie wasn't much of a gambler at all.

"You wanna hang out after work today?" Mason asked when he stopped by the coffee truck the following day.

"Can't," she replied as she made his regular drink. "It's tamale day."

"Tamale day?"

"A bunch of my family gets together to make a ton of Christmas tamales to give to friends and neighbors. It's tradition." She wasn't lying. It was tamale day. Her mother, sisters, grandma, and aunts were getting together to be part of a tamale-making assembly line. Except, by the time Natalie got off, there wouldn't be much for her to do besides help with cleanup. Still, she should at least make an appearance and try to participate in the family tradition, one that suddenly became quite important to her.

"I love tamales," he replied.

"Yup, me too. I promised my grandma I'd get there as soon as possible so I'll probably have to race to my mom's house as soon as it slows down around here."

He nodded his head in agreement.

"M-maybe I'll bring you some tamales when I come back next weekend." She mentioned this as a way to offer proof there were real tamales involved and it wasn't merely an excuse not to hang out with him. "You can eat something other than waffles for a change of pace."

He smiled, claiming his drink from her. "I'd like that."

Something about the whole interaction was unsatisfying. She called out before he got too far away. "I was thinking I might actually take a ten-minute break later today."

"Good. Breaks are important. You should definitely do that," he replied before leaving.

Ugh. It was as if he didn't care. Damn him and his damn meditation stall.

She tried hard not to let her grumpiness spill over to the next customers, a pair of kids, but she may have pushed the whipped cream nozzle with annoyance on their hot chocolates, giving them more than the usual amount. Good. Maybe they'd get cavities. And then she felt bad for wishing cavities on innocent kids and tilted the spout toward her own mouth, giving herself a healthy dollop because screw it.

During a quiet period, she put up a *Be back in 10 minutes* sign and walked to the barn. After all the trouble Mason went through creating a stall for her, it seemed a shame not to use it at least once. She weaved her way through families of Christmas tree shoppers and ducked into the barn.

Without heaters (or Mason because the man generated a lot of heat) the inside of the barn was chilly. She tucked her coat closer to her body, wrapping her arms tight around her. The barn was clean, no evidence of their date from the night before.

Her stall was shrouded in a makeshift curtain, her hand pulling it aside to slip inside. She stopped again, half believing what she remembered from the previous night was a dream, but it wasn't. He had done all this for her, and she loved it. Everything about him felt like a hug. Greed was settling within her, where she could believe all this was too much and, yet, she wanted more. The position felt dangerous. She wanted to scream. They should change the designation from meditation stall to screaming stall. No one would hear her. Natalie sucked in a deep breath, ready to release a frustrated shout—

The barn door creaked open.

She covered her mouth in case a scream escaped anyway. Was it Stan? She didn't want him to know she was nearby for fear he'd forget about his own break and force a long-winded conversation on her.

"Natalie?"

Mason. The relief sweeping through her was instantaneous.

She pulled the curtain back, fixing a hand on her hip. "What are you doing here?"

He stopped. "I—Sorry, did… Were you really going to meditate? I was watching to see when you'd come to the barn. I thought you were dropping hints earlier that you wanted me to, uh, see you during your break." His cheeks blushed pink as he twisted his knit hat within his hands.

As ridiculous as it was, her fingers had an urge to reach out and sooth the hairs sticking at odd angles, to take care of the guy. Instead, she tightened her grip on the curtain as if this was the single thing holding her control. "Well? What took you so long? Ten minutes isn't very long, you know."

Then he was there, sweeping her up in his arms. He kissed her well and good before setting her on the hay-couch. Like a clingy weirdo, she gripped his jacket within her hands, making it easier to press her face to his neck and breathe in the spicy citrus pine scent. It was better than any cologne. "You smell like my favorite tree, Prince."

"Yeah, I did that on purpose. You didn't fool me. I knew you were a sucker for Christmas tree pheromones."

She laughed because what else could she do? He wasn't wrong. She was the biggest sucker.

He brushed her hair, those hazel eyes taking their hold on her. "Hey, gorgeous. Did you have a nice evening yesterday?"

"Mm-hmm," she responded, unzipping his jacket.

"Yeah, me too." He shrugged from his coat, before his fingers went for hers, making quick work of it, pressing light kisses along her jawline.

"Oh, yeah? Were you with someone pretty?" The need to see him, to run her hand on heated skin, experience his broad chest again was consuming Natalie.

"Mm-hmm. I can't stop thinking about how she feels and the little sounds she makes."

"What? I don't make sounds."

He stopped, his eyes growing large, as though he'd been caught. "Oh…you thought I was talking about you?"

She pinched him. "Shut. Up." Natalie giggled when Mason tackled her, sending her backwards onto the hay with him looming over her.

"We're going to see about those sounds," he said, undoing her jeans.

"Come on, I only have five minutes left of my break. Nothing is going to happen in five minutes."

"So you're challenging me?" He pushed her jeans down enough to give himself access to her underwear, sliding his hand under the fabric and between her legs. His lips pressed to hers in a hungry kiss and…

He was right.

She did make whimpering noises.

Also, five minutes was enough time.

Natalie's head dropped as she clung to him, panting. His fingers slid against her. "Oh, God, Mas—"

The barn door yanked open. "No, Candy, it's not all right and it is a big deal!" Stan's voice echoed through the whole barn. Mason and Natalie froze inside their cow stall. Candy said something in response but not loud enough to understand the words.

"Oh, *I'm* the diva?" Stan said. "Why? Just because I don't want to be sharted on. I'm going to give that kid a gift all right. Santa's bringing that kid a big pile of diapers. Then he'll be crying." There was a pause. "No, Candy, he did it on purpose. That kid had no respect for me. I saw it in his beady little blue eyes. Well, I don't care how long the line is. Santa needs a break."

The barn door slammed shut and Stan continued muttering to himself as he walked to his stall. "Damn kid farting on my Carson City silk velvet."

Natalie pulled Mason closer to press her face into his chest because she was going to lose it. The more she had to keep quiet, to prevent revealing their hiding spot and compromised position, the harder it was to keep the laughter inside. A tremble went through Mason's body as he too was trying to hold it together. He at least removed his hand from her underwear.

There was a large sniff. "Good God! I can still smell it! What is that kid eating? Gonna charge those parents for dry cleaning."

Her snort was barely smothered in Mason's shirt as a silent laugh shook her shoulders. This was definitely how she was going to die today. Although, what she should be worried about was how long they were going to be stuck in the barn because there was no way she was sneaking out under Stan's nose. With Mason's help, she pulled up her jeans and redid the fasteners just in case they were caught, because every time he made eye contact with her, she almost lost it again.

Luckily, they only had to hold their composure for five more minutes before Stan left while pumping himself up with words of self-affirmation. As soon as the barn door slammed shut, the dam on Mason's and Natalie's mirth broke. She'd never laughed so hard in her life, tugging him closer to support her before she collapsed to the ground. His eyes crinkled to slits, tears slipping through the cracks as his face turned red.

"Oh my God," she said, wiping away her own tears. "I don't know if I'll ever be able to look at Stan's face again without busting a gut after this."

He plucked hay from her hair. "I better make sure everything is okay and he's not continuing to have a meltdown out there."

She was disappointed they weren't going to continue with their previous activity but, logically, getting back in the mood after that wouldn't be easy. They walked together toward the door, neither one in a hurry to return to work, and she clutched his arm for support in case the giggle fits took over again. "I better check to see if there's a line waiting for me. Looks like break time is over."

"There will always be more," he said.

Her heart lit because perhaps he was right.

Outside, he gave her a grin and said, "Have fun making tamales tonight."

"Yeah," she replied, regretting her earlier excuse. "I guess I'll see you later."

"Definitely." He pressed a light kiss to her lips before

walking toward the Santa booth.

Natalie flipped on her heels, ready to climb into her wonderful, dear horse trailer, seeing it with a whole new fondness. Who knew work days could be fun and unexpected and—

She stopped.

She'd walked from the barn, laughing, and holding his arm, kissing goodbye for the whole world to see without thinking twice about it, like it was a natural, everyday thing, as though everything could be simple and uncomplicated. But it wasn't.

Or…maybe it was.

Hours later she was still pondering the kiss, absentmindedly touching her lips throughout the day, wondering how a small goodbye kiss could affect her more than anything else, more than even things they'd done earlier that had gone beyond kissing.

But that goodbye kiss—that had been something else. Something new. Something she'd never known she wanted.

After work, Natalie drove to her parents' home in a dreamy daze, not remembering the trip at all. What had even played on the radio? Was it Christmas music? Non-stop commercials? She didn't know.

She was jerked from her daydreams when she walked through the door, loud conversations, and laughter streaming from the kitchen, and almost ran into Mia. "M, what are you doing here?"

"Your mom invited me. She was so sweet to remember I wanted to learn how to make tamales with you guys. You didn't get my text? Or was it really that busy at the tree farm today? You should have told me. I would have come out to help you. I hate thinking you can't even get away for a break or anything."

Natalie gave a nervous laugh, waving off her friend as she walked into the kitchen to greet the rest of her family. She tore off her winter outerwear feeling unbearably warm and hoping no one would notice any blushing coming from her direction. "Abuelita," she said, kissing the top of her grandmother's head. "Did you see the trailer for the new Chris Evans movie?"

Her grandmother set aside the corn husk she was spreading with masa and demanded Natalie pull out her phone and show her immediately. At first, showing the trailer with the rest of her family gathered around Abuelita's chair was a fun innocent distraction. When a shot of Chris Evans whipping a wet T-shirt over his head appeared, the rest of the ladies tittered. "Ay, Dios mío, chicas!" Abuelita said while fanning herself. Except things took an unfortunate turn when part of the trailer was covered with an incoming text.

> ***Mason:*** *Hey, don't want to interrupt tamale time but...*
>
> ***Mason:*** *I forgot to ask if you were doing anything Thursday night.*

This, of course, started a different type of tittering and the rest of the trailer was forgotten by everyone, except for Abuelita who kept Natalie's phone clutched in her hands and swatted away anyone attempting to reclaim it.

"Oh. My. God. Natalie. Who the hell is Mason? Are you dating someone?" Carla asked, before putting the spotlight on Mia as if she didn't trust Natalie's replies. "Is she dating someone?"

Her friend turned a panicked gaze to Natalie. Her stammering didn't help the situation one bit and neither did everyone talking at once trying to get answers.

"All right, stop. Stop!" she shouted into the chaos. "You guys are blowing this way out of proportion. It's just a guy I work with. It's a work thing."

Even Mariana, her used-to-be-most-favorite sister, scoffed and rolled her eyes. "Then why is Mia making that face?"

Her gaze whipped to Mia who suddenly schooled her features. "No, I'm not. I wasn't making a face. And, it's true. Technically...they do work together at Poinsettia Paradise."

Carla's mouth dropped open and she swatted Mariana. "It's that Christmas tree guy. See? I told you. Didn't I tell you he was gawking at her?"

"No, you said he was looking at you," Mariana replied.

"Yeah, probably because he thought I was her. We have some similarities as sisters. Except I might be a better match because he works with plants and I'm a floral artist so we probably have a lot in common."

"Excuse me? He was looking at you?" Natalie put a hand to her hip, ready to send the guy a batch of poisoned tamales.

"In her dreams," Mariana assured her. "No need to get jealous about it."

"I am *not* jealous."

Carla laughed. "Yeah, your eyes just bug out like that naturally, like you're about to She-Hulk and rip someone's face off."

"Can I please have my phone back?" Natalie asked. She had text messages to ignore. Besides, Abuelita had already watched the trailer twice at this point.

Her grandmother held out her phone with a sweet smile, which was deceptive, because as soon as the phone was in her hand, she saw a reply had been made to Mason. "What the hell?"

"Language, Natalie!" her mother said.

"She responded to my text message for me!"

"What?" the three younger women said together, scrambling to get behind her so they could see what was on screen.

All her grandma had written was *No*, plus the kissy face emoji. She didn't know her grandma even knew how to use emojis. *Ugh*! This would not stand.

"Buen trabajo, Abuelita," Mariana said.

"We can do that? Here, let me have it," Carla made a scramble for Natalie's phone and soon they were wrestling over the device. "Let me help you, hermana! I'm doing this out of love."

"All I want is a little privacy. Why can't you love me by leaving my business alone?" She yanked her arm, slipping from her younger sister's grasp, except the momentum wasn't enough to stop the phone from bashing the outside corner of her eye. "Ow!" This was followed by gasps. Her mother soon sat her down and put a bag of frozen hominy over her left eye and a plate of food on the table for her to eat. She gave her phone to Mia because out of all them, she trusted her the most. Mia was a manipulator, but she got people to do the dirty work themselves. She wasn't one to send sneaky text messages under the guise of someone else.

"Your young man looks like Chris Evans?" her grandmother asked.

"Sorry. He's a white guy but no." She wasn't about to tell all of them that he was better than Chris Evans because she could fully sink into his arms and he gave the warmest, best hugs and smelled like white fir Christmas trees—And now she actually missed the guy. Her life was a disaster.

"He responded," Mia said.

"About time," Natalie said flatly. "He probably wasn't sure how to respond to a kissy-face emoji and now thinks I'm clingy. Thanks, Abuelita."

"He said Thursday is board game night and he wants to know if you can come."

"Ooooo, like Twister? Not sure if you're flexible enough for that one, Nat." Carla wiggled her eyebrows suggestively.

"Shut up," she responded. There was no use in rolling her eyes when one was covered with a bag of frozen hominy. She turned to Mia. "Do you think he means Twister?"

"Okay, I said, *Like Twister?* and he just responded, *lol.*"

The women around the table all exchanged confused looks with each other. "What the hell does that mean? I hate texting with guys and all this damn flirty shit. I just want straightforward answers," she grumbled.

"Language, Natalie!" her mom said again.

"Wait, he followed up with, *I don't have Twister, but I can ask the group if you really want to play it.*"

"The group?"

Mia gasped, a hand going to her chest. "His friends. He wants you to meet his friends." The other ladies also aww'd at this including Abuelita.

"He has friends?" She felt herself shut down. Everything was moving way too fast. It was too much to meet these mystery gaming friends already. She and Mason were work acquaintances who sometimes did sexy things inside of empty barns. Now she had to meet other people?

Her friend raised an eyebrow. "Yeah. Most people have friends. I think it would be weird for a person not to have any."

"Ross didn't have any friends when you met him."

"Well, yeah, but…he's weird. See? Exactly my point and why I want him to be friends with Mason. Ross might really like going to a game night."

"I don't know."

"God," Carla said with an exasperated sigh. "It's just a silly game night with a bunch of friends. It's not a big deal. What's wrong with you?"

"Ay, mija, I have a good idea. What if you invite your friend here. His friends can come too. I'll invite the family and we can make it a big party with lots of food and stuff. I think there's Monopoly in the closet. Sounds like lots of fun, right?"

Natalie and her sisters did a slow turn to stare at their mother after her suggestion. "Yeah, no," Mariana jumped in. "Mom, come on. We don't want to scare the guy off already. You want him to meet weird cousin Eduardo at this stage? Let's give Natalie a chance here."

"Okay, I think everyone is getting way ahead of everything. There's no reason anyone has to meet anyone—"

"I told him you'd come!" Carla said.

"What? Mia! Why'd you let her have my phone?"

"Sorry. I just set it down for a second." Except she didn't look sorry at all.

"Oops!" Carla said, looking sheepish before giggling. "Abuelita just added the eggplant emoji."

Chapter Nineteen

THURSDAY EVENING, NATALIE stood at Mason's apartment door, holding a plate covered in tinfoil her mother insisted she bring. She considered not knocking, anxiety hitting her at full force. Taking a breath, she tapped on the door tentatively. There was laughter coming from inside. If no one noticed the knock, she could go home, eat tamales while drinking wine, and watch some trash TV. Tempting.

Before she could slip away, the door was flung open by Mason with the biggest grin on his face. "Hey, gorgeous. Come on in." She was swept inside, like a tornado. He helped remove her coat and scarf to hang on an entryway coat rack posted on the wall, while she balanced a plate of hot tamales.

She held her breath, waiting for a kiss hello, wondering if it would hit her the way his goodbye kiss had. But when he tilted his face closer, he frowned. "What happened? Is that a black eye?" His voice was laced with concern.

She touched the affected area. Natalie must have rubbed the makeup off on the nervous drive over. "Oh, yeah, I got in a fight with my sister."

"What?"

"It's nothing. It was an accident. We were fighting over my phone, and I accidentally knocked it into my face. I-I brought tamales." Before she could react, he brushed a soft kiss over the bruise. She swayed, her eyes shuttering closed.

"Come on. You can meet the rest of the group. Actually, the black eye is a good strategy. You can intimidate them with your toughness."

She didn't feel tough, more like a nervous puddle of softness, but she let him pull her into the dining room where the rest of the group had gathered at a dining table. They were going through a stack of board games while sipping on bottles of beer.

"This is Natalie," Mason announced. "That's Isaac, his husband, Damon, and Gemma, and Handsome Jay."

"Come on, Mase. Don't introduce me like that. It's just Jay." Except the man with the dark, perfect hair, tan, and dimples was indeed too handsome to be real. The nickname was fitting.

Mason leaned closer, saying, "He's married to Gemma so, to everyone's great disappointment, he's off the market."

Her eyes turned to Gemma who was also exceedingly pretty. "I brought tamales," Natalie said. Let the awkwardness commence. Isaac offered her a chair while Mason went into the kitchen, returning with paper plates, forks, and a beer for her.

"We were thinking Ticket to Ride was a good game to play with your first time joining the group. Have you played it before?" Gemma asked her.

"Oh, uh, no." In fact, she didn't recognize any of the games in the stack. Gemma's words surprised her, as if they were expecting her to keep returning and she was part of the group already.

"You don't mind if I break into this, do you? I'm dying to eat one of these tamales," Mason said, pulling off the foil and unleashing the steam underneath.

"Oh, yeah, I'll take one of those too." Jay held out a plate.

"These guys will inhale a whole plate of offerings before you have a chance to blink your eyes," Gemma warned her. "Don't be afraid to use your fork as a weapon." She pretended to stab her husband in the hand before spearing her own tamale and unwrapping the corn husks. Natalie laughed, taking a sip from her beer, beginning to relax. When Mason put his arm around her, she found herself tucking into him.

"This is really good. I'll eat your tamales any day," he said, pressing his mouth close to her ear. She didn't have the heart to mention she wasn't involved with these tamales, kind of wishing she didn't arrive home too late. After all the effort he made toward her, she was wanting to give back a little more.

As the game was set up, Isaac explained the rules. The game allowed the group to talk casually about other things or boisterously give each other a hard time. She really liked Mason's friends. Mia and Ross would fit in easily with them. *Great.* Mia's influence was working. But she was having fun, enjoying being included in Mason's world.

"Wow," Isaac said at one point, "It seems like you finally found someone who has no qualms about cheating, just like you, Mase."

She threw her head back and laughed. "Mason will tell

you, that when I cheat, I'll admit it. I think this is really just a case of beginner's luck."

Isaac shook his head as though disappointed, but his dark brown eyes glittered with humor. "Like boyfriend, like girlfriend. Those who cheat at board games together, stay together, I guess."

"Fake girlfriend, you mean."

Gemma laughed at this as she set a train piece on the board. "Fake girlfriend?"

She feigned shock. "What? Mason, you didn't tell your friends we were fake dating? They're going to think this is actually something real." She playfully bumped his shoulder with her own but, though she was teasing, there was a moment when the jovial expression on his face fell, his ears turning red. She had the awful feeling she'd said the wrong thing, possibly embarrassing him when all she was doing was having fun.

"Wait, what?" Isaac replied.

As much as she gave Mia a hard time about her people-pleasing charm, Natalie tried to channel her to rescue the situation. If there was one thing her friend was good at, it was making people feel good. She pasted on her best smile, laying a hand on one of Mason's broad shoulders while leaning into him. "Well," she said, as though preparing for story time. "I suppose that's simplifying things somewhat. Maybe he was too modest to tell you about the time he was Prince Charming, rescuing me from the attentions of Diva Santa with one tiny lie. Of course, I didn't really know Mason much at that point." His hazel eyes turned to her, his gaze hitting her directly in the heart. "But, since then, I've come to realize he's one of the best guys I've ever known."

"God. Stan is still there?" Jay chuckled. "Hon, we definitely have to go get a tree this weekend and I need to see Santa. He told me he used to be part of a knife gang."

"No, stop. I know that man tells a lot of stories, but that can't possibly be true. That's one Santa who could be knocked over by a strong breeze," Gemma said. "And I can totally believe he tried hitting on Natalie. Goodness, Mason! Why are you holding back all the good tea?"

"Let me tell you something. Mason is one of the best fake or real boyfriends you could ever have. The guy is the sweetest," Isaac said.

"He's definitely the sweetest," Gemma agreed.

"Hey," Jay interrupted. "You know Damon and I are right here. What about your spouses?"

"Come on, Jay. You already have most handsome. You can at least let me have sweetest," Mason said.

"Fine. I'll let you call me Handsome Jay if I get to call you Sweet Mase."

"Deal."

"Although," Isaac said. "How sweet can he be when he cheats at board games?"

Laughter again filled the dining room and Natalie relaxed. The group returned to good-natured conversation and she wove her arm through Mason's, leaning against him, and, she hoped, all was right with the world again.

"DID YOU HAVE fun?" he asked her after everyone else had

departed.

She stood in the entryway, trying to decide if she should put on her shoes and also leave. She didn't want to. "I did. I really liked the game, and your friends are nice." She wondered why they weren't touching yet. He stood opposite her, his hands stuffed in his pockets, and the urge to be touched by him was driving her wild with need. "I… If I come back for another game night, can I invite Mia?"

"Yeah, sure." His eyes studied her. Did he want her to leave? Was he not making a move because he was still hurt by what she'd said earlier? Natalie thought about apologizing but wasn't sure how to define what they had. She only knew she wanted more of whatever it was.

"Will you stay?" he asked, breaking through the quiet, his voice low.

Her heart beat heavily in her chest. "I have work tomorrow, and I'm opening, so I need to get up early."

"Got it." It's possible he took this for another one of her excuses. She always seemed to have one.

"But if you don't mind me waking up super early…" She let the rest of the sentence fall away, much like her resolve. Taking a step toward him, her hand tugged on the front of his shirt. Her wish was answered as he pulled her close, pressing her to his body, wrapping his arms around her. His mouth covered hers and he seemed to sigh into her. Natalie realized this was exactly where she wanted to be. Maybe she didn't have all the words right now, but she could give him something. She scraped her fingers through the hair along the nape of his neck, meeting his mouth and tongue with her own, giving his lips gentle bites. "I want you," she whispered.

In a single graceful move, he scooped her up, holding her to him as she clung to his shoulders, spreading kisses along his neck. He carried her to his darkened bedroom, gently depositing her on the bed. Her clothes were peeled away, his calloused hands brushing along her skin everywhere. She couldn't help shivering in anticipation as her own eager fingers helped rid him of his garments. Beneath her hands was the soft crush of chest hair and she wanted to giggle with giddiness, wanting him to press into her until she could hardly breathe because she loved the feel of it, the feel of him.

After he slid on a condom, he crawled over to her. "We're not in a barn. I want to take my time with you." He brushed gentle lips along her temple. "Tell me what you like."

"I..." Natalie couldn't remember ever being asked before, and he wasn't making it easy to think. A ball of emotion caught in her throat. Before any of it could escape and ruin everything, she blurted, "Kiss my boobs." The command was absolutely ridiculous. She expected him to laugh at her. If she'd thought about his question for any length of time, it probably wouldn't have been her first demand. She just wanted something to happen before she lost it completely.

But he didn't laugh. He inched down her body, hot, slow kisses following the same path, until he paid her small breasts ample attention, leaving tender kisses there, and gently tugging on her nipples with his teeth. Whatever he was doing, it was working, because she soon forgot all about being ridiculous, letting her head roll back and savoring his attention.

Her breathing increased heavily when he moved even lower, settling his face between her legs and using his tongue and mouth to tease her. She could barely stand it. The sensations of what he was doing to her were overwhelming as she arched her body, mumbling his name until she couldn't help but cry out. Natalie collapsed, placing a hand over her chest as she tried to catch her breath.

This man.

He was everything.

Mason crawled back up her body, kissing along her jawline. "Can I have you?" he said in a low voice.

"Yes," she whispered. Natalie didn't want to deny him anything.

With a groan, Mason eased into her. "God, you feel so good. I don't think I could ever get enough of you."

"Mm-hmm." She wrapped herself around him, kissing across his eyelids.

He pulled out before pushing back in, moving slowly at first, proving he meant it when he said he actually wanted to take his time with her.

At one point, his breath was hot on her ear. "You're worth it," he said. "You've always been worth it."

She squeezed her eyes shut, convinced this would help in preventing the heart attack that was sure to follow because her chest was squeezing itself too tight.

"Did you hear me?"

She could only nod.

"Good."

Natalie reopened her eyes, feeling a spark relight inside

her. Re-energized she began to push against him, giving into him as hard as he gave to her, watching as his eyes darkened with intensity as she scratched and playfully bit him as only a villain could. His fingers gripped her tighter as he pushed harder, his face pressing into her neck until he groaned loudly and collapsed.

In between heavy pants, he said, "There will never be a sweeter honey than you."

And, yes, it was completely sappy, but she couldn't stop the smile from forming on her lips. "Well, you are the expert."

A soft chuckle escaped him.

The moment was complete bliss and she wanted to laugh her ass off before doing it all over again with him. She was almost devastated when Mason rolled off her, removing the weight of him, as he padded into the bathroom.

But, good God, she'd never experienced sex quite like that. How was she ever supposed to recover and go back to her life the way it was before?

After she'd returned from her own bathroom break, Mason pulled her onto the bed again, wrapping her in blankets and cuddling into her, releasing a sigh of complete contentment. "I *really* like you," he said into her shoulder.

She ran her fingers along the arms holding her, enjoying the feel of him. "Yes, I think that's pretty obvious now."

He brushed the hair from her neck, pressing a kiss there. "I know we kind of had a conversation about this before, but… Surprising as it sounds, you were right. I'm not the type of guy for flings. I get attached. I can't help it. We both know if this thing between us becomes a relationship, you're definitely going to be the stronger one out of the two of us. And I've already put myself on the hook here, waiting for whatever you're willing to give me."

Natalie didn't give her standard answer. For the first time, she paused. As much fuss as she gave about not wanting to get attached, something was different. She didn't want to give him up. She may get something from her trips to Tahoe, but she didn't get anything close to this. Perhaps there was something to be said for allowing herself to become familiar with a person, to let him become familiar with her. Justifications were being created in her mind. Why couldn't she continue to see him? As Mia had said, the only person standing in her way was herself. As long as she kept her head and heart on a leash, maybe she could survive and be okay. The temptation of it all had been born and she ached to grasp hold.

Mason continued rambling. "I guess what I'm trying to say is that maybe if some charming, good-looking guy strolls into the coffee shop—"

She smiled to herself. "What do you mean 'maybe'? That happens all the time. One of them is a regular. Orders the same drink every time."

"Okay, *when* some charming, handsome guy strolls into the coffee shop and asks you out, maybe you'll say no because you only want to be with me, just like I want to only be with you."

Natalie flipped around until they were facing each other, popping her head on a bent elbow as she studied him. "I see. Can I at least ask what this imaginary handsome, charming man's name is?"

"Does a name really play that much into your decision-making process?"

"Sexy people have sexy names. I'd like to know what I'm dealing with here."

His brow furrowed as though he was giving it serious thought. "Alejandro."

She snorted a laugh. "Alejandro?"

"That was the sexiest name I could think of off the top of my head."

"Okay, so Alejandro walks into Pony Expresso with his piercing green eyes and sparkling, perfect smile, sees me with my messy hair, tired eyes, and smudged makeup, is instantly swept away, and asks me out? Did I get it right?" The whole situation was way too close to what happened when she met Stephen, and—unlike that first time—her ex no longer sounded appealing in the least. But she didn't want to think about him, not when she had Mason right here who was a hundred times better.

"Well, shit. Now he sounds too handsome and you guys have the potential to bring beautiful children into the world. That was my fault for naming him Alejandro in the first place."

Natalie ran a finger along his chest. "I guess I would say, *Sorry, Alejandro. You're too late. I'm currently seeing someone.*"

There was a pause in the room. "Really? You're okay not having a sexy man-god like Alejandro?"

"Of course. My imaginary Italian boyfriend, Valentino, is way sexier."

Mason plopped onto his back in a dramatic fashion with a groan. "You know what? I know when I'm beat and can't compete."

"You can, because you're real and they're not. I mean, sure, your name is Mason Lavigne and it sounds like you should be the owner of a fancy hat shop in the French Quarter, but I still like it. And you can't tell me you don't get gorgeous gardeners coming into the nursery from time to time."

Natalie pulled herself to a sitting position, straddling Mason's body. She cupped her breasts with her hands and said, "Okay, just imagine I'm some blonde bombshell named Carlotta with actual boobs." Her voice switched to breathy and husky. "Hey there, big boy. I'm looking for a good pollinator, and you look like just the man who can help me out." She shimmied her shoulders for added flirtiness, flicking her hair back.

He barked a laugh, running a hand across her thighs. "A good pollinator? What does that mean? Is she looking for bees?"

"I don't know. I don't know that much about gardening so sue me. And does it matter? She's looking at you like you're a sandwich she wants to devour."

"What kind of sandwich?"

"Um. Ham and cheese."

"That's probably the unsexiest sandwich you could have come up with."

She released a frustrated growl because the thought of any real-life Carlotta was making her crabby. "Whatever. I already hate Carlotta and damn if I want to give her too much credit when it comes to creative sandwich options."

Mason cleared his throat, getting into character, as his

hand slid to her waist. "I'm sorry, ma'am—"

"Oh, yes, that's good. Always call them ma'am. The Carlottas of the world hate that."

"I'm sorry, ma'am. But we don't sell bees here. And I am not a sandwich."

Laughter spilled out of her as she dropped to his chest, snuggling into him. "That was really smooth."

"But not as smooth as Alejandro."

"Forget about that guy. He's a sucky tipper and keeps staring at his reflection in the window."

"I'll make sure to leave a double tip next time."

"Who knew the invention of Alejandro would bring about such positive results? I should have conjured him up a long time ago."

"Okay, but the point is, we don't need Alejandro or Carlotta, right? It's just you and me." He wrapped his arms around her, holding her close, and she'd never felt this safe and secure before.

"Just you and me," she repeated, closing her eyes, and letting a moment of peace settle over her soul.

Chapter Twenty

BEFORE SETTLING INTO sleep, Natalie had set the alarm on her phone for 6AM. Mason's internal clock woke him at 5:30 for some reason. Maybe he wanted a few quiet moments to appreciate her pressed against him, breathing deeply, her head resting on his chest. He resisted the urge to touch her too much, not wanting to wake her.

The time before Natalie had stepped into his life seemed like a decade ago. How he'd managed to get to this point, one where he'd won her over and was on the receiving end of her affection, didn't quite seem real. It was like when he first discovered his love of bees. Once he got past the fear of being stung, Mason felt he could do almost anything. She made him want to do more.

Such as breakfast.

He could make her breakfast. He had never been much of a cook but that didn't mean he couldn't do something. Did he have anything in his fridge? He couldn't make her waffles because he didn't own a waffle iron, nor did he have any eggs, which he was pretty sure were an ingredient of waffles…and pancakes, and omelets—pretty much anything belonging in the breakfast category. What time did grocery stores open?

He was still debating this in his head when the alarm on her phone beeped from its spot on the nightstand. Mason reached over, shutting it off, hating that it meant she would be leaving his bed soon.

The morning was dark, but she stirred, groaning her annoyance.

He brushed her hair from her face and pressed a soft kiss to her forehead. "Hey, gorgeous. It's time to get up. You want me to make you something?" He'd get creative if necessary. Who said you couldn't eat a peanut butter sandwich for breakfast?

She snuggled closer, her arms tightening around him. "That's okay. I don't wanna go to work. You're so cozy and warm."

He knew how Natalie felt because she was cozy and warm too. It was as if his heart had finally found its spot in the world, and all he wanted to do was sink right into her and make love to her the whole day.

"What?" she said, becoming more awake, tipping her head to him.

Mason may have said that last part out loud. Instead of repeating it, he said, "Can't you call in sick or something?"

"I'm the opening manager. Who am I going to call in sick to? I absolutely have to go to work this morning." Her voice was matter-of-fact and determined, much to his dismay, but then it switched to a lower tone. "But I also need you to sink right into me and make love to me, so you'd better make it fast."

He certainly wasn't about to argue and did just that.

THANKFULLY, IT WASN'T too much later when he saw her again. That morning, he stopped by Placerville Hardware, the shop where he'd been finding most of his ornaments. Part real hardware store and part kitchen/gift shop, he was usually able to find what he needed, (unless he was looking for an ornament with an inner tube). Today, he put two new ornaments on her tree: a small battery-operated candle and a train engine.

"Being sneaky again?" she asked beside him, holding a drink for him to take.

"I never tried being sneaky. Do you see me wearing a disguise?" He took a sip from his cup. "Besides, if I wanted to win over my girlfriend, she better know it was me who was decorating her tree. I don't want Alejandro getting the credit."

"Hmm," was all she said, but she didn't resist him pulling her to his side as they studied the tree together.

"The tree is still looking fresh. Someone's doing a good job watering it."

"You do realize I have to store all these knickknacks after the tree comes down, right? They're going to spend the majority of the year inside of a box, which is why this is a waste of money." But she reached out to gently adjust the red train engine ornament, so it hung straighter on the branch.

She still didn't get it, even after he'd whispered in her ear the night before. When it came to her, he didn't consider anything to be a waste. "I don't care. I want to fill your tree with hundreds of ornaments, until you're not even sure there's a tree under there anymore."

"Hundreds? That's going to take a long time."

"Exactly." Hopefully, it would take forever. "Can we talk about Sasquatch?"

A confused expression drifted across her face. "What? Why?"

"Because the hardware shop had a really cute Sasquatch ornament and I want to buy it for your tree, but I can't start throwing random ones on there now."

"Stop. There's no way I'm going to encourage this, especially for a silly Sasquatch ornament. All right, you need to leave now. I have work to do."

"Okay, I'll see you tomorrow at the farm… Unless you need to see me sooner?"

She rolled her eyes. "I think I can survive one night. I'll see you tomorrow and no Sasquatch ornaments. Stop trying to force something just because it's cute."

When he tipped his head to her, she kissed him goodbye, and he had never had a day start better.

THE LAST WEEKEND of Poinsettia Paradise was smooth sailing. He even heard his dad bragging about how well the season was going to Charlie. Christmas was still a week and a half away, but unlike other Christmas tree lots, the farm only sold trees for a limited time, ending the season early. The last weekend was busy, and Mason found himself trying to keep up with demand and not spending as much time as he'd liked escaping into the barn with Natalie. In fact, besides a few times he was able to sneak away to get his Mexican hot chocolate, they didn't spend any time together.

He couldn't complain too much because, on both Saturday and Sunday, she came home with him. He enjoyed exploring his girlfriend's body, familiarizing himself with what set her off and all the sweet sounds she made. Nothing made him happier.

"So, now that the season has wrapped up for you guys, are you just allowed to be lazy for the rest of the year?" she asked him as they sat in bed, sharing a bowl of peppermint ice cream.

"It's quieter but there's usually greenhouse prep that needs to be done, and planning for spring planting for the nursery. But this year is kind of different so I'm not exactly sure." With his dad wanting to retire, there may be things changing in his future. They hadn't talked much about it lately, so he wasn't sure what was going to happen now and thinking about it stressed him out. "I don't suppose this is also the quiet period for the coffee business. You can take time off, and we can spend Christmas somewhere warm and tropical." He kissed her bare shoulder before taking a spoonful of the ice cream she offered him.

"I wish. My parents would probably flip out if I miss the family's Christmas Eve get-together. However, they owe me after my uncle basically forced me to drop my usual December Tahoe vacation in order to work at your place."

"You take a trip to Tahoe every December? Do you ski or do professional snow tube racing or something?"

"Ha! No. I-I just go to get away from everything. Take a

week for myself."

"You go by yourself?"

Her spoon scraped the edges of the ice cream in a slow circular manner, her concentration deep. "Yeah."

"You don't get lonely?"

"I usually made a friend or two when I was there."

He wasn't sure what she meant by *friend* and he was afraid to ask if these were men. Not because Natalie shouldn't be able to do whatever she wanted, but rather he couldn't stop himself from being a little jealous of any man who got attention from her, even those in the past.

It was quiet for a moment or two. Only the sound of the metal spoon hitting the glass bowl filled the air.

"Do you regret giving up your trip?" he asked.

"No. I thought I would but..." She looked at him. "It's funny how things turn out, right? I've never eaten ice cream naked in bed before, never knew there was anything to it, and now I don't want to eat ice cream anywhere else. It's that good." She took the last bite, closing her eyes to savor it, and any weird jealousy he had evaporated because she was right. Anything in the past, whether in her life or his, didn't matter in the grand scheme of things because sometimes a person just didn't know about something until they did. And those other guys should be jealous of him because he had her and they didn't.

He took her empty bowl, setting it on the nightstand. "So you're doing this big Christmas Eve family thing?"

"Mm-hmm. What does your family do for Christmas?"

"Most of my extended family is in Arizona. So for the holidays it's usually just my parents and me. I usually go over on Christmas Day. My mom makes duck for dinner. It has to be quieter than your family thing."

"Oh, for sure. You guys have duck? I don't think I've ever had duck before? Sounds fancy. They sell that at the Grocery Outlet?"

Mason chuckled. "I don't know where she gets them. You can come if you want."

"Oh, no. I don't want to invade your family's holiday—"

"Come. I want you to meet my parents."

"I've already met them."

"That doesn't count. I want you to meet them as my girlfriend." He kissed her shoulder again, his lips traveling to her neck.

"Oh." She was quiet for a brief time before finally saying, "Okay."

"You can bring a little noise to break up our normal quietness."

"*Excuse me*? Are you saying I'm noisy?" But she laughed as he pushed her into the bed and began to kiss her with more intention, his hands sliding across her body.

"I keep telling you, you're not quiet, but I like that about you," he murmured against her skin. "I love your shoulders. You have the best shoulders."

"I love your shoulders too." Natalie slid her arms around his neck, her fingertips chilled from holding the ice cream bowl. He shivered when they touched him. "Do you want to come to my family's Christmas Eve bash?" she asked.

He stopped, staring into her beautiful brown eyes. "Really?"

"My family is curious about you."

She'd told her family about him? "Yeah, okay."

"Okay," she said.

This was it for him. He'd finally found it.

Mason loved her.

Absolutely. Completely.

Chapter Twenty-One

"HE'S COMING OUT of the garage, right?" Natalie asked. Her mother flung an exasperated arm in the air, showing that she couldn't care less if her husband made an appearance on Christmas Eve, before continuing to chop tomatoes for salsa.

"Is everything set for the dishwasher delivery?" Natalie asked Mariana, who had taken the lead on the gift for their mother.

"Yeah, don't worry. It's already at Tío's and he's going to bring it by tonight. Carla bought a big red bow to put on it and everything. It's all going to be fine."

Her sister had the calm, in-control energy she needed this evening. Natalie was becoming anxious, in particular about inviting Mason to join them. When she'd asked him, it had felt right but she was becoming less sure. Was it too soon? Even her "ex-fiancé" had never come to a family get-together, thank God. Unfortunately, she'd already mentioned Mason's invitation to her mother who then mentioned it to everyone else. They were acting as if the Pope and everyone else at the Vatican were coming because suddenly there wasn't enough food. It didn't make any sense, considering there was always plenty of food and Mason was only one additional person. There was no point in reasoning with anyone.

Mason also appeared to be excited to attend, sending her texts and asking how he should dress and if he should bring anything. The last one was answered with a resounding *NO* because the last thing they needed was more food.

Apparently, the only one nervous about the whole situation was her because, holy cow, Natalie was really doing this. She was trying to be in a relationship, and both liked it while being absolutely terrified as she waited for the other shoe to drop. She was afraid, as soon as the holidays were over, reality would hit and the relationship would return to pumpkin form or whatever the Christmas version was.

"Hola, Papá. Feliz Navidad," she said with all the gentleness of confronting a lamb, approaching his recliner where he was bundled in a blanket and listening to music on the radio. She gave him a hug and kiss on the cheek.

"Hey, baby. You bring back my truck."

"Yup. Filled it up, not a scratch on it. Thanks for letting me borrow it. You're the best father a girl could have."

"I haven't seen you as much lately. You met your mother and sisters for lunch, and you didn't invite me. No one ever invites me because your mother hates me."

She pushed down her aggravation at the insinuation her father was purposely left out of things. Especially because the *lunch* was here at the house and it happened when she dropped off a couple of gifts since they were already wrapped and in her car. Her mom feeding her while she was here was happenstance and a common occurrence. "I've been busy working. You know Tío has had me working extra these last few weeks. You can complain to him and see if he'll give me a double vacation."

She deserved it, plus a promotion to partnership. Also, if she got double time off, a tropical vacation with Mason could be an actual possibility. It would allow their relationship to exist in a daydream state for a little longer.

"You work too much," her father agreed.

"Right? I agree. But I'm happy to spend today with you and the rest of the family. You know Tina is going to be here with the baby soon." If there was one thing her father was a sucker for, it was babies. He adored them. The few times he perked up and looked happy was when he was able to gush over a baby, whether it was her cousin's or a stranger's. "Oh, and I invited someone over because I want him to meet you."

Her father's mood lifted. "You invited a friend? To meet me? Is it a boyfriend?"

"Mm-hmm," she replied. "His name is Mason and I met him working at the Christmas tree farm. He's really nice. You'll like him." She couldn't imagine anyone not liking Mason. She had no doubt he'd win over both of her parents easily.

Her father's happiness flickered away. "How come I haven't met him before?"

She rolled her eyes but kept her smile in place. "It's brand new. Only Tío Enrique knows him. You come inside, and when he gets here, I'll introduce him to you first because you are mi papá. Okay?"

This did the trick and her father stood, letting her lead him into the house. As soon as they entered, Enrique was there to pat his brother on the back and other people shouted their holiday greetings as if her father had returned from a long trip. It was the type of reaction he loved, and she was willing to do whatever she could to humor him today.

Enrique answered the door when Mason arrived. Her uncle was confused at first until he figured out that the business arrangement with Daniel may have jump-started an additional arrangement of a different sort. He gladly welcomed Mason with a pat on the shoulder and handshake, ushering him inside.

"This is Mason," she said, bringing her father over as promised. "Mason, this is my dad."

He was dressed in a nice button-down shirt with dark pants. He'd had a haircut and beard trim, the cleft in his chin becoming slightly more visible again. Mason smiled easily, although he appeared somewhat overwhelmed with an audience building around him. She probably should have warned him this could happen, especially when word went out about Natalie having a boyfriend for the first time in forever.

"Hi. Nice to meet everyone. Here, I brought this for you." He handed a large, luscious pink and red potted poinsettia plant and a small jar to Miguel.

Her father took the items, studying the label on the jar. "Honey?"

"Oh, yeah, that's a small gift from my beehive. It's from my stash I harvested this past year. It's a good one."

Her father looked at the jar again and then to Mason, his expression amazed as though he'd been gifted with liquid gold. "You brought this for me?"

"Well, you and anyone you want to share it with. Maybe not any bears." He grinned, before bestowing a friendly wink in her direction. If she was the type, she would have swooned. Prince Charming was exactly what was needed at this moment, and she couldn't stop her heart from swelling, wishing they were alone so she could fling herself at the man.

Her father transferred the items to one arm, taking Mason's elbow with the other. "Come. Come. Are you hungry? First, we eat and then we will visit Tina's baby. Todos, él es el novio de Natalie. He brought me honey."

While other people fawned over him, Mariana leaned close to her. "Good job, Nat. Looks like you brought home a winner. He brought a bigger poinsettia than Carla brought home from work, and Dad's introducing him to Mom like it's nothing." It was true. Miguel brought him to her mother and Mason had to lean down for her to hug. The older woman practically beamed in happiness at the introduction. Things got better when her father handed the poinsettia over to Abuelita because *she likes gardening*. Miguel kept the honey for himself though.

"Everything is going to be fine. Right, Mari?" Natalie asked.

Mariana gave her shoulders a squeeze. "Yup. Don't worry. I'll help keep an eye on the battlefield and make sure the ceasefire is being honored."

Mason was brought to one of the tables, and she had to fight through the crowd in order to sit beside him. Obviously, he was being given the royal treatment, but she was his girlfriend and was owed some courtesy. It wasn't long before a bowl was plopped in front of Mason while the rest of them fought to get their own.

"Hey, gorgeous," he said as soon as she was able to get settled beside him, and she may have swooned again, her gaze flickering away and her cheeks warming. She had to fight off a girlish giggle. Who had she become? Natalie had no idea, but she didn't appreciate her sister, Carla, staring at her while leaning her chin against her palm with a smile on her face.

"Shut up, Carla," she said.

"What? I'm just thinking about Luis." Her sister pushed her bottom lip in a pout. "I miss him. I should call him back." She pulled out her phone, which Mariana snatched away.

"Nope. We're not going through this again."

"Mari, it's Christmas! Give it back, you brat!"

Abuelita patted Carla's hand, whispering something to her, which settled her sister down but didn't remove the pout from her face.

Mason leaned toward Natalie. "What kind of soup is this?"

"It's pozole rojo. It's like a stew with pork and hominy." She reached toward the colorful pottery bowls one of her relatives had set in the center of each table filled with cheese, chopped cilantro and onions, and sliced radishes, sprinkling them into her soup. He followed her lead. "I'm pretty sure one of my aunts brought roasted turkey breast and some gravy. Our meals are a mix of traditional American holiday and Mexican food. Either way, you're not going to leave hungry."

"Oh my God, this is so good. I will happily die right

here," he said. There was a real possibility he would die because of the way her relations kept attempting to push food on him, well past the point of reason. She took charge in fighting them when he whispered to her that he didn't think he could eat another bite.

"Mamá, seriously, stop. You're going to make him sick."

"He's a big man. He needs a lot," her mother said. "I will pack some food for you to take home, okay?"

"Sorry," she said to Mason.

"Why? I'm not. This is one of the best nights of my life."

As soon as the eating slowed, Enrique snuck out of the house with his sons and they soon returned, wheeling a brand-new dishwasher on a dolly. Mariana and Natalie jumped up to dash to their mother and place their hands over her eyes while Carla hurriedly grabbed the giant red gift ribbon to plop on the front. As soon as the surprise was revealed, with much flourish from the family, Rosa cried out in happiness, tears flowing down her face as she rushed to each daughter, squeezing their cheeks and pressing kisses to them. Natalie couldn't remember a happier night in her life. Finally, a Christmas that truly felt like magic.

After the gift was properly fawned over, her mother excitedly approached Mason and said, "You like board games, right? We have Monopoly. You want some hot chocolate? I'll make you some hot chocolate." She placed an old dusty box with split corners on the table.

"We don't have to play Monopoly," she said to Mason, not wanting him to feel obligated.

"Oh, fun! I want to play," Carla said. Soon a couple of her other cousins joined in.

"Come on, Natalie. It'll be fun." Mason removed the lid from the box.

"Okay," she replied, a smile spreading across her face because her heart was so light that evening. But her good mood also clearly put her off her game, as everyone snatched a playing piece before she had a chance to choose.

"Here, Nat, you get to be the old shoe," Carla said, plopping it on the table in front of her. "It suits you."

"Gee, thanks," she replied flatly.

"Here, I'll trade you. I was actually looking for the shoe and somehow accidentally grabbed the car." He swapped pieces with her.

"You guys know this game isn't a co-op, right," her sister said. "You guys can't go into buying Boardwalk together."

Natalie wasn't listening to her sister. How could she when she was taken by him? She pulled him to her and kissed him sweetly, partly to irritate her sister but mostly because she wanted to. All her previous nervousness and apprehension from the day flitted away. This was real. What she had with Mason was something substantial, not fleeting. She didn't understand how, after all her fighting and running away from relationships, she'd gotten so lucky to have a great guy who adored her and fitted in with her family. Natalie couldn't remember why she'd been so worried in the first place.

This had to be exactly how Mia felt with Ross. Maybe happiness in a relationship was possible after all. She should send her best friend a text to let her know she was right about everything and she was forgiven for all past attempts at manipulation.

"Okay, gross," Carla said about the kiss, but her eyes crinkled in amusement. "Before we start playing we need to set up a few house rules. First rule, no kissing between players, unless you want to see me vomit all over the game board. Second rule, no teams. It's everyone for themselves. All those in favor, raise your hands."

Her sister and cousins raised their hands outvoting her and Mason easily. Natalie didn't blame them—it wasn't too long ago she would have voted the same way. She shrugged nonchalantly because she'd sneak her boyfriend away for more proper kissing later. Plus, her sister didn't make any rules about not touching Mason, which she was planning on doing, both above and below the tabletop.

She didn't want the evening to end and, luckily, it was tradition for the family to stay up as late as possible, trying to make it to midnight so they could swap gifts with each other. The only ones that didn't make it were Abuelita, who was currently dozing in a recliner while wearing a Santa hat, and the baby sleeping in a pop-up crib.

The sparkle of the evening began to wear off when Natalie noticed grumbling coming from the kitchen. She shot a panicked look to the couch where Mariana was chatting with a cousin, trying to be subtle as she tipped her head in the direction of the argument. Getting the message, her sister excused herself and went to find their parents.

Whatever Mariana did, it wasn't enough because soon her parents were full-on arguing because her father was determined to swap the dishwasher tonight, while her mother didn't want to worry about her kitchen turning into messy chaos while the party was in full swing. Also, she didn't trust Miguel would do it right and, as a mechanic, he took great offense to this. The only saving grace was they were at least fighting in Spanish, but it didn't take someone fluent in the language to know their conversation wasn't friendly. Natalie wanted to cover her face and fade away, especially when Mason leaned in to whisper, "Is everything okay?"

"Oh yeah, they, uh, always do this."

"Always," said Carla who was busy counting her money to buy a property card and not the least bit fazed by the argument.

"It's fine," she reassured him while also trying to reassure herself.

Her father then exclaimed, "Why do you hate me? It's Christmas. I want to do this for you and you won't even let me share the bed with you. You say I need to sleep in the guest room but I am not a guest. No one knows what I go through being married to such a hateful woman." Then her father went into the garage, slamming the door behind him.

Natalie couldn't even look at Mason, let alone say anything. She felt herself shut down as a dark cloud descended over what was once a merry get-together. The game continued but all the joy had gone out of playing. She didn't even react when he took her hand in his.

When the game finished, he said, "I better get going. I don't want to wear out my welcome and it's getting late." Her other relatives stepped in and invited him to watch a movie with them, but Natalie wasn't among them. At this point, she was looking for her own excuse to go home. She walked Mason to his car, holding a Tupperware of food her mom made for him.

"Thanks for making sure I made it safely to my car," he said, pulling her closer as they stood beside his vehicle, wrapping his arms around her in a hug.

"Yup."

"Are you sure you don't want to come home with me?"

"I better not. I should help my mom clean up and then there will be presents."

He pulled back, concern etched in his features. "Is everything okay?"

How could she tell him today was nothing but an illusion? She allowed herself to get caught in a dream and, like most dreams, it was beautiful and comforting and full of promise. But her parents brought her right back to the reality of the situation. Everything faded. She didn't know why she thought a new dishwasher, a new boyfriend, a new anything would fix things. It was all a bandage because the underlying ugliness was still there and nothing would change it. She was probably headed for the same fate because what made her so special? It wasn't something anyone could escape.

But she couldn't tell him all this, so she replied, "It's fine. I'm just tired. It's been a busy season and I think it's starting to hit me."

He soothed a hand over her hair. "Okay. I'll see you tomorrow."

"Yeah. Sure. Tomorrow."

He brushed his lips over hers, but she didn't do anything to further the kiss.

She held a little of herself back and hoped he didn't notice.

Chapter Twenty-Two

"HEY, MOM." MASON'S mother stood at the stove and he had to step over a sleeping Bentley in order to wrap her in a big hug, kissing the top of her head. "Why is this dog always in the way? Do you need help with anything?"

"Oh, hi, sweetie. Would you mind finishing the salad for me? Your dad started to cut up the veggies, but then I think he got distracted by something else. What time is it? Is Natalie arriving soon?"

"Yeah, she texted me about fifteen minutes ago that she was on her way." Despite leaving Natalie's parents' house feeling as if there was something wrong, he tried to push it aside, accepting her reasoning that she was tired.

Today was Christmas and the day came with some bittersweet feelings. He should feel happy and content but there was that one moment, while he stood at the bathroom mirror brushing his teeth, where he considered this was likely the last Christmas spent at the farmhouse with his parents. Who knew what the next year would entail. Would he be flying down to Arizona to spend part of the holidays there or would they travel to Placerville? There was a lot that was still unknown.

"So, you really like this girl, huh?"

He chuckled. "Oh yeah. I'm pretty sure this is the one I'm going to marry." Movement caught his eye. Glancing up, Mason did a double take. There was Natalie standing in the kitchen entry with his dad beside her. He hadn't heard the doorbell ring or anything. Now he stood there, with a vegetable peeler frozen in his hand, his previous words echoing loudly in his ear. "Natalie."

Bentley jumped to awake, scrambling to greet her, which had his mom turning around. "Oh. Hello. Welcome." His mom went to his girlfriend, giving her a quick hug. "Mason, you should take her coat." This did a good job of snapping him into action.

"My mom insisted I bring over some cookies," she said, offering a Tupperware filled with cookies that were rolled in powdered sugar to his mother.

While she smiled softly at his parents, something about her was reserved, as though some of her normal light was tucked away somewhere. He didn't consider his conversation with his mom as anything bad but Mason was kicking himself for opening his big mouth anyway. Their relationship was still in that new, fragile state and he didn't need to give her an excuse to already run away from him. He couldn't lean over and say, *Forget what you heard. I was just kidding*—not with his parents there. She might not believe him and for a good reason. He hadn't been kidding. Either way, there wasn't much he could do about it now.

He tried to pretend everything was fine, peeling her jacket off and taking her scarf. Beneath the outerwear, she wore a deep green sweater dress made of the softest material and her hair fell in loose waves. He couldn't stop himself from pulling her into a hug, brushing a kiss along her temple, but she didn't fold into him as normal.

"It smells good. Do you need help with anything?" she asked, removing herself from his arms.

"Dinner is just about done. Mason, can you set the table please?"

Once dinner was ready, they loaded up their plates with duck, mashed potatoes, green bean casserole, and bread rolls. She answered his parents' polite questions. They asked if she had any siblings, how long she'd been working for her uncle, and if she had any other hobbies or interests. As much as his parents worried about him finding himself another Dakota, they were warm with Natalie and appeared to genuinely like her. The glow in his chest returned as he draped his arm across the back of her chair, feeling a sense of pride.

"I like to read or hang out with my best friend. One of my sisters and I train for the El Dorado 10k marathon every year. It's probably time for me to give up those waffles Mason keeps feeding me."

"Is this the same sister who's an EMT?" his mother asked.

"Yes, that's right."

There was a lull in conversation as the eating continued. He never realized how quiet his family dinners were until experiencing Natalie's holiday events.

"The duck is really good. Thank you so much for inviting me," she said to fill the void.

"Oh, thank you. You're so sweet. I'm so happy that you and Mason hit it off. I had been trying to get him to sign up for one of those dating bachelor shows—"

"Mom," Mason warned, his cheeks heating. His mom was joking, kind of, but Natalie didn't know that. He slid her a glance. She returned it with some of her old spark lighting her eyes for the first time that day.

"What?" His mother was oblivious to the fact he was embarrassed. "There's no reason you couldn't have been on one of those shows. You're tall, and women like men who are tall. Plus, you're handsome. Don't you think he's handsome, Natalie?"

"Mom, come on. Stop."

"Yes," Natalie agreed. "Very handsome."

"Well, it certainly doesn't matter now. He's found you and you're a very lovely young woman. And you know Mason is natural husband material. He's so helpful to have around. You do want to get married someday, don't you?"

Oh God. Regardless of how he felt toward her, they didn't need this kind of pressure. He might have been able to laugh it off as his mother being a mother if Natalie hadn't overheard him in the kitchen earlier. It made his accidental slip even worse.

Mason cleared his throat, his brain working furiously in an attempt to change the topic before his mother brought up grandbabies, making the whole conversation even more awkward. "I'm also happy to not be a contestant on a reality show nor have to fight over other contestants like Alejandro and Valentino for someone like Natalie. Here, have some more bread rolls, Mom."

"So, uh, Mason said you guys were soon going to move into spring planning for the nursery." Natalie appeared uncomfortable, tearing her roll into pieces.

"Yeah," his father answered before changing his mind. "Actually, I keep forgetting. No, we're not. After we're gone, that's going to be someone else's responsibility."

"Gone?" she asked.

Mason opened his mouth to answer but his father beat him to it. "Yeah, we're moving to Arizona soon."

She shot him a confused look, her brow furrowing. "Oh, I didn't know."

He tried to lighten the mood again, leaning toward his girlfriend and said, "You can see why my mom is so eager to influence my love life right now."

To his dismay, she didn't crack a smile, focusing on her plate instead.

After the food was cleared away, his parents turned on the TV for the traditional viewing of *Miracle on 34th Street.* He put an arm around Natalie's shoulders on the couch, but she kept her arms wrapped across her stomach and was tense, even as he played with the ends of her hair or dropped a soft kiss onto her shoulder.

"What's wrong?" he said after she bid his parents goodbye and they walked to her car.

"Nothing. I—"

"I know that's not true. I can feel it when I touch you. You're obviously bothered about something. You can tell me."

She leaned against the driver's door of her vehicle, closing her eyes, and sighing. His stomach dropped. Mason could fix this. He'd reassure her that he wasn't about to pop the question. She didn't need to freak out when he wasn't rushing her into anything.

"I knew it," he said. "I felt it right here." He put a hand on the back of her neck, gently massaging it. When her eyes opened again, they were glossy. The sight of those dark velvet eyes swimming in tears set a deep fear in his gut. "What's wrong?"

"Are you moving to Arizona?"

"What?" He was taken aback but also filled with relief. This wasn't about him saying he was going to marry her. He laughed, pulling her to his chest.

"Stop laughing at me." The words were muffled against his chest, but the irritation came through.

He leaned back. "No, I'm not moving to Arizona. My parents are. I'm staying right here. Is that what's been bothering you? Although it makes me feel good that you'd get this upset at the thought of me leaving."

Her face didn't soften; the annoyance was laced in the creases of her forehead. "This isn't funny."

"Yeah, it kinda is. Come on, don't you think I would have mentioned it if I was planning on moving to another state?"

"Stop it. Just stop." She shoved a hand against his chest as though she meant it.

"What's going on?"

"I can't do this, Mason."

"You can't do what?" The cold, unsettling feeling had returned to his chest.

"This. Us. This is my fault, okay? I just thought… I'm not sure, but I know that I'm just prolonging the inevitable. Maybe not this time but there will be something else. And I don't want to keep waiting for something bad to happen. I'm sorry. But it was never going to end the way you thought it would."

Mason's laughter vanished. He was confused but still kept a small amount of hope alive that this was a simple misunderstanding. "Is this about what I said in the kitchen? I'm sorry, okay? I-I wasn't thinking."

She shook her head, the tears returning to her eyes. "You don't need to apologize. You haven't done anything wrong."

"Then why does it sound like you're breaking up with me?" Frustration and aggravation crawled along his skin and he rubbed roughly at his head.

Natalie leaned against her car, running a tired hand across her face. "You want to get married? Have kids someday? All that traditional stuff, right?"

Was this a trap of some kind? He studied her trying to guess the right answer, the one that would get him back into her good graces.

"I'm not trying to trick you. Even if I hadn't heard you in the kitchen, I already knew."

He relented. "Yes."

"Yeah, and your mom was right. You're, like, prime husband material."

"I… Is this what's wrong with me?"

She took his arm, gripping him. "There's nothing wrong with you. Okay? You're allowed to want these things and you should be able to have them. I want you to have them. The part that's wrong is me."

He released a bitter laugh. "Okay, so we're doing the 'it's not you, it's me' thing."

She sighed. "I'm never going to get married."

"What? Why?"

"To be honest, I don't want to ever find myself stuck in a situation like my parents. Their love died and now they only hate each other. Before you came along, I didn't want to be in a relationship, fake or real. And I knew better than to start anything with you, but you're just that likable. I went against myself. But I don't want to keep leading you on, making you think that I'm going to eventually give you what you want, when I can't."

This whole conversation was bonkers to Mason. "Natalie, honey, we've only been together for a few weeks. All this stuff you're worried about, if it were to happen, is way down the line. I'm not rushing anything. I'm not expecting to become a husband next month. I just want to be with you."

"But why should you waste your time on me?"

He snapped because it was clear he wasn't winning. "Because I love—"

"No, you don't!"

Mason brushed a hand across her cheek, hoping this would be a link, allowing him to hold on to her. "I do. With all my heart, Natalie Gonzalez-Torres. And if you don't ever want to get married, okay, fine. But let me be with you. Please."

Natalie wiped a tear away. "You don't love me. You can't. You may feel something, but it's not love, Mason. Whatever you think it is, it isn't real."

"You're going to tell me what I feel?"

"You said it yourself. We've only known each other for a

few weeks. No one actually loves someone that fast, and, even if they do, there's no way it's going to last. Do you think your parents are still madly, deeply in love? Do you ever notice them showing affection—a hug, a kiss, anything with each other? Today when we were watching a movie, they didn't even sit next to each other. I'm telling you, everything fades. And all you end up with is cold, drab January. I'm not going to be stuck, Mase."

"Come on, Nat—"

"These are my problems, not yours. I don't want you to stop believing. I like that you still believe. I don't want you to settle for the horse blanket on the ground. You deserve so much more."

Mason couldn't see anything beyond his own heart crushing into a pile of dust.

Natalie gave him one long look, her own eyes glistening with unspent tears. "It seems like you forgot after all." She pointed to herself. "Villain."

Chapter Twenty-Three

WHEN SOMEONE TAPPED on her office door, Natalie did her best to smother her heavy breaths and delicately dry the corners of her eyes with some commercial toilet paper from the supply closet. It wasn't the best choice as the paper wasn't the softest. Her skin was becoming raw. "Yeah?" she called, hoping whatever it was wouldn't require her to leave her office.

"It's Mia."

Dammit. She cleared her throat, hoping it would be enough to make her sound in total control and not on the verge of losing it. "I'm really busy. Can I just talk to you later?"

"What are you busy with?"

Double damn. She struggled inventing something believable, which shouldn't be difficult to do, but it was as if she suddenly forgot what her job entailed. "I'm doing payroll."

"Let's stop beating around the bush. I was in Ross's office, and I could hear you crying."

It was debatable how many tears had to be present to warrant the definition of crying. She swung open the door anyway. "I'm fine. I wasn't crying."

Her friend's expression revealed horror. "God. What

happened to your eyes?"

"What?" She touched the corners, trying not to flinch at the sensitive pain from it. "Allergies."

Mia pushed her way inside and shut the door, which only served to remind Natalie of the one time Mason had done the same thing. She reached for the toilet paper again.

"Natalie. Stop. You haven't been answering my texts. I'm not going to let you just shut yourself off from everything."

"I'm not. I'm at work, okay? I can't just drop everything when you text."

"I texted last night."

Last night, she drove home from Mason's parents' house and proceeded to cry her eyes out. The last thing she was worried about were text messages.

Mia looked at her with such sympathy while rubbing her arm, she couldn't hold it together anymore. The tears sprang forth and she leaned into her friend who held her close.

"Talk to me."

"I…ended…things…with…him." Each word was a struggle as she sobbed.

"Okay. You want to tell me why? It seemed like things were going great and you really liked him."

"I do really like him."

"Then why did you end things?"

"You already know there's no point."

"Do I know that? You may say it, but it doesn't mean that I've accepted it."

"You know I can't do relationships and I'm never going to get married so…" She hiccupped and should be embarrassed about all the snot soaking into Mia's shoulder, but, at the moment, she didn't care.

"You're doing this to yourself. I know you joke around and call yourself a villain but the only one you're constantly punishing is yourself. You're your own worst enemy. You don't have to do this. You can take a breath and just be with Mason. Stop jumping ahead to the very worst possibilities."

"B-but if I get sucked into this even more and I end up like my parents, it's going to hurt worse. Mason hating me is going to make me cry."

Mia pulled away, studying her as she wiped tears from her cheek. "Nat, you're already crying. I understand you're scared. I know this can be terrifying but…you're already stuck, both by a past that you can't change and a future you can't predict. Sometimes all we have is right here in the present and you have to take advantage of what you've got. Regrets are made of days where we had a chance of doing something but chose not to."

"It was just so much easier when I didn't have to worry about this, when I could just go to Tahoe and do whatever."

Mia's brows drew together, her mouth setting in a line. "Easier for who? Certainly not easier for me. I hate those trips."

"What?" She was taken aback as her friend had always been nothing but supportive. Had she been missing something the whole time?

Now Mia was getting teary-eyed. "I hate them. I'm your friend. I will do almost anything for you, except help you bury dead bodies because I don't have the constitution for it, but those trips cause a lot of stress for me. You don't think I worry about you? I worry that maybe you're going to meet up with someone who isn't a good person, who might do something to hurt you. Not only am I going to feel completely helpless being so far away but then I'm also the one hiding it from your family and they'd probably be extremely angry with me being a part of this. And I don't have much of a family here in Placerville as it is, Natalie. I don't want to lose you or them."

"You don't have to worry, I always take—"

"Don't tell me not to worry! People have feelings and, I hate to tell you this, but you can't control other people's feelings. What I feel is what I feel. And I don't care what you and Ross say about my abilities to persuade. The truth, Natalie, I can't persuade anyone of anything that they didn't already want to do in the first place. So, yeah, I can't stop you from taking these trips or doing whatever you're going to do with Mason. You're going to do what you want. But you also can't stop me or your parents or Mason from having feelings or opinions either. The number of things in the world you have actual control over is very, very small. So why would you even choose to give up one of the things you can control?"

Natalie wiped a hand across her eyes. "It's fine. You can hate me. Mason hates me—"

"You don't get it! This has nothing to do with hate. It's about love. I love you. I want you to be happy. And I'm pretty sure Mason loves you too."

There was no way Mia knew about his earlier confession and yet she somehow knew anyway. "He can't love me. And, even if he did, what's going to stop it from fading?"

"Let me show you something." Mia pushed Natalie into

her office chair before retrieving her phone and scrolling through it. "There's this picture. And before you get mad at me, I only took it because I had a feeling I was going to need it, so you can finally see what I'm seeing from my perspective. Ah, here it is. Are you going to tell me that whatever this man feels for you isn't real?" She turned the phone around and it was a picture from inside the horse trailer. Mason was leaning against the order window while Natalie made him a hot chocolate.

"When did you take this?"

"The day after you went snow tubing with him. The fact that you didn't even notice I took a picture should tell you something right there."

"Which is what? That I was concentrating on my work?"

"God, Natalie, can you take off the damn blindfold for once?" She wasn't like this very often, so when she did act blunt, one couldn't help but pay attention. With two fingers, Mia enlarged the picture on her phone, giving both a closer view of Mason and herself.

As much as she wanted to keep fighting her best friend over who had the most accurate perspective on situations, she was way too exhausted to create an argument. Instead, she took a good look at the photo. As she expected, Mason's face was tilted upwards, gazing at her with a soft smile on his lips as though he'd never adored a person more. She wanted to cry all over again because she knew he adored her. She'd seen this expression from him several times and could feel it in the way he touched her, talked to her, in basically everything.

The real surprising thing was her own image. Her cheeks

were flushed, probably due to the cold, but she wore a large smile as though he had said something she found amusing. Her hand was halfway in the process of brushing a strand of hair away from her cheek. Her eyes were downcast but she radiated happiness. She hardly recognized herself, especially with how she felt today. All those times Natalie wondered what Mason saw when he looked at her, she finally saw it for herself. If the people in the picture were strangers, she'd admit she saw two people who were completely smitten with each other.

"You don't get to decide for him how he feels or what he's willing to do for you. All you have is a single choice and that is, what are you going to do with his love? And how do you keep love from fading? You put everything you have in it and fight like the villain you are."

NATALIE HAD BARELY recovered from her conversation with Mia when her uncle stopped by.

"Is everything okay?" he asked.

"Oh, yeah, it's…just allergies, I think. My eyes have been really dry lately."

Her uncle gave her an odd look, even his mustache tilted in concern. There was no way he believed her, but she didn't have the energy to care. Regardless, Enrique proceeded ahead. "I know I said we'd wait until after the new year to discuss your position, but I think we can have the conversation now."

"What? Really?" She had a sudden moment of doubt.

Could she actually do this? Was she ready?

"Yeah, I'm starting to look ahead at when I want to retire, and what I think we should do is go through the process of hiring a new manager to free up your time. You can work with me to learn more of the responsibilities that I deal with like insurance, vendor contracts, that sort of thing. You take over those things and I'll give you a percentage of the business. Maybe not 50/50 right away but we'll work up to it when you start taking over the business more. Plus, if you want to expand the business with the coffee truck, I'll let you have free rein on that. How does that sound to you?"

"Really?" she asked again. After planning this for so long, she was having trouble believing it was happening.

"Yes, really. I'd be proud to have you as a partner."

Natalie burst into tears again.

"Are you really that happy?"

"Uh-huh, sure. Thank you, Tío." Except it was hard to be truly happy when she was also miserable. Whatever she thought she'd feel at this moment wasn't there. It was almost as if her heart was so empty it was lost at feeling anything.

"Have you changed your mind? Do you not want this anymore?"

"No, I do."

"But these don't look like happy tears."

"I'm fine. It's just that..." She'd never discussed personal issues with her uncle before. She blurted her thoughts before she could change her mind. "Is the story really true? Did my parents fall head over heels for each other in a week?"

His forehead furrowed. "Why are you asking this?"

"I don't know. Besides my mom warning me not to be

like her, she never wants to talk about it. I'm just supposed to trust her that doing anything close to what she did is an automatic disaster. And maybe it's true, maybe they did really love each other back then, but whatever they were, I can't see any of it, and all I worry about is that I'm going to end up just like them. That fear is currently sabotaging one of the best things in my life, and I can't get past this."

Now that she'd started, she couldn't hold any of it back. If she wanted to be a real partner with her uncle, it should be built on honesty. "Also, I'm sorry. I was never going to Tahoe to gamble. Instead, it was just to get away and meet…dates. But I was worried that everyone would judge me so I let everyone believe I liked to gamble. You're the only one in the family who knows the truth and I don't want you to lose respect for me but…" She couldn't finish. The avalanche of words blubbered from Natalie, along with tears. She realized this could make her uncle regret everything, not because she believed she did anything wrong, but because it made her look like a mess, which was not good business partner material.

Her uncle's arms went around her, pulling her to his chest gently. She was so exhausted, so emotionally drained, Enrique was the only thing keeping her from heaping to the floor. "Natalie. Eres mi familia. That doesn't change ever. Comprendes?"

She nodded.

"Talk to me."

She took a breath and told her uncle everything. There was no point in hiding anything about Mason, about her worry about becoming her parents. He listened to all of it in silence.

"This is really what you think? All marriages will become unhappy? You will become your mother?"

Natalie didn't have the heart to call her uncle on his own marriage, to ask if he was still in love, because either he'd say no and she'd feel horrible for her aunt or he'd say yes, and she wasn't sure if he was honest. Their marriage was a quiet one, so she didn't know what was true. Instead, she nodded her agreement.

Her uncle sighed, leaning his tall body against the office wall behind him. "The story of your parents is not what you think. What you have with Daniel's kid is not the same and let me tell you why. You are not your mamá or your papá. Like you, they were young, but they were much younger than you are now and did not think about their decisions. You think about everything. Why do you think I've always wanted you for Pony Expresso? You're smart. You don't like to be rash.

"Most importantly, you are not in a relationship for the same reasons as your parents. The essence of their story is true. They eloped after knowing each other for a week, surprising all of us. But maybe a bit of the story is left out because it's not so good."

Natalie held her breath. "But you know the truth?"

"Of course. I am his brother. I was there. The marriage happened because of jealousy, and your mamá didn't see it because she was too in love. When they met at that party, your father had recently broken up with a girl named Christina. But he realized he made a mistake. He loved Christina, wanted to be with her forever, thought he could win her back. She was also at the party and already had a new novio, and had no interest in your father anymore. This made Miguel angry and he thought, if he could make her jealous then maybe she'd come back. When that didn't work, he wanted to punish her for choosing someone else."

"What in the telenovela hell? He got with Mom in order to make another woman jealous?"

Her uncle shrugged. "Yeah. But Rosa didn't find out about Christina until after the wedding. She became angry. She's still angry. Understandably, she wanted to punish him."

"How angry could she have been? My parents have three kids."

"I can't speak on that. Sometimes things just happen and, you know, she became pregnant with you soon after the wedding. The family and the church forbid them to divorce and so here we are."

"But they're miserable. Why should they continue to be miserable?"

"Could they get divorce if they really want to? Sure. But part of me thinks they use it as an excuse because they want to punish the other. They're used to being miserable. They don't know how to move past it. As weird as it is, maybe they're scared not to be miserable. But that is not you and Mason. I saw it at the party. You want to make each other happy, not miserable. He sees that you don't want to be an old shoe and he gives you the car. This is what love looks like; this is how I love your tía. It isn't big declarations and bouquets of roses, although she deserves that too. You think because you're smart you see how things are, but you don't see everything."

Perhaps Enrique was right. Natalie didn't always see everything, or she chose not to. The latter was worse because she used it to make decisions she shouldn't have made, hurting both Mason and herself. She wanted to cry all over again. As much as she tried to avoid it, she'd allowed herself to become as stuck as her parents but in a completely different way. Choosing to be miserable because she was used to it rather than take a scary risk.

"I'm sorry for lying and I understand if you don't want me for a business partner."

"Natalie, I want you to be a part of this business if you want it. Do you?"

"Yeah, I do."

"Then it is not just my business, it is *our* business. And, like we do in our family, when there is reason to celebrate, we have a fiesta."

Despite having good news on a professional front, Natalie didn't feel much like celebrating. She probably wouldn't until she figured out how to fix her personal life.

Chapter Twenty-Four

THE CARDS IN Mason's hands didn't make any sense. It wasn't that he hadn't played this game before. He had at least a dozen times at this point. It was more that his brain didn't work well enough to make sense of what he held in his hand. These past couple of days made it hard for him to make sense of a lot of things.

He didn't even want to do board game night but, after his friends heard about Natalie, they insisted on getting together with him. Unlike their usual sessions, the group at the table was uncommonly quiet. They were waiting for him to do something, like play some of his cards…or cry. It could have gone either way.

Mason had half expected his friends to rag on him about being unlucky in love once again. They hadn't. Also, unlike the Dakota situation, they didn't immediately complain about Natalie or tell him he was better off without her. Maybe they sensed he didn't want to hear it. Mason wouldn't be able to stand listening to how horrible Natalie was, because maybe his brain wouldn't let him believe it yet.

"Are you going to go, Mase?" Gemma asked.

"Oh, yeah, I…" He squinted at his cards, concentrating harder, but it was of no use. "Sorry, I-I can't. I just don't…"

He leaned an elbow on the table, hiding the top of his face with the palm of his hand. An arm went around his shoulders, coming from Gemma. "I'm sorry," he said.

"Oh hell," said Isaac. "It's not just you. I really liked her too. I'm just as disappointed as you are. I got sucked in and was rooting for you guys. I feel like we all got dumped."

"Yup," Damon said in agreement.

"I don't know how I could have been so wrong. Am I just really bad at this? I really thought she was it."

Gemma sighed. "Maybe you're not wrong. Maybe you're just wrong about the timing. You have to let her figure some things out, just like you need to figure your own shit out."

"Geez, Gem, cut the guy some slack." Jay said. "He probably feels bad enough. We all do."

"I'm only giving him the truth. And here's another one. You can't force someone to be ready for you, and sometimes people aren't ready."

"How the hell do I know when someone's ready?"

"You listen to her."

Mason didn't say anything because he was trying hard not to cry. He didn't want to admit he hadn't listened to Natalie very well. Her words had struck him out of the blue and he hadn't been prepared. It was hard to listen beyond his own pain. The hurt was so loud, a freight train could blast through his apartment and he wasn't sure if he'd hear it.

Not that he considered Gemma wrong. He'd known his friend to be insightful and right about most things. It must be hard for Jay to be constantly wrong, but he didn't feel too badly for the guy because he at least had someone. Mason had no one. Well, he did have his friends. He had his bees at least. And Mason was lucky his parents were still in great health. They were moving because they wanted to, not because they were abandoning him.

Regardless of how it played out, he didn't consider one minute he spent with her to be a waste. He couldn't stop himself from loving her any more than he could use his mind to stop his heart from beating. Gemma was probably right in that Natalie had her own stuff to deal with and one holiday fling wasn't going to change everything.

His life was something Mason had to figure out on his own with or without Natalie or his parents.

A FEW DAYS later, he went to see his dad at the farm. It was time for him to face the situation head on and really think about what he wanted in life. He found his father and Bentley near the barn, pouring wood pellets from a forty-pound bag into a giant bin.

"You need help with that?" he asked, stepping in to grab the bag, but his father shooed him away.

"I got it. I'm not that feeble yet," Daniel insisted.

"I know."

He took a breath, ready for an honest conversation with his dad. "I just want you to know that I'm always willing to step in when you need me to. I know that what happened with Dakota really damaged that trust, and I suspect this is the reason you've held off on retiring lately. You've been waiting on me just as I've been waiting on you to forget. And I'm really sorry. It was selfish, and I want you and Mom to have the life you want. I should have done more to prove myself to you, and asking you to forget about me stealing from the company isn't really fair."

His father's eyebrows lifted in concern. "You know I love you, right? I do know that you're sorry and have been really trying to make up for that bad decision. I've seen it. Don't think I haven't noticed. Both your mom and I love you and want to give you everything we have."

Mason swallowed the lump in his throat, fighting past it. "I appreciate that but I think we should talk about the business."

A proud smile spread on Daniel's face as he patted his arm. "I don't think you have anything to worry about, Mase. If you want the business, it's yours. You did really good this season. I'll talk to Charlie about it."

His heart thumped with a tiny beat of joy at the pride his dad would trust him enough with his legacy, but he tamped it down. "I, uh, was actually just talking to Charlie and I think you should sell it to him. He has the money, which you and Mom need, and he loves this business almost as much as you guys do. He'll be good for it."

His father's smile melted away as his brows drew together, as though trying to decipher Mason's words. "You don't...want the business?"

He rubbed a hand along his jawline. "I think you were right about me before. I'm not ready. I thought I was ready for it but these last few weeks have had me thinking about other things and what I might be more interested in. You're right that I can't explore anything else if I'm under the weight of owning the business. Logically speaking, I think we both know Charlie is the one who should run it. I need to figure out my own shit."

"What are you going to do?" His father frowned, looking concerned. "Is it the bees?"

Mason laughed. "It's not a hobby. It's not a passing interest. Yes, I love the farm and the nursery, but I really think I can do something here. And, maybe like you, I have this new drive to build up something with my own hands and not just be handed a legacy but create my own. I've talked to Charlie and he's going to let me keep the hive here and give me some manager shifts, but I've decided to go back to school, take some courses in business and agriculture. I can also use the money I make from selling honey to start expanding the hive. I don't know how it's all going to work out but now that I have this idea in my head, I have to pursue it. This is what I want to focus on."

Daniel nodded, pulling him into a half hug with a few rough pats on his shoulder. "Okay. You'll figure it out. I'm proud of you. I will always be proud of you."

Mason hadn't done anything of any significance, so he wasn't sure what his dad had to be proud of yet, but a new determination lit inside of him and this was at least something. He was about to leave but changed his mind, turning to his dad again. As long as they were having honest conversations, he might as well go all the way.

"Can I ask you something? Do you and Mom still love each other?"

"What the hell kind of question is that?"

"I don't know. I…just noticed you guys don't really show a lot of affection."

The older man set his hands on his hips, looking toward the farmhouse in the distance. "You know your mom wasn't set on doing this nursery thing or living here in Apple Hill. She liked the area fine—it is pretty after all. She's just always been more of a city girl, liked having lots to do, always feeling restless like you. She did it for me."

"Do you think she has regrets? Nat—Somebody told me love fades. Is it true?"

"I haven't always been one hundred percent sure about your mother's feelings toward me all the time. There are moments when she looks like she wants to smother me with a pillow. But do I love her? Hell yeah. Does love fade? Probably for some it does. But, in my experience, love is like the seasons. Sometimes it's a little drier or a little colder. And other times it'll be so warm you want to bask in it. It's an ebb and flow, something that needs to be cultivated and taken care of just like a plant. It's not something you can race toward, grab it, and then that's it—you're done. If you're lucky enough to find someone, you'll never be done, and if you want to thrive in it, you'll find your love in the little things, the things no one notices but you two, rather than big showy displays. Your mother came here for me. She started this nursery business for me. It's because she loves me. And because I love her, I always want to do whatever I can to make her happy. This is why we're moving to Tucson. Does that answer your question?"

"Oh, uh, yeah." It answered more than he'd expected. Perhaps Mason had seen being in love as some sort of end game, some kind of achievement he could latch on to and that would be it: he would be set for life.

He was walking back to his truck when his phone vibrated with a message and, seeing Natalie's name, his heart leaped inside his chest. Mason stopped in his tracks. He never expected to see her name on his phone ever again. He opened her message.

It consisted of a graphic of an invitation to a New Year's party at the coffee shop. The only words she had included to him was, *Hope you can come.*

He stood there and stared at it, wondering if it was sent by mistake, wondering if he should respond and if he did respond, what would he say? Mason concluded it was indeed a mistake because why would she invite him to a party after everything? He almost put his phone away, to ignore it, because his heart still hurt.

Except, the organ was a lot more stubborn than he originally thought. There was a faint beat of optimism. Maybe it wasn't a mistake. Maybe Gemma was correct and Natalie was telling him something else. Was she ready? The more time that passed, the stronger this optimism got.

Only, he didn't want to make a mistake.

Because when it came to her, it was either forever or nothing.

Chapter Twenty-Five

PONY EXPRESSO WAS packed but not with the usual customers. Most of it was her family and friends of Enrique. The celebration party was being held in the evening after closing. Perhaps this was why everything felt weird.

After her honest conversation with her uncle, she sensed a weight had been lifted from her shoulders. It certainly didn't solve everything. Her parents were still the same as they had always been. In fact, they got into a small argument when they first arrived. She saw them, or her place between them, differently. Both her parents loved her and her family. This had always been true. And, in spite of her frustration with them, she loved each of them. But she couldn't change them. She accepted her parents' issues were theirs and they didn't have to be hers. This new perspective pushed some of the stressful parts of her life from her heart as if it was making room for other things.

She was doing her best to enjoy the New Year's party that was also celebrating her new official business position, but something was missing—or, rather, it was someone who was missing.

Natalie had sent Mason an invitation but never received a reply in return. She didn't blame him. She'd been in the wrong and had treated him horribly. And, yet, there was one tiny bit of hope, a small spark in the dark, that maybe he'd see her invitation for what it was: a chance for her to apologize and maybe get things right for a change. She had hoped he'd somehow be able to look past all the hurt she'd caused, and still want to see her.

Except the party had been going for an hour and a half and there hadn't been any sign of Mason.

Nothing.

Natalie did her best to plaster a smile on her face, pretending she'd never been happier, doing her best to side-step any inquisitive questions about Mason's whereabouts. She did her best to concentrate on Mia who was chatting away about some funny incident that happened during a photography job she had done recently for the Parks and Rec Department of Placerville, when a figure outside the shop caught her attention.

It was him.

He had come.

Natalie, heart hammering, sucked in a breath.

"What's wrong?" Mia asked before following her line of vision. "Oh," she said with understanding, but Natalie barely heard.

He walked past the shop windows with his hands stuffed in his jacket pockets, shoulders hunched as though this helped block the winter wind, but he wasn't in a hurry, as though it was a casual stroll on Main Street. He stopped at the door, his hand outreached, but seemed to change his mind, hand dropping. It lifted once more, before dropping for good. He turned, returning to his previous path.

He wasn't coming.

He'd tried but couldn't do it.

Natalie became desperate, pushing past relatives as she made her way to the shop entrance and outside. The air was biting, she didn't have a jacket, but she didn't feel the cold, only potential devastation. "Mason."

He stopped before slowly turning to face her. "Hi."

She rushed to cover the steps between them. "You're not going to come in? We have food and drinks and stuff. I even have a new drink for the occasion." She was rambling nonsense, but she couldn't help it.

"Yeah, I'm not really up for it. I'm sorry. I thought I could do this, but I'm not so sure it's a good idea."

She latched on to his arm, afraid this might be her last chance, cursing herself for every time she had put up a roadblock between them in the past because experiencing it on the other side sucked. Natalie realized it was now or never. "Listen. I'm really sorry about everything. I just got scared that I was going to repeat past mistakes, and I took it out on you because it was easier than facing how much of a disaster I am. All I did was create more of a disaster because maybe I'm so used to it, it feels normal. But I'd rather choose something different this time. I'd rather choose you."

His expression didn't ease, instead he appeared more conflicted. "You're not the only one who's scared. I've been scared about a lot of things, but you were the one thing in my life that I felt sure of. And then, completely out of the blue, you dropped me. How am I supposed to be able to move forward knowing you can do that to me again? I don't know if I'm strong enough."

He'd made his decision. He wasn't going to give her another chance. Natalie rubbed a hand across her cheek to wipe away a tear before she straightened her spine, pulling herself together.

"Come on." She grabbed his arm again, encouraging him toward the door.

"Natalie, I don't think—"

"There's something I want to show you." Thankfully, he let her lead him inside the shop where he received greetings and cheers from her family. This gave her some hope. As Mia had told her, a person couldn't be persuaded if they didn't want to do something in the first place. Perhaps he hadn't shut the door completely; there was still a part of him that wanted this, wanted her. If she had to shove her shoulder against the door and push her way inside, she was going to try.

She took him to the Christmas tree, which still stood in the corner of the shop. Despite her best intentions for prolonging the white fir on life support, its needles were drying out. Natalie hadn't the heart to toss it yet as she'd become attached.

She pulled him closer so they could block out the crowd and they could talk with some privacy. "Look, I'm not a sentimental person. For much of my life most of this stuff hasn't mattered to me. And then you came along and—Well, maybe I've been settling for fake Christmas trees my whole life because it's easier, less messy. You made me realize how much I was missing out on the real thing. You've made me a real Christmas tree type of person, and not because I think everyone needs a real Christmas tree to celebrate the holidays or that people can't celebrate in their own ways, but I want this for you. See? I added some ornaments."

She pointed to them through unshed tears. "There's a barn. A poinsettia. And a stack of board games, and a cool Diva Santa. Oh, and my grandma helped me make this one out of felt because I couldn't find one at the hardware shop. It's supposed to be a waffle. It's not very good and I stuck myself pretty bad while sewing it." She presented her bandaged pointer finger as evidence.

Mason's gaze went to the bandage before returning to the ornaments hanging on the tree, his mouth slightly open, completely speechless. Finally, he said, "Why?"

"Well, because I love you and this makes you happy. You're worth all the effort and bandaged fingers. And I hope it's not too late and you think I'm still worth it even after I royally screwed up."

"I thought you didn't believe in love."

"Don't you think if I could change my stance about Christmas trees, I can do the same in regards to love? The Christmas tree and bee lobby have finally won me over. It's a new year, Mase. I want to start it off right."

The silence between them stretched and she grew nervous again. Then he said, "One thing I haven't changed my mind on is that I'm still okay with never getting married. If you don't want any of the traditional stuff, but you still let me love you, then I don't care."

"Maybe we can take it one step at a time. Neither one of us needs to rush ahead, and we can just enjoy the journey we're on. We'll take it slow. It gives me some time to figure out my mess."

"And I can figure out my mess."

For the first time, a smile spread across her face. "Oh, you have some too?"

"God, yes. But it doesn't hurt to have a bright spot in the middle of it." He took her hand, pressing a kiss to her bandaged finger. "You make it all worth it."

She wasn't sure how to react, and she burst into tears, drawing the attention of nearby partygoers but Natalie didn't care. She and Mason were in their own private world, and he was all she noticed. She catapulted herself into his arms, trusting him to catch her as she threw her arms around his neck.

"I don't think there's going to be anything drab or gray about January this year. Maybe this was the secret all along."

She believed him because Natalie felt the same way. "Happy New Year. I love you, Mason Lavigne."

"I love—" but she pressed her mouth to his in an eager kiss. She knew he loved her. She'd seen it from him a dozen times already.

Her family cheered in the background, there was even a celebratory shrill whistle, like they were watching the end to a satisfying movie. She knew her parents, along with the rest of the family, would be happy to have Mason back because she was gloriously, undeniably happy. The previous emptiness she'd felt at the beginning of the evening was filled. Now it was a party, one she hoped would happen again and again.

She slowly pulled away from Mason, gazing at him, his cheeks flushed pink and his eyes crinkling in joy.

"You," he said, to finish his previous statement.

"Come on. You need to try this new drink I made, and Mia wants you to befriend her husband, Ross."

"Sure," he said, taking her hand and allowing her to lead him through the crowd to the counter. "What's this drink?"

"It's a honey cinnamon latte. I'm calling it Honey Bee Delight even though my uncle hates it and thinks it's cheesy."

Natalie went behind the counter, grabbing a sharpie to draw his name on a paper cup before making the drink. "I'm using the honey you brought Dad. Really had to wrangle that out of him. Hopefully, you'll like it…although you might not. It's an acquired taste, I think."

"Maybe you'll need more of that honey or you'll consider selling some in the shop to customers."

"I'll talk it over with myself and if I make a convincing argument, I'll let you know. I am the boss now.

She handed him the drink, licking a drop of honey from her finger. Mason studied the cup where she'd used a red sharpie to draw hearts and poinsettias around his name.

"I'm never going to be able to throw away this cup now," he said to her.

She rolled her eyes but couldn't help smiling. "Yes, you can. There will be plenty more where that came from. By the way, I'm coming home with you tonight."

He raised an eyebrow. "Is this why you're giving me caffeine? Is this still considered taking things slow?"

"Yes and yes. I'll make sure after the damn party is over to walk to my car very slowly. I think anyone would consider that taking things slow." He grinned at her, and she bit her lip to keep her own smile from escaping. "Will you just shut up and drink that?"

Mason took a generous sip but was unable to hide the slight grimace passing across his features.

"You don't like it?"

"No, I do. Although, I think maybe you're right and it's an acquired taste. I need another sip is all. Is the honey for me and the cinnamon for you?"

"Yup. A little sweet, a little spice. What other combination sounds like paradise?"

He smiled. "I think it's perfect."

It was better than perfect.

It was them.

Epilogue

One year later

"THIS IS A horrible wrapping job," Natalie said as she took the gift from him.

She wasn't wrong. Mason was the worst gift wrapper in the world, using way more wrapping and tape than was necessary, but he got the job done. He didn't let her teasing bother him. Mostly, because what she said was true but also because they were sharing a quiet Christmas on their couch, beside their white fir Christmas tree, inside their living room. While there were still things considered hers and his separately, he took great joy in knowing that many things were now theirs.

As much as they had planned to take things slow (he was even willing to wait years if necessary) things didn't seem to work out that way. After Mason had helped move his parents and Bentley to Arizona during the summer, he returned to bad news and good news. The bad news was a text message notifying him of a rent increase on his apartment. The good news was his girlfriend throwing herself at him, dragging him to the bedroom and tearing off his clothes soon after his return to Placerville.

"You missed me, then?" he had said after making love to

her.

"What makes you think that?"

"My suitcase is still in the entryway."

"Isn't that normal? It takes me a week to unpack my suitcase when I come back from a trip."

"Well, maybe I'll just keep it packed. I might be moving again since my rent's going up."

She eyed him, before her gaze flitted away. "Or you can move in with me?"

"I could. But what about taking things slow?"

"How much longer is on your lease? Like a month? We'll just slowly move your stuff over during the course of a month. A plate one day, a cup the next. I'm pretty sure most people would consider that slow."

Either her argument was convincing, or he really loved her. It could have gone either way. "Yeah, you're probably right about that," he had responded.

In the end, they'd moved most of his stuff to her place in the course of a day because both of them were busy with work and school and just general stuff. Plus, who had the time to do a bunch of back-and-forth trips when using one moving truck was way more convenient? When his friends volunteered to help him move, with the promise of pizza and beer, things happened a lot faster than planned. Not that Natalie or he ever complained about it. Everything was taken in stride as though this was meant to be. Considering all the adjustments he'd had to make in a year, it was as if his life was in a constant state of change anyway. What was one more?

On top of this, he was dividing his time between taking

classes at the local community college, maintaining his beehives, and picking up shifts at the nursery. Natalie was busy working with her uncle. They were considering getting a better coffee truck with a more permanent spot in the city, plus working with Lana at special events. This didn't leave a lot of free time between them. Living in the same apartment guaranteed time together, and there was something to be said about coming home to someone. They could eat a quiet meal, while streaming a show on Netflix, and he could take pleasure in just being with her. His father had been right. It was the quiet moments where he found true contentment.

"Will you just open it already?" Mason said as Natalie stretched out unwrapping the gift he had handed her.

They had already spent Christmas Eve with her family, staying until the wee hours. They came home and decided to open the small gifts they had for each other before getting some rest. They were flying soon to spend time with his family in Arizona.

She finally pulled off the wrapping and laughed. "A waffle iron? Your Christmas gift is me making you breakfast?"

"Well, when you put it like that—"

"How else am I supposed to put it?"

Okay, she may have a point. He hadn't thought this through and perhaps it wasn't as romantic as he originally thought. "I, uh, gave you a waffle iron to show that I'm going to make you waffles."

"You can barely make pancakes."

"I'm getting better."

She laughed again. "Okay. I will let you make me waffles. I might even help. Here's your gift."

Natalie handed him a small box wrapped more neatly than his. She nervously pulled on the ends of her sleeves until they mostly covered her hands. He mimicked her by pulling on the tape very slowly to unwrap.

"Will you just unwrap the damn thing before I break your damn hand off?"

"Good grief. You're a violent Christmas grinch—do you know that?"

"Villain," she said automatically.

He removed the rest of the paper to reveal a small plain cardboard box. Opening it revealed a Christmas tree ornament, specifically a Sasquatch wearing a Santa hat. Since they'd brought home their tree, Mason had provided her with special Christmas ornaments he picked throughout the season whenever he came across one reminding him of her. While they didn't have a whole tree filled with ornaments, they were well on their way. Mason planned to take years making this happen. "Aw, honey. You remembered that I wanted a Sasquatch ornament. I love him. He looks exactly like me."

"Actually, that's on purpose. I had it custom made. See? You're even wearing the same white T-shirt and blue plaid pajama bottoms. Take off the paper on the front."

He studied it again and saw where Natalie had taped a small piece of wrapping paper to the front of the ornament. Peeling it away revealed Sasquatch holding a heart and it read, *Marry Me*.

"You know," she said, "I was thinking. Maybe after we get back from Arizona, we can do a small trip to Tahoe, just you and me. It could be a fun getaway since I'll still be on vacation and your classes haven't started yet."

He lifted his gaze to her, not quite hearing everything she had said. "What?"

"It's just an idea. I feel like we've both been so busy, and it's been a long time for me so it might be kind of nice."

"Natalie, I… Did you just ask me to marry you?"

"Oh, yeah, I did. Once I make up my mind about something, that's pretty much it. I know we said we'd take things slow, but if we take a while to plan the wedding, like maybe we hire a vendor every other month, that probably counts as slow, right?"

He scooted closer, pulling her legs until they draped over his lap so he could get as close as possible, breathing her light scent of sweet mint and jasmine. "Yeah, I'd say that would count as slow." He brushed his lips over hers, nibbling, tasting, completely reveling in the feel of her. She made a little groan in her throat as he deepened the kiss, her fingers already traveling under his T-shirt.

"Or we could elope in Tahoe?" she said. "Save ourselves a lot of effort."

"Mm-hmm," he replied, his hands already sliding along her torso. "Or maybe there's something in between. Something small but both our families can be there."

"Okay. I guess you're worth a little bit more effort. If that's what you want." She sweetly kissed the corner of his mouth. "Marry me?"

"Yeah," he said, pressing another kiss to her. "But you're still not getting that dick pic."

She laughed, pulling him closer. "Well, then I guess I'll just have to be satisfied with the real thing."

The End

Acknowledgments

This being my second published book, you'd think I'd have this whole writing thing all figured out. But writing a book is never easy, each one coming with its own share of struggles. Luckily, I'm fortunate enough to have wonderful people pulling me through the process. And no amount of thanks on my part ever seems to be enough to express how grateful I am…but I will try my best.

First and foremost, I'd love to thank everyone on the Tule Publishing team. Not only did they see the potential in me to pick up my stories in the first place, but they have an amazing group of people who take my messy words and make them sparkle—from editing to the final book version and beyond. I'm so glad to be working with such a supportive team of people.

I also want to give special thanks to my agents, Ashley and Kelly, who help keep me from spinning out of control. Your patience with me means everything and I feel fortunate to have you in my professional life.

Beta readers and writing friends are an essential part of the writing process, not only for pointing out where the story can improve but also by providing much needed encouragement. I want to thank Frank Tybush, Leumas LLewtnac, Sarah Smith, and Natalie Wolicki for being so kind as to give me feedback when I need it.

I love my Romance Fight Club ladies! Denise, Allie, Beth, and Janelle thank you so much for being a group that provides the best advice and the best laughs. May we continue fighting over book boyfriends for a long time. P.S. The Victor trophy is mine!

Also, to my fellow Tule sisters, Mia, Denise, Lisa, Kelly, Heather, Stacey, and Rebecca, I'm so happy you welcomed me into your group. Being able to glean information from your experiences has been so helpful in my writing journey. You all are seriously the best.

To my husband, thank you for always being my first and biggest cheerleader when it comes to my books. Being able to spitball ideas with you during our afternoon walks always provides sparks of inspiration even when you create impossible writing challenges for me. Diva Santa will always be a character we created together.

And, lastly, I'd like to thank friends, family, and readers. Thank you so much for giving this new writer a chance to share a world of her own creation. I will always be so grateful for your support.

Love in El Dorado series

Book 1: *Striking Gold*

Book 2: *A Poinsettia Paradise Christmas*

Book 3: *Lucky Strike*

Available now at your favorite online retailer!

About the Author

Janine Amesta is a California girl who now lives in the high desert of Oregon with her husband and their cat, Hitchcock. She studied screenwriting in college, but her moody thrillers always had way too much flirty banter. She's a master at jigsaw puzzles, skilled at embroidery, and critiques bad movies on Twitter.

Thank you for reading

A Poinsettia Paradise Christmas

If you enjoyed this book, you can find more from all our great authors at TulePublishing.com, or from your favorite online retailer.

TULE
PUBLISHING

Milton Keynes UK
Ingram Content Group UK Ltd.
UKHW010719311023
431661UK00004B/269

9 781961 544154